GUNS IN THE GALLERY

GUNS IN THE GALLERY

A Fethering Mystery

Simon Brett

CRÈME de la CRIME

This first world edition published 2011
in Great Britain and in the USA by
Crème de la Crime, an imprint of
SEVERN HOUSE PUBLISHERS LTD of
9–15 High Street, Sutton, Surrey, England, SM1 1DF.
Trade paperback edition first published
in Great Britain and the USA 2012 by
Crème de la Crime, an imprint of
SEVERN HOUSE PUBLISHERS LTD.

British Library Cataloguing in Publication Data

Brett, Simon.
   Guns in the gallery. – (A Fethering mystery)
   1. Seddon, Carole (Fictitious character)–Fiction. 2. Jude
   (Fictitious character : Brett)–Fiction. 3. Fethering
   (England : Imaginary place)–Fiction. 4. Women private
   investigators–England–Fiction. 5. Detective and mystery
   stories.
   I. Title II. Series
   823.9'2-dc22

ISBN-13: 978-1-78029-015-7 (cased)
ISBN-13: 978-1-78029-517-6 (trade paper)

All Severn House titles are printed on acid-free paper.

Severn House Publishers support The Forest Stewardship Council [FSC],
the leading international forest certification organisation. All our titles that
are printed on Greenpeace-approved FSC-certified paper carry the FSC logo.

Typeset by Palimpsest Book Production Ltd.,
Falkirk, Stirlingshire, Scotland.
Printed and bound in Great Britain by
MPG Books Ltd., Bodmin, Cornwall.

To
Roger and Louise,
with thanks

ONE

The human mind is very selective in its retention of information. Carole Seddon had walked along the parade at Fethering more times than she cared to remember, but she'd never before been really aware of the Cornelian Gallery. Of course, she knew it was there, but she had never thought it might have any relevance to her own life. As she passed the frontage on a daily basis, usually with her Labrador, Gulliver, on the way to his walk on Fethering Beach, she had paid scant attention to the gallery's window displays.

This, like many things in Carole's life, was a product of her austere middle-class upbringing. Her parents' lives had been dedicated to keeping below the level of any parapets that they might encounter. By their scale of values, one of the worst social offences was 'drawing attention to oneself' – or, even worse, 'showing off'. Though they'd never articulated the view, there was a tacit assumption in their household that most artistic expression was a form of showing off. And to their cash-strapped, penny-pinching, post-war minds, the idea of spending money on art belonged in the disapproving category of 'frittering'. During her upbringing, Carole had lost count of the sentences she had heard from her mother which began: 'Fancy frittering your money away on . . .'

It was, of course, impossible to go through life in complete ignorance of art. Carole had been given a very basic grounding at school, and on foreign trips had paid visits to famous galleries where she had dutifully gazed at famous paintings, waiting in vain to feel the responses such images were meant to prompt. In common with other areas of her life, aesthetic appreciation was one in which her emotions were not easily unlocked.

And, though with the passage of the years she had in some ways mellowed, Carole Seddon would still never have entered the Cornelian Gallery with a view to buying a work of art. The only adornments on the antiseptically clean walls of her house, High Tor, were a few landscape prints her parents had inherited from an elderly aunt. They had been part of her life for so long that she no longer noticed them – and would indeed have been hard put to say from which countries the scenes they represented came.

But the reason why Carole Seddon went into the Cornelian Gallery that Monday morning in late April was printed on the glass door she pushed open. 'FRAMING SERVICE'. She had something she needed to get framed.

It was a photograph of her granddaughter. The birth of Lily to her son Stephen and his wife Gaby had been an important contributory factor in the thawing of Carole Seddon. And after her joyless upbringing, her rigid career in the Home Office, her tense marriage to, and ultimate divorce from, her husband David, there had been quite a lot in her to thaw. The process had been begun by her friendship with a new neighbour Jude, who had moved into Woodside Cottage, the house adjacent to High Tor, and the thawing could still at best be described as a 'work in progress'. Though Carole's personality had relaxed considerably, she was still capable of regression, clamming up her emotions at some social challenge or imagined slight.

The photograph of Lily had been emailed by Gaby. Though initially slow to embrace computers, once she had bought a laptop Carole Seddon had quickly become hooked on the technology. There was something in its unemotional efficiency that struck a chord in her probing, analytical mind. She had catalogued all of her pictures into directories and subdirectories with the same scrupulous attention to detail that had character-ized her work in the Home Office.

Carole had also devoted some time to mastering the skills of Photoshop and ensured that no images were finally saved until they had been cropped and enhanced to look their absolute best.

There was no one in the Cornelian Gallery when Carole entered, so she had a chance to take in its contents. The interior was not large, and much of the floor space was occupied by small tables, displaying what she could only think of as 'knick-knacks'. There were notebooks, bookmarks, notelets, *Ex Libris* stickers, pens, pencils, erasers, sharpeners, all decorated with familiar images from the world of art. Carole wondered how the tortured mind of Van Gogh would have responded to the knowledge that his iconic sunflowers might one day provide the cover for a slab of Post-it notes. He'd probably have cut off the other ear.

On one side wall hung a collection of West Sussex landscapes – the South Downs, local beaches – whose style looked vaguely familiar. Closer inspection revealed them to be the work of Gray Czesky, a self-appointed *enfant terrible* of an artist, whom Carole had met in the nearby village of Smalting. She winced as she remembered the prices he charged for his chocolate-box watercolours.

One painting on that wall was clearly by another hand. Central to it was the instantly recognizable outline of Eros, but the statue was set in an unfamiliar Piccadilly Circus. Everything was covered with snow, not the pristine white of the newly fallen, but that tarnished grey of the thaw's first day. The bleakness of the scene, of red London buses sloshing their way up towards Regent Street, was evocative of the comfortlessness of shoe-soaking slush.

The opposite wall hosted a display of framed relief works in copper, bronze and bright enamel colours. Twisted torsos apparently grappling each other or wrestling with winged dragons. Undoubtedly 'modern' art, thought Carole with a knee-jerk sneer. And real dust-traps, added the compulsively house-proud element of her personality.

On the remaining wall of the gallery were what looked at first sight like a sequence of Christmas tree designs, a series of upturned, arrowhead shapes in a variety of textures and colours. They puzzled Carole at first. She suspected further excesses of modernity and had only just identified them as samples of frame corners when the door at the back opened to admit the gallery's owner.

As she did with many other people in Fethering, Carole knew the woman's name and a certain amount about her life, but the two of them had never actually had a conversation. Bonita Green was a small woman one side or the other of sixty, whose style of dress hadn't changed a lot since she had been an art student (at 'the Slade', according to local gossip; though local gossip wasn't quite sure what 'the Slade' was).

And even back then her fashion sense had had something retro about it. Her lifelong sartorial icon appeared to have been the French *chanteuse* Juliette Greco. Summer and winter Bonita always dressed in black, V-necked black jumper, tight black slacks (there was no other word for them) and black trainers. Her brown eyes were outlined in black and her hair, improbably black and with the fluffiness brought by much dyeing, framed her face in a long page-boy cut. Perhaps as a student, she had had a sexily *gamine* quality, but age and two children had spread her contours considerably. Still, Bonita Green was so much a part of the Fethering landscape that people stopped noticing her. And no one ever voiced the thought that she might look faintly ridiculous.

'Good morning. Can I help you?' Her voice was affectedly sultry, matching the incongruity of her appearance.

She knew who Carole was just as well as Carole knew who she was, but they both maintained the Fethering convention of being complete strangers to each other.

'I was looking for a frame for a photograph.'

'Is it a standard size? We have a big range of ready-made. Or will you want a frame specially made for it?'

'Well, I'm not sure.' Carole Seddon reached into her handbag and produced a large envelope containing the precious picture of Lily. She withdrew the photograph slowly, trying to stop herself from hoping for a reaction of amazement at the beauty of its subject.

She got none. Bonita Green was interested only in dimensions. 'Doesn't look standard,' she said, before checking the edges with a transparent plastic ruler. 'No, if you want to keep it this shape, you'll have to have a frame made.'

'What do you mean, "if I want to keep it this shape"?'

'Well, it's clearly been worked on in Photoshop. You could crop it again to get it to a standard size.'

'That is the size I want it,' said Carole with an edge of asperity. The gallery owner hadn't exactly gone as far as to criticize her Photoshop skills, but had been too close for comfort to such a social lapse. 'It is a rather special photograph for me.'

'I'm sure it is,' said Bonita Green, still insufficiently in awe of Lily's beauty. 'Had you any thought of what kind of frame you'd want?' She gestured to the Christmas trees of samples behind her. 'As you see, we have quite a wide range to choose from. I would have thought, for an image that size, you would need the frame to be at least *this* thick. But as to colour or finish, of course that's up to you. What did you have in mind?'

Carole was somewhat distressed to realize that she didn't have anything in mind. Her intention had been to get Lily's photograph framed. She hadn't given any thought as to how it should be framed. Characteristically, she felt annoyed by her lack of preparation.

'Presumably you've decided where you're going to put it? So you'll probably want to consider the decor of the room, so that it tones in with the colours there . . .?'

'I think I'm probably after something neutral,' Carole replied safely, at the same time hating herself for taking the safe option. She had a vision of her neighbour, Jude, selecting something exotic and multi-hued.

Bonita Green's hand moved to the relevant display. 'These are the blacks, whites and metallic finishes. And if you want decorative motifs on the frame, there's a wide selection of additional—'

'No, I think just plain, thank you,' said Carole.

She eventually opted for a colour which Bonita Green descried as 'gunmetal', but which she herself would have called 'grey'. It was appropriate. The colour matched Carole Seddon's helmet of hair, and there was sometimes a grey bleakness in her pale blue eyes. Slender, with a good figure – though she would never have thought of it in that way – she was in fact a good-looking woman in her fifties. But she didn't like drawing attention to herself. She maintained her parents' tradition of keeping below parapets.

But in fact, by choosing the unobtrusive from the framing options, Carole had selected something rather stylish. Bonita approved her choice, and the approval sounded more than the automatic blandishment of a shop-owner. 'You don't want a frame that's going to distract from the colours of the photograph itself,' she said. That was probably the nearest Carole was going to get to a compliment on her granddaughter's beauty.

Colour was not the only decision that needed to be made.

There were also choices available in material, finish, mount and glass. Carole opted for a wooden frame with an 'antique' gunmetal surface, an Ice White mount and White Water glass. This last was the most expensive, but she let herself be persuaded of its superiority over other glasses. Again, Bonita Green seemed to approve of her selections and that gave a small boost to Carole's fragile confidence.

The cost of the work was considerably more than she had anticipated, but she managed not to blench, reassuring herself that only the best was suitable for Lily. Then came the question of how long the work would take. Would the photograph have to be sent away?

'No, all our framing is done on the premises,' replied Bonita Green. 'Just a moment.' She moved towards the door from which she had emerged and called out, 'Spider, could you just come here a minute?'

After a moment, a large man lumbered into the gallery. He wore blue overalls, spattered with a Jackson Pollock of paint and glue drips. The remarkable thing about him, though, was his hair. Dyed black, swept back in a quiff with long straight-cut sideburns, it had the complete Elvis Presley look. And in fact Spider's bulk helped to make him look quite like the deceased superstar, in his late Las Vegas diamanté Babygro incarnation. He loomed over his employer, a presence that was at the same time protective and slightly threatening. Carole tried very hard – and not entirely successfully – to avoid looking at the hair.

'Spider . . . this lady . . .' The gallery-owner maintained the local convention of ignorance. 'I'm sorry, I don't know your name.'

'Carole Seddon.'

'May I call you Carole?'

'Please.'

'Thank you. And I'm Bonita.'

This was a very important moment in Fethering protocol. Though the two women had both known each other's names for years, from this moment on they would be able actually to use them.

'And this is Spider, who does all my framing.'

'Good morning.'

The big man nodded acknowledgement. Bonita Green lifted up the photograph of Lily. 'Carole wants this framed. We should have everything we need in stock. I know you've got a bit of a backlog at the moment . . .' The big man nodded again. 'So when do you reckon we can promise this for?'

There was a silence. He seemed to have an aversion to speech and Carole wondered if he was actually dumb. But at length, slowly he articulated the word, 'Thursday.'

'What sort of time would that be, Bonita?'

'First thing. If Spider says Thursday, he means he'll have finished it on Wednesday.'

'So I might be able to pick it up on Wednesday?'

'No. I usually close the gallery round four thirty. Spider often works on after that, sometimes Fridays and weekends as well. Isn't that right?'

With a nod of confirmation and farewell, the taciturn framer went back into his workroom.

'Oh, very well,' said Carole. 'First thing Thursday I'll pop in. What time do you open?'

'Ten thirty. Ten thirty every day, except Sunday and Friday, when we're closed.'

The Calvinist work ethic within Carole could not repress the thought that ten thirty to four thirty was a fairly undemanding opening schedule. And taking Fridays off. But then again she knew very little about Bonita Green. Perhaps the woman was lucky enough to have a private income, and maybe the Cornelian Gallery was nothing more than a wealthy woman's hobby.

'Anyway, I'd better be off. Would you like me to pay now or pay a deposit or something?'

'No, that'll be fine. Settle up when you pick the thing up on Thursday.'

'Well, that's very good of you.'

'Oh, if you were a complete stranger, I'd ask for payment upfront. But because you're local . . .' said Bonita Green, thus deflating the Fethering convention that they didn't know anything about each other.

'Thank you so much, anyway, and I'll—'

But Carole's parting words were interrupted by the

appearance from the back of the gallery of a man in his early
thirties. He had floppy brown hair, and was dressed in an
expensive pinstriped suit. The tie over his white shirt was of
that lilac colour favoured by politicians.

'Good morning, Mother,' he said breezily.

'Morning. Giles, this is Carole Seddon. My son, Giles.'

They exchanged good mornings.

'I was actually just leaving.'

'And has my mother given you an invitation to our Private
View?'

'No, I haven't, Giles.'

He shook his head in mock reproof. 'Dear, oh dear. Where's
your entrepreneurial spirit? I thought we agreed that you were
going to hand out invitations to everyone who came into the
gallery.'

'Well, yes, but I—'

Ignoring his mother, Giles Green reached behind the counter
and produced a handful of printed cards. 'Something you won't
want to miss, Carole. Friday week. It'll be *the* event of the
Fethering social calendar. Have you heard of Denzil
Willoughby?'

Carole was forced to admit that she hadn't.

'Only a matter of time. He's going to be very big. Big as
Damien Hirst in a few years' time, I'll put money on that.
And he's showing his new work here at the Cornelian Gallery.
So there's a chance for you, Carole, to be in at the beginning
of something really big. Right here in Fethering you will have
the opportunity to snap up an original Denzil Willoughby for
peanuts . . . and then just sit back and watch its value grow.'

'Well, I don't often buy art, I must say.' Don't *ever* buy art,
if the truth were told.

'Then you must simply change your habits,' asserted Giles
Green. 'It's too easy for people to become stick-in-the-muds
in a backwater like Fethering. But things're going to change
round here. Isn't that, right, Mother?'

'Well, Giles, I'm not sure—'

'Of course they are. Here, Carole, you take two of these.
Bring a friend.'

Carole Seddon looked down at the invitations which had

been thrust into her hand. The image on the front looked like an explosion in an abattoir. And the Private View to which she was being invited was called 'GUN CULTURE'.

TWO

' I t's not my sort of thing,' Carole protested, looking down once again at the Cornelian Gallery invitation.

'How do you know what's your sort of thing until you've tried it?' asked Jude, a smile twitching at her generous lips. A well-upholstered woman of about the same age as Carole, she had a body which promised infinite comfort to men. As usual, her blonde hair was piled untidily on top of her head and she was dressed in swathes of brightly coloured layers. She and Carole were ensconced in their usual alcove at Fethering's only pub, the Crown and Anchor. In front of them were their customary glasses of Chilean Chardonnay.

'Well, *art.*' Carole infused the word with a wealth of contempt. 'I mean, my life's always been too full to have time for the excesses of art.'

'You've been invited to a Private View that lasts two hours. You don't have to stay the full two hours. If you're not enjoying it, you can leave after half an hour. Is your life so full that you can't spare half an hour?'

'Well . . .' It was a question to which Carole really didn't have a very good answer. Except for when Stephen, Gaby and Lily came to see her, or she went to visit them in Fulham, there weren't that many demands on her time. There was taking Gulliver for his walks on Fethering Beach, of course . . . and diligently removing impertinent motes of dust from the surfaces of High Tor . . . then sometimes the final few clues of *The Times* crossword proved obdurately difficult . . . but Carole could always find a spare half hour. Too many spare half hours, she thought during her occasional moments of self-pity.

'I'm sure it'll be fine for *you*,' she went on. It was true.

Jude had the knack of slipping easily into any social environment. 'You're used to dealing with arty people. I wouldn't know what to say to them.'

'You'd say to them what you'd say to anyone else. Anyway, they're not going to be very arty. I mean, if Bonita's inviting everyone who comes into the Cornelian Gallery to get a photo framed, it's hardly going to be the Royal Academy's Summer Exhibition, is it? There'll be half a dozen people connected with the art world and, apart from them, all the usual Fethering faces. Nobody's going to be quizzing you on your knowledge of Renaissance painting or your view of the Impressionists. It's not going to be trial by ordeal.'

'No, but . . .' The trouble was, if you were Carole Seddon, every social event was trial by ordeal. Even ones where there was a good chance she might enjoy had to be preceded by hours of agonizing over whether she would make a fool of herself or wear the wrong clothes or commit some other *faux pas*. She had the shy person's rather arrogant assumption that she – and her shortcomings – would be the focus of everyone else's attention.

'I'm sorry,' she repeated finally, 'but I really don't think it's my sort of thing.'

'What's not your sort of thing?' asked the rough voice of Ted Crisp. He was the landlord of the Crown and Anchor, and he'd just brought over to their table the day's Lunchtime Specials they had ordered, two seafood risottos. Ted was a large scruffy, bearded man, always dressed in faded sweatshirt and jeans. When he'd taken over the lease, he'd just been thought of as a large scruffy bearded man; but now the Crown and Anchor was gaining something of a reputation as a gastropub, he was regarded as a 'local character'. People who'd watched too many television food programmes assumed that his scruffiness was some form of 'retro-chic'. Which it certainly wasn't. Ted Crisp had always been like that. And any chic he had was the chic he had been born with.

'Oh, nothing,' Carole replied to his question, but Jude undermined her by saying, 'We were talking about art.'

'Art, eh?' Ted echoed. 'I heard a story once about a burglar who broke into the house of a modern artist, and while he was nicking the stuff, the owner came back. Burglar got away, but the artist just had time to do a lightning sketch of him. Took it to the police, and now they're looking for a man with nineteen purple legs and a couple of poached eggs on his head!' He let out a great guffaw. 'You have to laugh, don't you? Well, no, clearly you don't, but I do . . . otherwise it goes all quiet.'

'What a loss you were to the stand-up circuit when you gave it up,' observed Carole.

He grinned at her, knowing she was only teasing. Carole still found it incongruous that she should be sufficiently relaxed with a publican to be on teasing terms with him. Nor could she suppress a sense of daring incongruity from the knowledge that she had once had a brief affair with Ted Crisp.

He pointed down to the Cornelian Gallery invitation on their table. 'You two going to that then?'

'Yes,' said Jude.

'I don't think so,' said Carole.

'Be good eats there.'

'Oh?'

'Event being catered by none other than the Crown and Anchor, Fethering.'

'Then that's another reason for us to go,' said Jude. 'Your outside catering business seems to be taking off in a big way, Ted.'

He shrugged, always embarrassed by references to the burgeoning success of his pub. His lugubrious, laid-back style was better suited to commiserations about failure.

'But it's true,' Jude insisted.

'Well, if it is, it's nothing to do with me. Down to Zosia, all that is.'

At the mention of her name, a blonde pigtailed girl behind the bar looked up and waved at the two women. Zosia had come to Fethering from Warsaw a few years before to investigate the circumstances of her brother's death. She had stayed and her perky efficiency had totally transformed the running of the Crown and Anchor. Though Ted Crisp had been initially grudging about having a foreigner behind his bar, even he would now admit that he'd be lost without Zosia.

'Anyway, better leave you two ladies,' he announced. 'There's a queue at the bar.' There was. The pub was filling up with tourists as the April weather improved. 'If I think of any more art jokes, I'll be right back.'

'No hurry,' said Carole, teasing again.

For some minutes silence ensued, as the two women tackled their excellent seafood risotto. The Crown and Anchor's chef, Ed Pollack, really was going from strength to strength. With him running the kitchen and Zosia the bar, the reputation of the pub was spreading even beyond the boundaries of West Sussex.

Carole and Jude finished their food at the same time and both sat back, taking long swallows of Chilean Chardonnay.

'Jude, do you know Bonita Green?' asked Carole.

'A bit.'

'Does that mean that she's been to you for *healing*?' She could never quite keep a note of scepticism out of the word. To Carole's regimented mind her neighbour's practice of alternative therapies would always come under the heading of 'New Age mumbo-jumbo'.

'No,' Jude replied with a grin. 'That's not the only way I meet people, you know.'

'Of course not. Well, I met her this morning.'

'For the first time?'

'For the first time when we exchanged names, yes.'

Jude couldn't resist another grin. She never failed to be amused by her neighbour's social subterfuges.

'So what do you know about her?' Carole went on.

'Just that she's run the Cornelian Gallery for many years. I think she'd trained at the Slade a long time ago and worked full-time as an artist. At some point she got married and had a son, maybe there was another child, I'm not sure. And the husband . . . I can't remember . . . she either got divorced or was widowed and I think it was round then she started the gallery.'

'I met the son this morning. Do you know him?'

'I've met him casually.'

That was the way Jude met most people. Complete strangers found themselves suddenly in conversations with her. She was very easy to talk to, a good listener, so genuinely interested

in other people that she very rarely needed to volunteer much
information about herself. Carole Seddon felt a familiar pang
of envy. She couldn't think of any occasions in her own life
when she'd done anything *casually*.

'What do you know about him?'

'About Giles? Not a lot. Had some high-flying City job, got
made redundant a few months back. And I think his marriage
broke up round the same time. Local gossip has it that he's
moved back in with his mother on a temporary basis.'

Again Carole felt peeved that she didn't seem to hear the
same quality of local gossip as her neighbour did. But she
supposed that to access it she'd have to change the habits of
a lifetime and start talking to people she hadn't been introduced
to. The kind of people to whom she gave no more than a
'Fethering nod' on her morning walks with Gulliver.

'Where does Bonita live then?'

'In the flat over the shop.'

Carole pictured the High Street frontage of the Cornelian
Gallery in her mind's eye. 'Can't be much room in there for
two of them.'

'No, I gather it isn't an ideal arrangement.'

Carole was alert to the implication. 'You mean they don't
get on?'

'I wouldn't say that, but I can't think it's an ideal situation
for any mother in her sixties suddenly to have a son in his
thirties around all the time.' Her neighbour waited patiently,
sensing that Jude had more to tell. 'Also I gather Giles has
plans to work with Bonita in the business.'

Carole pointed to the invitation on the table. 'Hence this?'

'I'd say so, yes. Denzil Willoughby is rather different in
style from the artists Bonita usually exhibits.'

A nod from Carole, as she looked at the twisted images on
the invitation and mentally compared them to the innocuous
watercolours she had seen on display in the Cornelian Gallery.
'Well, you seem to know quite a lot about them,' she said, an
edge of sniffiness in her tone.

Jude smiled. 'I could tell you some more.'

'Oh?' Carole didn't want to sound too eager.

'There's another reason why Giles Green wants to be

down here. His new girlfriend lives near Chichester.'

'Do you know her too?'

'I've met her. Girl called Chervil. I know her sister Fennel better.'

'Chervil? Fennel? What happened? Did their parents have an accident with a spice rack?'

Jude giggled. 'I don't know. There's certainly something hippyish about them. The parents, Ned and Sheena Whittaker, demonstrate that other-worldliness which only the very rich can afford. They have this big estate near Halnaker. Butterwyke House. And they're always experimenting with the latest ecological fad. Solar panels, wind turbines, organic gardening, they've done the lot. But, as I say, they can afford it, so good luck to them.'

'Is it inherited money?' Carole was always intrigued by the very basic question of what people lived on.

'No. The Whittakers made their pile in the nineteen-nineties' dot-com boom, and were lucky enough – or possibly shrewd enough, though I think it was luck – to get out before the whole thing went belly up. The result is they've got shedloads of money.'

'And did you meet them through your healing?'

'Yes. Ned put Fennel in touch with me.'

'Ah. Right.' Carole didn't expect any more details. Jude was always very punctilious about client confidentiality. And while she continued to see Fennel Whittaker, a beautiful and talented artist with a crippling medical condition, she would never divulge the secrets of the sessions the two of them had shared in the front room of Woodside Cottage.

'So Giles Green has a thing going with this Chervil?' asked Carole.

'Yes. She used to work in the City too, but she's moved back down to Butterwyke House to help her parents in their latest business venture.'

'Which is?'

'"Glamping".'

'What on earth is "glamping" when it's at home?'

'The word's a contraction of "glamorous" and "camping".'

'There's nothing glamorous about camping,' said Carole

with a shudder. She remembered all too well the damp misery of holidays under canvas on the Isle of Wight with her parents. And equally watery experiences in France with David and Stephen, when they made yet another attempt to do things that they imagined normal families did. The awful smell of musty damp canvas came unbidden to the nose of her memory.

'Well, there's quite a vogue for it now, Carole. Wealthy City folk getting what they imagine to be a taste of country life. Totally authentic experience . . . yurts with wood-fired stoves . . . not to mention gourmet chefs and sometimes even a butler thrown in.'

That prompted a 'Huh' from Carole. Though she didn't vocalise it, another of her mother's regular sayings had come into her mind. 'More money than sense'. Amazing how many things that could be applied to in the cushioned world of West Sussex.

'Would you like to see it?' asked Jude.

'See what?'

'The glamping site at Butterwyke House.'

'Why?'

Jude shrugged. 'Interest. I'm going up there on Saturday. You're welcome to come if you want to.'

'Why are you going there?'

'Amongst the services offered to the happy glampers are a variety of alternative therapies. Sheena asked if I'd be interested in providing some of them. She's suggested the idea to Chervil. So I'm going up there to have a look round, see if it'll be suitable for me.'

'Do you need the money?' asked Carole characteristically.

Another shrug. 'One can always use a bit more money.'

This prompted another recurrent question in Carole's mind. What did Jude live on? Her lifestyle wasn't particularly lavish, and she never seemed to be hard up. But was there really that much profit to be had in the healing business? These were things that should have been asked when her neighbour first moved into Woodside Cottage. They now knew each other far too well for such basic enquiries to be made. Whenever she introduced someone new to Jude, Carole was always tempted to prime them beforehand to ask the relevant questions. But somehow it never happened.

'Anyway, why should I come with you, Jude? You're not proposing I should masquerade as an acupuncturist, are you?'

'No, I just thought you might want to have a look around.'

'But how would you explain my presence?'

'It wouldn't need any explanation. I'd just say, "Carole's a friend of mine. She wanted to have a look round, so she came along with me".'

'"Have a look round"? That sounds like snooping.'

'Only to you it does. Look, Ned and Sheena are running this glamping as a commercial business. For all they know, you're a prospective client. You might want Stephen, Gaby and Lily to stay there at some point.'

'Oh, I don't think so. Camping and Stephen never really did get along.'

'Well, as I say, if you want to come with me to Butterwyke House on Saturday, fine. If you don't, equally fine.'

It was far too casual an arrangement to match Carole's standards, typical of her friend's vagueness in social matters. If the owners of Butterwyke House had actually invited Jude to take a friend along, that would have been entirely different. Carole was rather intrigued by the suggestion, though.

'Anyway, what we need now,' announced Jude, 'is two more of those large Chilean Chardonnays.'

'Oh, I don't think we—'

'Yes, we do,' said Jude as she sailed magnificently up towards the bar.

THREE

Carole Seddon arrived at the Cornelian Gallery on the dot of ten thirty on the Thursday morning. As she prepared to leave High Tor, Gulliver had got very excited, thinking he was going to get another walk. When it was clear that wasn't on the cards, he went off and lay down reproachfully in front of the Aga. Soon be time to switch that off for the summer, thought Carole. Gulliver wouldn't like his source of warmth being removed either. His lugubrious expression seemed to anticipate future annoyances.

The gallery door had a sign on it saying 'OPEN' and it gave when Carole pushed, but there was no one inside. Everything looked exactly the same as it had on the Monday. Maybe the odd Monet pencil sharpener had been sold, but all of the framed artworks were still in place on the walls. It was a long time, Carole began to think, since business had been brisk in the Cornelian Gallery.

She looked more closely at the Piccadilly snowscape on the wall and wondered why it intrigued her. The buses struggling up Regent Street were old-fashioned double-deckers, and the clothes of the red-faced people in the streets suggested the work had been done some thirty years before. There was something unusual about the sludginess of the scene, a quality which should have been depressing, but was perversely uplifting. She noticed the painting was signed in the corner with the initials 'A.W.'

Carole waited, not quite sure what to do. Had there been a bell on the counter, she would have rung it. Someone more relaxed than Carole Seddon would probably have called out 'Hello!' or 'Anyone there?' or even 'Shop!', but she only aspired to a couple of loud throat-clearings. There was no response.

The silence wasn't total, though. Sounds emanated from the closed door at the back of the gallery. Presumably Spider was there, working longer hours than his employer. Really, Carole reasoned, it was him she needed to see rather than Bonita. Spider was the one who was actually framing her photograph, after all, so it'd make sense for her to collect it from him.

Carole moved forward and tapped on the connecting door. The sounds from the other side abruptly ceased, but there was no answering voice. She tapped again, then boldly pushed the door open and stepped forward into the framing workshop.

It was a large space, probably twice the size of the gallery in front, full of machinery most of whose functions Carole could only guess at. The one she could identify was a huge guillotine mounted at the end of a large table. Fixed to one wall was a cabinet making a grid of deep pigeon holes, containing lengths of different framings. Against another different grades and sizes of glass were stacked. Like Spider's overalls, every space was splattered with paint and glue. There was a haze of white dust and a mixture of smells, among which newly cut wood predominated.

In the centre of the workshop stood the considerable bulk of Spider. The expression on his face suggested he didn't like having his inner sanctum invaded. He said no word of greeting to the intruder.

'I'm Carole Seddon. I was in here on Monday with a photograph to be framed. Bonita said it would be ready today.' He still said nothing. 'Is it ready?'

After a silence, he conceded two words to her. 'It's ready.'

'Well, Bonita doesn't seem to be around, so if I could just pick it up and sort out what I owe you . . .'

'I don't deal with the money,' said Spider slowly. 'Or the packing. Bonita does that.'

'Oh, I don't need the photograph packed. I only live just up the High Street.'

'Bonita does the packing,' Spider repeated. 'I don't, like, want the responsibility. If something gets broken.'

'I'm sure the photograph won't get broken between here and where I live? I wonder, could I see it . . .?'

Spider gave this proposition a long moment's thought. Then, apparently unable to see any harm in obeying it, he bent down to a rack of his recent work and extracted the framed photograph.

He had done a brilliant job. Lily looked wonderful. Carole couldn't wait to have the picture hanging in pride of place on her sitting room wall.

'Oh, that's terrific! Thank you so much. Are you sure I can't just settle up with you and—'

'Bonita deals with the money,' he insisted. His tone was not aggressive, but it couldn't be argued against. Carole wondered for a moment whether it was just she who prompted this reticence in the framer. But, though normally ready to detect the smallest slight, she quickly decided that it was just Spider's manner, a form of shyness perhaps, that he would display to whoever he met.

His body language made it clear that he wanted to be alone, but Carole lingered. Rather than asking her to leave, Spider turned pointedly back to his work. He picked up two pieces of wooden frame whose ends had been cut diagonally and lined up their edges together on one the bench-mounted machines. He depressed a foot pedal and a slight thump was heard. Then he picked up the two pieces of frame, now conjoined into a right angle.

'Sorry, but what is that machine?' asked Carole.

'Underpinner,' came the minimal reply.

'And what does it do?'

'Underpins,' replied Spider with, for the first time, a slight edge to his voice. Carole continued to look expectantly at him, so he provided a reluctant explanation. 'Fixes the joint, like, with vee-nails.'

'Vee-nails?'

'Shaped like a vee.' Spider turned round the L-shaped section of the frame and showed the metallic heads of the rivets embedded deeply into the joint.

'Oh, I see.' Carole moved her hand across to the metal plate of the underpinner. 'So the vee-nails pop up through—'

'No.' Spider immobilized her hand in a tight but surprisingly gentle grip. 'Don't go near that. Could do you a nasty injury.' Then, suddenly embarrassed by the contact, he released his hold.

'What do all the other machines do?' asked Carole, emboldened by the moment of intimacy.

To her surprise, Spider readily answered her question. She decided that he was just deeply shy, but talking on the subject of his work he relaxed considerably. He was almost gleeful as he demonstrated to her the Morso mitre-cutting machine, which produced exact forty-five-degree angles at the touch of a foot pedal. He showed her the glazing gun, which used compressed air to shoot metal 'points' into the back of a frame to fix glass and mounts in place. He then moved on to the mount-cutter and the vacuum press for mounting and heat-sealing prints and photographs. And he was starting to describe the ancient and laborious process of mixing gesso and rabbit-skin glue to make mouldings for picture frames, when the demonstration was interrupted by the appearance of Bonita Green.

Immediately Spider clammed up. Again Carole did not think his silence arose from any animus against his employer. He was just embarrassed to be seen in communicative mode, and moved silently back to his work.

The gallery-owner quickly sorted out the credit card transaction to pay for Spider's work. She was delighted, she said, that Carole was so pleased with the job done and if any more framing was needed . . . well, she knew where to come.

But her customer couldn't help noticing that Bonita seemed distracted. The Juliette Greco black was a little smudged and the eyes it circled were red. The woman appeared to have been crying.

FOUR

'There's a long tradition of mankind seeking out the simple life,' said Ned Whittaker. 'One only has to think of Virgil's *Eclogues* and *Georgics*. Then of course there are English pastoral poets like James Thomson with *The Seasons*, and later the back-to-nature writings of Henry David Thoreau. I feel that what we're doing here at Butterwyke House is a part of that continuing process.'

Carole tried to avoid Jude's eye. The twitch of a grin from her neighbour might have a destructive effect on her own straight face. Neither of them had expected to hear 'glamping' described in such ambitiously literary terms.

As Ned Whittaker pontificated, he stood in the Georgian bay window of his home's magnificent sitting room. Manicured lawns stretched away to an invisible ha-ha, beyond which sheep safely grazed. From the window, nothing could be seen that did not belong to the Whittakers. And here was the owner extolling the simple life.

Only in his late forties, Ned had a slim, well-toned body. His short grey hair, rimless spectacles, checked shirt and lazy cords gave him the look of a minor academic. His voice retained the South London twang of his modest upbringing. There was about Ned Whittaker a boyishness, which he cultivated.

His wife Sheena was a plump, comfortable blonde who had spread sideways a bit. The couple had met at school, then she'd become a hairdresser and they'd married when they were both nineteen. The wedding had been quickly followed by the birth of two daughters and at that stage the family had lived in a modest rented flat. Ned had worked as a sales assistant in a gentleman's outfitters.

His success, he always maintained when asked about it, arose completely from 'being in the right place at the right time'. And that was true. A colleague at the shop where he worked had proposed to him the then novel idea of selling online, getting members of the public to order clothes through their computers. At the time Ned knew virtually nothing about IT, but his friend did, and that was what mattered. What Ned brought to the party was a very good buyer's eye for sourcing cheap garments from the Indian subcontinent.

The business had been a success right from the start. Within three years profits had increased a hundredfold. Ned and his partner didn't have a conscious strategy for the development of their company; it was just that whatever decisions they made seemed to generate more income. It was as if they could not help themselves from making money.

And in that heady time bigger rivals looked with a degree of envy at the newcomers' success. Some of the major High Street names had been slow off the mark developing their online businesses and saw the advantages of buying off the shelf a company that was already up and running. A bidding war developed. As the figures offered became more and more astronomical, Ned Whittaker had been against selling out. He didn't think they had yet reached their own full potential. But his partner, who had always been the commercial brains behind the company, said it was time to move on, and Ned graciously gave his consent.

Early in 2000 the takeover deal was made, leaving Ned Whittaker and his partner with more millions than they would ever have time to spend. Within weeks the dot-com bubble burst and one large High Street chain was left with a very expensive white elephant and thousands of angry shareholders.

The Whittakers than started spending their legitimately gotten gains. Butterwyke House was one of their first purchases. Once they were established there, they were recognized by local charities as potential sponsors and quickly joined the ranks of the Great and Good of West Sussex. They became generous benefactors to the arts and medicine. As a result, they were invited to all kinds of local events, where they met a lot of other people whose main – and in some case only – point of interest was their wealth.

Sheena, who had developed a woolly attraction towards ecological concerns, encouraged her husband to invest in a variety of worthy green projects. And Ned devoted much of his time to filling in what he regarded as the deficiencies in his education. He read widely, and if his assimilation of all he read was not always very deep, he did not let that prevent him from filling his conversation with frequently inapposite quotations and references.

Jude, who had encountered the couple a few times, knew that they could occasionally court ridicule with their unworldly innocence, but had no doubt that their hearts were in the right place.

Carole was reserving judgement. In spite of her earlier demurral, as the week had progressed there had been less and less doubt that her curiosity would prevail and she would join her neighbour on the visit to Butterwyke House.

They were in the sitting room that Saturday morning waiting for Chervil Whittaker. Ned had said that his younger daughter was really taking over the new glamping part of their activities and it would make more sense if she were to show them round the site. 'Obviously Sheena and I could do it, but it's really Chervil's baby. I think she's just out shopping or something.'

At that moment he and his wife had exchanged a look, which told Carole and Jude that, whatever was delaying their daughter, it wasn't shopping. But they didn't mind waiting. They were in a lovely room and provided with excellent coffee and shortbread biscuits. These had been produced by

an efficient young woman in a bright print dress. Though
she didn't wear uniform and was addressed by her first name,
there was no doubt that she was staff. And the immaculate
appearance of everything outside and inside suggested that
Butterwyke House had quite a lot of staff.

Conversation with the Whittakers was no strain. Sheena was
one of those people who clearly didn't like silence. She chat-
tered on about local events and the new season of plays at
Chichester Festival Theatre, to which she and Ned were
substantial donors. Her husband occasionally chipped in with
some literary reference; each time he did so Sheena smiled
with admiration. From the way they looked at each other, it
was clear that they were still very much in love, an appearance
that charmed Jude and made Carole characteristically
suspicious.

After a while they heard the sound of a car scrunching to
a halt on the gravel outside, then the front door opening. From
the hall a young woman's voice, much more expensively
educated than her parents had been, said, 'I don't care what
you do, but just don't mess things up for me.'

Another young woman's voice, similarly educated, replied,
'I have no intention of messing things up for you. What you
do is your own business.'

'If it's my business, Fen, then why the hell do you . . .?'

The first voice, perhaps becoming aware that their conversation might be overheard, dried up. Ned Whittaker cleared his
throat, ill at ease for the first time since Carole and Jude had
arrived. 'Morning, girls!' he called out. 'We're through here.'

There was a moment's silence, then in the sitting-room
doorway appeared a tall girl with long, highlighted blonde hair.
Only a slight sharpness of her features prevented her from
being beautiful. She was probably mid-twenties, slender and
gym-toned. A designer polo shirt and jeans showed her figure
off to advantage.

'Hi,' she said.

'This is Chervil.' Ned introduced Carole and Jude. The girl
gave the latter a knowing look. 'You're the one Fennel's had
sessions with?'

'That's right.'

'I was thinking Jude might be able to offer some healing services for the glampers,' said Sheena.

Her daughter had clearly not heard this idea before. She thought about it, and then said 'Cool.'

'I thought it'd make sense if you were to show Carole and Jude round the site,' said Ned.

Again Chervil thought about the suggestion before saying, 'Yes, good idea.'

Both Carole and Jude received the strong impression that the girl's parents were slightly in awe of her, slightly nervous as to how she might react to their ideas. It was only a hint in the atmosphere, an anxiety not to upset her.

Now she knew what was happening, Chervil Whittaker turned the full beam of her blue-eyed charm on to the visitors. 'I'm ready when you are. It'd be a great pleasure to show you round.'

As they went through the hall, the three of them encountered Fennel Whittaker who was texting a message into her iPhone with some vigour. Though physically very much in the same mould as her sister, Fennel had long black hair and brown eyes. She too wore jeans, with a floppy cardigan over a black T-shirt.

The moment she saw Jude, the girl abandoned her texting and went across, allowing the older woman to enfold her in her arms. Carole felt a familiar pang. She knew she would never have a tiny fraction of the instinctive empathy her neighbour had with people. Jude's very presence was a kind of therapy.

'How're you doing?' she asked.

'Oh, you know . . .' replied Fennel.

'Hang on in there.'

As the girl nodded wryly, Carole observed the effect this exchange had on her sister. There was a tug of annoyance, even petulance, at the corner of Chervil's mouth. Her expression reflected the tone of the girls' earlier overheard conversation.

'Come on, we'd better be going,' said Chervil.

As she disengaged herself from Jude, the loose sleeve of Fennel's cardigan slipped up her arm. Carole saw, on the inside of the wrist, the parallel lines of white scar tissue from old razor cuts.

FIVE

A large field had been given over to the new glamping project. Like everything else on the estate, the site was very high spec. A gate had been set into the surrounding walls, so that visitors would not have to use the imposing lion-guarded main entrance of Butterwyke House. A gravel drive led from the lane outside to a paved car park, from which York stone paths led to the individual camping units. New trees had been planted, so that in time the setting would be well shaded from the summer sun.

The accommodation came in the form of yurts, 'genuine ones imported from Mongolia,' Chervil Whittaker assured Carole and Jude. They were quite large, circular structures, squat with a conical roof shaped like a coolie hat. The framework was wooden, and its lattice wall sections and ceiling poles were covered with felt, 'made from the wool collected from the Mongolian tribesmen's flocks of sheep.' The result was a semi-permanent building, 'warm in winter and cool in summer.'

Chervil Whittaker's presentation was very slick. Whatever it was she had previously done in the City, the experience had trained her well. Only when she got on the subject of the Buddhist symbolism of the yurt did her knowledge become a little shaky. And she wouldn't have had a problem with the average potential yurt-renter. But in Jude she had encountered someone who did know quite a lot about Eastern religions.

'The crown of the yurt,' Chervil was saying, 'or *toono* in Mongolian, takes the form of the Buddhist *dharmacakra*.'

'And what's that when it's at home?' asked Carole, who didn't have much time for any religion but the Church of England (and she didn't even believe in that one). She certainly thought that Eastern religions were for their ethnic adherents superstition and for any Westerners who subscribed to them sheer pretension.

'The *dharmacakra*,' replied Chervil, 'is a circular symbol.'

'Representing what?' asked Carole.

'What do you mean?'

'A symbol can't just be a symbol, can it? It's got to be a symbol *of* something.'

'Oh.' But Chervil Whittaker was only momentarily nonplussed. 'It's a symbol of the circularity of life . . . sort of, how what comes around goes around.'

'It's not quite that, is it?' said Jude gently.

'Oh?'

'Well, Chervil, the *dharmacakra* is one of the *Ashtamagala* symbols, isn't it?'

'If you say so.'

'And it's one of the eight auspicious symbols of Tibetan Buddhism.'

'Right.'

'Really it's the Wheel of Law, representing *dharma*, the Buddha's path to enlightenment. And its symbolism as a wheel depends on the number of spokes it has. Eight spokes represent *Ariya magga*, the Noble Eightfold Path. Twelve spokes represent *Paticcasamuppada*, the Twelve Laws of dependent Origination. And twenty-four spokes—'

'Yeah, well, whatever,' said Chervil. Then a marketing thought struck her. 'Hey, Jude, maybe you could write a little piece about this stuff . . .? Then we could print them up and add them to the welcome pack we put in the yurts for our guests. We're thinking of having on the welcome packs the logo "Deeply Felt".'

'Why?' asked Carole.

'"Felt". That's what the yurts are made of – Felt.'

'Ah,' said Carole.

'But would you be up for writing something about the Buddhist bit, Jude?'

'Sure. If you think—'

'We'd pay you, obviously.'

'Oh, I don't think I'd need paying for something like that.'

'No, of course we'd pay you,' said Chervil firmly. The

Whittakers had so much money that they liked to dole it out for every service, however minor. Paying for things gave them a sense of security. 'Yes, I think that'd be good,' she went on. 'I think a lot of the people who're likely to come here will have spiritual needs . . . you know, they'll want time in the country really chilling out and getting their heads together.'

Carole could not prevent a wince of annoyance crossing her face at the mention of these two alien concepts.

'You say "people who're likely to come here",' observed Jude. 'Does that mean the site isn't open yet?'

'We open officially next week. Last month we've had friends staying, testing everything out, seeing all the facilities work as they should.'

'And what kind of facilities do you have?' asked Carole.

Chervil smiled confidently. 'I'll show you,' she said, and led them to the painted door of one of the largest yurts.

The central space was large and, though quite a lot of light came through the circular, spoked smoke vent at the crown of the structure, Chervil switched on the lights. Clearly the back-to-nature experience included electricity.

It also included a large wood-burning stove in the central area, perfectly appointed bathroom with toilet, and a fully equipped kitchen featuring a state-of-the-art gas cooker. Everything was so new and top of the range that Carole and Jude wouldn't have been surprised to see an Aga in there. On the walls hung framed pictures of various Buddhas.

'They won't be exactly slumming, will they?' said Jude.

'Certainly not. What we're offering here at Walden is pampering rather than slumming.'

'Walden?' echoed Jude.

'That's Dad's input. From something he read, I forget what it was.'

'*Walden, or Life in the Woods*,' said Carole, with something of the tone of a school swot, 'was the name of the book written by Henry David Thoreau, chronicling the two years of his life he spent practising self-sufficiency and simple living in a cottage near Walden Pond.'

'Gosh,' said Jude. 'How on earth do you know all that?'

'I found it on Wikipedia,' admitted a somewhat shamefaced

Carole. 'There was a clue in *The Times* crossword to which
the answer had to be "walken" or "walden". "Walken" didn't
make sense, so I googled "walden". Hence my exhaustive
knowledge of Henry David Thoreau.'

'Well, that would figure,' said Chervil. 'That must be why
Dad chose the name: "simple living".'

Jude looked around the lavish interior of the yurt and
refrained from commenting on the irony of those last two
words. 'So if I were to do therapy sessions, how would it
work? Would I come and visit the people who required them
in their individual yurts?'

'Oh no,' said Chervil. 'We have a special place where
we'd do the therapy sessions.' Keeping silent to maintain
the drama of her revelation, she let them out and along a
path to the largest yurt of the lot. Opening the door, she
announced with a flourish, 'This is the Spa and Treatment
Area.'

Her *coup de théâtre*, seen through a short passage, was a
complete state-of-the art gym in a circular space smaller than
the exterior circumference of the yurt. It was floored with
gleaming white ceramic tiles. Off this area, doors led to other
rooms labelled 'Plunge Pool', 'Hot Tub', 'Steam Room' and
'Sauna'. Chervil pointed to three doors without signs on them.
'Those'll be the treatment rooms.'

She opened one to reveal a pleasant space containing an
electrically adjustable massage table and other equipment.
Once again, everything was top of the range and brand new.
'Would you be able to work somewhere like this?'

'Looks fine,' said Jude.

'In our preliminary brochures we're offering "a range of
alternative therapies".'

'Like what?'

'Reiki, Hatha yoga, homeopathy, acupuncture, reflexology,
bach flower remedies.'

'I don't do any of those.'

'Oh?' Chervil Whittaker sounded severely disappointed. 'Do
you do hot stone massage?'

'No.'

'Why? Don't you believe in any of them?'

'No. I've tried some of them and I have friends who use them very successfully, but I'm not qualified in any of them.'

'Oh? Does that matter?' Chervil's priorities were evidently different from Jude's. She just wanted a range of therapies available for her potential customers, and didn't seem too bothered by their practitioners' level of competence.

'I think it does a bit,' Jude replied.

'So what therapies do you do?' the girl asked.

This was a question to which Carole had often wanted an answer, but she now knew her neighbour too well to ask it. How convenient that Chervil had done the job for her. She awaited the reply attentively.

'I'm a healer,' said Jude. 'I channel energy.'

Well, what on earth does that mean, thought Carole, who had been hoping for more specifics.

But the answer appealed to Chervil Whittaker's marketing instincts. 'I like that,' she said. '"Healing . . . Energy-channelling". They'd look really good in the brochure. What does it involve, Jude?'

'A mixture of techniques which I've worked out over the years.'

'Massage?'

'Sometimes.'

'Laying on of hands?'

'In a way.'

'Wow!' The girl was getting very excited. 'We could call it "Total Healing". Lots of people would go for that.'

'What kind of people?' asked Carole. It was another question to which, as a natural sceptic in such matters, she had wanted an answer for a long time.

'Well, people who feel kind of that they've got something wrong with them, but they don't know what it is, so they'd like to have some kind of therapy that covers everything.'

'"One size fits all"?' Jude suggested.

'Exactly that!' Chervil Whittaker was ecstatic now. 'This could be a real winner. Now, how would you rather be paid? Per session, or would you like us to put you on a retainer?'

'I'm sorry, but I haven't said that I'll do it yet.'

'But surely you will?' Something in Jude's face gave the girl pause. 'Why not? Aren't the facilities up to scratch?'

'The facilities are absolutely fine. Best I've seen for a long time. But I don't do healing as a kind of add-on leisure activity.'

'Oh?'

'I do it for people who I think need it, to help people who are genuinely suffering.'

'Some of the people who come here might be genuinely suffering.'

'And so they could have healing rather in the same way that they might have a session in the hot tub or the sauna?'

'Yes.' Chervil nodded with enthusiasm.

'Hm. I don't think that's for me, I'm afraid.'

'Why not? You'd get paid well over the odds.'

'I don't do it for the money.' That prompted a predictable snort from Carole. Jude smiled wearily at her neighbour as she tried to explain. 'Healing is a kind of gift. When I do it, it takes an enormous amount of energy out of me. And it doesn't work unless I believe totally that the person with whom I'm working is in genuine need of my services.'

'Oh.' But Chervil was only cast down for a moment. 'Well, some of the people who come here might be in genuine need of your services.'

'Yes. And when you have some that you think genuinely are, then give me a call and I'll come and make an assessment.'

'Right.' The girl still seemed upset that anyone could want to resist taking their share of the Whittaker millions. 'Are you sure you don't want us to put you on a retainer?'

'Positive.' There was a silence while Chervil seemed to turn something over in her mind. Then she said, 'So you think my sister is in genuine need?'

'What do you mean?'

'I know Fennel's been coming to you.'

'Yes.'

'And her need is genuine?'

'As opposed to what?'

'As opposed to her just play-acting, doing the *prima donna* routine, trying to monopolize our parents' attention?'

Aware of the underscoring of bitterness in the words, Jude replied gently, 'I think her need is genuine.'

'And do you think you can help her?'

'I hope so.'

'I hope so too. I've been living with her throwing hysterical fits all the time ever since I was born.'

'Well, as I say, let's hope I can help her.'

'Hm.'

Carole decided that a new direction in the conversation might be timely. 'I gather you used to work in the City, Chervil?'

'Yes.'

'But you decided to get out of the rat race?'

'A bit of that, yes. And I really got excited about this Walden project. Now my boyfriend's living down here too, so that's fine.'

'Giles Green.'

'Yes.' The girl looked curiously at Carole. 'Do you know him?'

'I've met him briefly. I was in his mother's shop; you know, the gallery.'

'Oh yes? And did she mention that I was his girlfriend?'

Carole realized she had got herself into something of a social cleft-stick. She hadn't heard about the relationship between Giles and Chervil in the Cornelian Gallery. It had been Jude who'd mentioned it. And now she was in danger of looking as if she'd been gossiping about the girl behind her back. (Which of course she had. Gossiping behind people's backs was the principal pastime of the Fethering community.)

'No, no. Bonita didn't mention it.'

'No surprise there,' said Chervil.

'Oh?'

'Bonita Green doesn't approve of my relationship with Giles.'

'Why not?'

The girl shrugged. 'I think she got on rather dangerously well with his wife. Soon to be ex-wife, I'm glad to say. Or then again, maybe she's just one of those mothers who think no girl is good enough for her son.'

*   *   *

On the way back to Fethering in her prim Renault, Carole said, 'You missed a trick there, Jude.'

'Oh?'

'Turning down that retainer Chervil was offering. It would have been very nice for you to have a regular income coming in.'

Jude sighed. 'You just don't get it, Carole, do you?'

And it was true. Carole didn't.

SIX

Neither of them had mentioned it when they met at Butterwyke House, but Fennel Whittaker had a session booked with Jude at Woodside Cottage for the Monday morning. The girl arrived on the dot of ten – she was obsessive about timekeeping – and Jude could tell from her expression and body language that her mood was bad.

But initially nothing was said beyond greetings and conventional pleasantries, as Jude uncovered the massage couch in her cluttered sitting room. The curtains, almost terracotta in colour, had been spread across the windows and the sunlight diffused through them to give the space a warm, orangey glow. Without being told, Fennel Whittaker stripped down to her underwear and, once a length of paper sheet had been unrolled for her, lay down on her front on the couch.

Jude's attitude to healing was instinctive. She adjusted her treatments according to the needs that she sensed in individual clients. Though she had trained in a variety of alternative therapies, she did not subscribe to any one to the exclusion of others. Her approach was mix and match. The important element in any healing was channelling energy. How that end was achieved varied from client to client.

With Fennel, Jude had quickly realized that they should start each session with a traditional massage, for which she rubbed a little aromatic oil on to her hands. The young woman's frame was full of tension. The gentle force of Jude's hands could ease that, and also feeling the contours of the girl's body gave an insight into what was happening in her mind.

As ever, while she massaged, Jude talked. What she said was relatively unimportant. If the client wanted to contribute to the conversation, fine. If not, equally fine. What was important was Jude's tone. Together with the magic wrought by her hands, the soft warmth of her voice helped to put the client at ease, to make them more receptive to the therapies that followed.

That morning Fennel was disinclined to talk. No problem. Jude chatted casually about the visit she and Carole had made to Butterwyke House on the Saturday. She observed, but did not comment on, a new tautness in the girl's body when mention was made of the Walden experiment. The tension increased when the name of her sister Chervil came up.

When Jude finished the massage, Fennel was lying on her back, considerably more relaxed than she had been when she entered Woodside Cottage. Jude wiped the oil off her hands with kitchen roll and said, 'Are you happy lying there or do you want to sit up?'

'Lying's cool,' said the girl drowsily.

'Did you bring some of your recent artwork?' This was a suggestion Jude had made at a previous session. Fennel Whittaker was a talented artist. She had started at St Martin's College of Art, but had been forced to give up the course halfway through her second year. The cause had been a complete mental breakdown. She had suffered two before as a teenager, but the one at college had been the most severe.

In fact, she was lucky to be alive. Living at the time in a Pimlico flat her parents had bought, Fennel had made a suicide attempt, washing a great many painkillers down with the contents of a whisky bottle. She'd also cut her wrists, but fortunately missed the arteries. It was by pure chance that Chervil had dropped into the flat, found her sister unconscious and summoned her father. The incident had been followed by six months' hospitalization for Fennel in the most expensive private clinic the Whittakers' money could buy.

She had emerged on a strong regime of antidepressants, which did seem to improve her condition . . . so long as she took them. But Fennel Whittaker was still the victim of violent mood-swings and seemed to be permanently on the edge of another complete collapse.

In her manic phases, however, she produced a lot of art and, from what Jude had seen of the stuff, it was very good art. For that reason she had suggested that Fennel should bring along some examples of her recent work to their next session, in the hope that the paintings might offer some clues as to the the causes of her depression.

'In the carrier by the sofa,' the girl replied lethargically.

Jude picked up the bag. 'Do you mind if I have a look at them?'

'Be my guest.'

She shuffled out a handful of paintings. They were water-colours that had been done on ordinary copy paper which had curled a bit as they dried. But though the medium was a subtle one, there was little restraint in the images depicted. The predominant colours were dark, deep bruise blues, slate greys interrupted by splashes of arterial blood red. So violent were the brush strokes that at first Jude thought she was looking at abstracts. But closer scrutiny revealed that the paintings were representational.

Each picture showed the body of a woman, young, shapely, but twisted with pain. Their features were contorted as they struggled against restraints of chain and leather, the red gashes of their mouths screamed in silent agony. But a defiance in their posture and expressions diluted their bleakness. There was suffering there, but also a sense of indomitability. Tormented as they were, Fennel Whittaker's women would not give up anything without a fight.

'And these are recent works?'

'Yes. All done since our last session.'

A week then. 'You've been busy.'

A shrug from the massage couch. 'When I've got ideas I work quickly.' But the way she spoke was at odds with her words. She sounded apathetic, drained, only a husk of her personality remaining after the threshing storm of creativity that had swept through her body.

'Well, they're very good,' said Jude. 'A lot of pain there.'

'Yes,' Fennel agreed listlessly.

'Don't you get a charge from knowing that you're doing good work?'

'I do while I'm actually painting. I look at it and it feels right. Every brush stroke is exactly where it should be. I feel in control. Then I look at it a couple of days later and . . .' She ran out of words.

'And what?'

'And I think it's derivative crap. I can see the style I'm imitating and I'm just deeply aware of all the other artists who have done it better over the centuries, and all the artists who're even doing it better now.'

'Have you always had that kind of reaction against your work?'

'Usually.'

'And does it ever change?'

'How do you mean?'

'Do you ever come round to thinking what you've done's rather good again? Do you recapture the feeling you had while you were actually painting it?'

Fennel Whittaker sighed. 'Has happened. There's some stuff I did during my first year at art college . . . before I . . . you know . . . I felt pleased with it . . . and one of my tutors, Ingrid, who I really rated, she thought it was great. Yes, some of that's bloody good.'

'Doesn't knowing that cheer you up?'

'No. It makes me feel worse, if anything.'

'Why?'

'Because I look back and I think: God, the girl who did that had a lot of talent! Unlike the girl who's looking back at the stuff. Whatever it was I may once have had, I think I've lost it.'

'You do know that a lot of creative artists suffer from bipolar tendencies?'

'Yes. It doesn't help much to know that, though. Doesn't stop me thinking that my work's crap . . . along with everything else in my life.'

Jude was silent for a moment, trying to decide what therapies she should use for the rest of the session. For the time being, though, she reckoned talking was doing Fennel as much good as anything else would.

'Is there anything specific that's made you feel down at the moment?'

'There's never anything specific. It's just . . . everything.'

'Are you sure about that?'

'What do you mean?'

'I know I've asked you this before, but are you sure there wasn't something in your past, something that happened that triggered the depression?'

'And as I've answered before, no. What are you hoping I'll say – that my father interfered with me when I was a child?'

'I wasn't suggesting that.'

'I know you weren't. Anyway, the answer to your question remains the same as when you last asked it. I think the depression is just something knotted into my DNA. A dodgy gene, like . . . I don't know . . . being born with red hair perhaps?'

'And there's nothing that's happened in the last few days that's got you particularly depressed?'

Fennel looked up, alert to a slight change in Jude's tone. 'What makes you say that?'

'Just when we were at Butterwyke House and you and Chervil came in, it sounded as if you'd been having a row.'

'Not a row. It's just the way sisters are, always sniping at each other.'

'When Chervil was showing us round Walden, she seemed a little bitter about you.'

'What? Complaining I was monopolizing our parents' attention?'

'Yes.'

'Huh. I don't know where she gets that from. If she genuinely thinks I'm going through what I go through simply to score points over her, then I wish she could have a couple of days of depression, so she knows what it feels like.'

'And she doesn't?'

'No. Chervil's never had a negative thought in her whole life. Eternal Bloody Pollyanna. Chervil's fine. Never been any problems with her. She's always been our parents' golden girl. Always done everything right.'

'What about relationships?'

'She's never lacked for male attention.'

'That wasn't what I asked. Do her relationships last?'

'Till she gets bored with them, yes. Chervil never risks getting hurt. When a relationship is ending, she always sees to it that she's the dumper rather than the dumpee. And she never dumps a boyfriend till she's got another one lined up. Chervil hasn't spent more than a week without a boyfriend since she was fourteen.'

'Whereas you . . .?'

The bark of cynical laughter which greeted this enquiry was more eloquent than words would have been.

'My sister's guiding principle is: love 'em and leave 'em. Chervil rather prides herself on being a *femme fatale*.'

'And what about her current relationship? With Giles Green.'

'Oh, you heard about that. She seems quite keen at the moment. Early days, though. Let's see whether he's still on the scene in a couple of months.'

Jude was interested in this display of sibling rivalry. Chervil had said it was Fennel who monopolized their parents' attention. Fennel effectively described her sister as their favourite. Something to be explored at some point, perhaps. But not in this session, Jude decided.

'Going back to your relationships, Fennel . . .?'

'Huh.' The girl let out a long, cynical sigh. 'How many ways do you know of saying the word "disaster"?'

When she had first got her laptop and started exploring its capacities, Carole Seddon had been very sniffy about Google. Sniffiness was in fact her default reaction to anything new. And there didn't seem something quite natural about being able to access information so easily. How much more civilized it was to consult her shelf of reference books when there was something she needed to check for *The Times* crossword. Everything she needed was there between hard covers: *The Shorter Oxford English Dictionary, Roget's Thesaurus, Chambers' Biographical Dictionary, The Oxford Companion to English Literature* and *Brewer's Dictionary of Phrase and Fable*. References to things she couldn't find in those volumes didn't deserve to be in any self-respecting crossword.

But the appeal of Google was insidious. And the speed with which it delivered information was undeniably impressive. Increasingly Carole was seduced by the simplicity of keying a word into a search engine rather than flicking back and forth through the pages of a book. Soon she was hooked. If anyone had asked her about her addiction (which nobody did), she would have justified it on the grounds that, now she had a grandchild, it was important to keep up with developments in information technology. But she knew that the excuse was really mere casuistry.

In fact Carole was spending more and more time online. When checking facts, one thing did so easily lead to another. The speed with which data could be sorted appealed to her filing cabinet mind. There seemed to be websites out there to deal with any query one might have. And though she kept piously reminding herself that the answers provided might not always be verifiably correct, the process remained intriguing.

Carole even – and this was something she would not have admitted under torture – used an online crossword dictionary to solve stubbornly intransigent clues in *The Times* crossword. You just had to fill in the letters you had got, put in full stops for the missing letters and, within seconds, all the words that fitted the sequence would appear. Using the device went against the very spirit of cruciverbalism, but then again it was seductively convenient.

There was no surprise, then, that on the Thursday, the day before the Cornelian Gallery's Private View, Carole Seddon found herself googling Denzil Willoughby.

Considering that she had never even heard his name a fortnight before, he had a remarkably large presence on the Internet. Spoilt for choice, she decided to start with his official website.

On occasion in her life Carole had begun sentences with the words 'Now I'm as broad-minded as the next person . . .' And in Fethering that was probably true. Most residents of the village shared a comparable breadth of mind. But by the standards of the world at large, their gauge was not very broad.

And certainly not broad enough to encompass some of the images on Denzil Willoughby's website.

Now Carole knew that the urges to reproduce and defecate were essential features of the human condition, but she'd never thought that either should have attention drawn to it. And certainly not in the flamboyant way that the artist highlighted them. Not only did he commit the cardinal sin of 'showing off', he compounded the felony by being vulgar.

Carole wondered whether Fethering was ready for Denzil Willoughby.

SEVEN

'The history of art is the history of great talents being discovered in the most unlikely and humble places. And places don't come much more unlikely or humbler than the Cornelian Gallery in Fethering.'

A few people at the Private View found Giles Green's words amusing. Denzil Willoughby certainly did. The permanent sneer on his face transmuted effortlessly into a sneering smile. Gray Czesky, the ageing *enfant terrible* of nearby Smalting, also thought the remark warranted a snigger. So did Chervil Whittaker. From the adoring way she looked at Giles and drank in his words, every one of them was wonderful to her ears.

Her sister did not look as if she would ever be amused by anything, least of all if it came from Giles Green. Jude looked anxiously across the room, sensing Fennel's mood and wishing it could be appropriate just to go across and enfold the girl in her comforting arms. But she knew that wasn't the sort of thing to do at a Private View. She was also worried by the grim determination with which Fennel was drinking. Jude knew what medication the girl was on and she knew it didn't mix well with alcohol. That was, assuming Fennel was taking her medication. If she wasn't, the alcohol still wasn't going to improve her mood.

Ned and Sheena Whittaker seemed unaware of what their older daughter was doing. They had arrived separately – Fennel in a Mini, her parents in a Mercedes – but had hardly even greeted each other. Perhaps they'd had some kind of row, but Jude thought it more likely that Ned and Sheena just felt relaxed, their anxiety about their elder daughter's mental health allayed by being at a public event.

They laughed at Giles Green's words, but it was an uneasy laughter. Jude suddenly realized that the older Whittakers were in fact very shy. Their huge wealth had moved them into circles where they would never have dreamed of going, but they had never lost the gaucherie of their ordinariness. Social events, even as low-key as a Private View at the Cornelian Gallery, were still a strain for them.

The person who was disliking Giles's remarks most seemed to be his mother. Bonita Green didn't find the disparagement of her gallery at all funny. She had put a lot of work into building up her business and many of the people at the Private View were from her carefully nurtured local contacts. She didn't want them to hear the kind of things that her son was saying. Alienating her client base could undo the efforts of many years.

There was a woman standing next to Bonita whom Carole had been introduced to earlier – to her surprise – as Giles Green's wife, Nikki. She was around forty, tall and slender, with blonde highlights in her hair. In fact, she looked strikingly like a fifteen-year-older version of Chervil Whittaker. Had Giles Green, like so many men, just replaced his spouse with a newer model?

'Soon to be ex-wife', Chervil had said, but the woman's mother-in-law made no mention of any rift in the marriage when making the introduction. Carole doubted whether Nikki Green's invitation to the Private View had come from her husband. Had Bonita just been stirring things?

And yet there seemed to be no awkwardness between husband and wife, even though Chervil was all over Giles. Maybe they were one of those couples, which Carole read about but rarely encountered, who were genuinely 'grown-up' about the failure of their marriage.

Like his mother, few of the local contingent at the Private View were very amused by Giles's words. It was all right for them to criticize Fethering – indeed, doing so was one of their most popular pastimes – but woe betide the outsider who voiced the tiniest cavil about the place.

Nor did the locals seem very appreciative of the art on display. As Carole knew from his website, Denzil Willoughby's approach to his work was confrontational. Though too young – and probably not talented enough – to feature in the famous 1997 *Sensation* exhibition, the artist followed very firmly in the grubby footprints of Damien Hirst and Tracy Emin. For Willoughby, all art produced before his own was cosy and bourgeois. In the personal statement on his website he derided the 'mere representational skills' of the Old Masters, the 'shallowness' of the Impressionists and the 'glib simplicity' of most contemporary art.

For the Private View – and perhaps for the duration of the exhibition – all of Bonita Green's display tables had been moved through to Spider's workshop. Though the Christmas trees of framing samples kept their place on the back wall, the other paintings, the Gray Czeskys and so on, had given way to Denzil Willoughbys. The only one left on display, Carole noticed with interest, was the slushy snowscape of Piccadilly Circus. She pointed out the oddity to Jude, who was also impressed by the picture's quality.

The Private View's main exhibit, which took over much of the central space in the Cornelian Gallery, was what looked like a real medieval cannon on a wooden stand. Every surface of the metal had been plastered over with newspaper photographs of black teenagers. These, according to the catalogue presented to everyone at the Private View, had all been victims of gun crime in English cities. The piece was called *Bullet-In #7*.

When she and Jude had arrived for the Private View – she would have never entered on her own – Carole had looked at the decorated cannon in quiet disbelief. Then she had read in the catalogue that the work 'reflected the fragmentation of a disjointed society in which the *machismo* of disaffected youth bigs up the potent phallicism of firearms.' When she saw the

price being asked for the work on the sheet that they had been
given with their catalogues, she assumed the wrong number
of noughts had been printed.

After the first shock, Carole had murmured to Jude, 'I can't
somehow see that in my front room, can you?'

The neighbour had giggled. The thought of *Bullet-In #7* in
any Fethering front room was unlikely. The idea of it amidst
the paranoid neatness of High Tor attained new levels of
incongruity.

'Still,' Carole went on, 'full marks for effort, I suppose.
Just building a cannon that size must've taken hours.'

'I don't think so.' Before Carole could stop her, Jude had
rapped against the artwork with her knuckles and been
rewarded by a hollow sound. 'Fibreglass. He bought it
ready-made.'

'But where would you buy a ready-made fibreglass cannon?'

'Prop-maker. Lots of stuff like that gets built for television
and movies.'

'So if Denzil Willoughby didn't even make the cannon,
where is the art in what he's done? He's just bought something
and put it on show with his name attached.'

'Ah, no. When he bought it, the cannon didn't have photos
of murdered black kids on it.'

'And is that what makes it a work of art?'

'Of course it is. Carole, you might come across a fibreglass
model of a medieval cannon . . .'

'It doesn't happen very often to me in Fethering,' said her
neighbour sniffily.

'No, but if you were to come across one, then you might say
to yourself, "Oh, look, there's a fibreglass model of a medieval
cannon" and think no more about it. You wouldn't have the
vision to cover it with pictures of teenage victims of gun crime.'

'No, I certainly wouldn't.'

'But Denzil Willoughby did have that vision. Or "concept",
if you prefer.'

'So rubbish like this is "conceptual art", is it?'

'I guess so. Denzil Willoughby thought of the concept of
juxtaposing a medieval cannon with images of murdered black
teenagers.'

'And is *that* what makes it a work of art?' Carole repeated.

'I'm sure he'd say it was.'

'But what do you think?'

Jude shrugged. 'If you can say something's a work of art, and get people to hand over money to possess it as a work of art . . . then I guess it's a work of art.'

'Huh. The day you catch me frittering my money away on something like that, Jude, you have my full permission to have me certified.'

'If that moment ever comes, I can assure you I will,' said Jude with a twinkle. She looked round at the other exhibits, most of which were actually in frames and hanging from the gallery's walls. 'Maybe you could see some of these fitting in better in High Tor . . .?'

She had expected this would prompt another 'Huh', and she wasn't disappointed. The actual frames were the only parts of Denzil Willoughby's smaller works that Fethering residents would have recognized as art. The contents of those frames were startling and ugly. In keeping with the *GUN CULTURE* theme, the images were composed of weaponry parts; a rifle bolt here, a trigger there, the butt of a pistol, a sawn-off shotgun barrel. Mixed with these oddments of metal were more photographs, whose highly coloured violence was too graphic ever to have appeared in newspapers. And the components within the frames were set on misshapen blocks of shiny blood red, a brain-like porridgy white and a brown that reminded Carole of things she didn't want to think about too deeply.

Needless to say, these creations all had titles like *Butt-Naked #3*, *Chamber Pot-Shot #12* and *Telescopic Site-Specific #9*. And the prices on the printed sheet were no less ridiculous than the one quoted for *Bullet-In #7*.

Yet, in his welcome to the Cornelian Gallery Private View, Giles Green kept harping on about the works' 'investment value'. Carole Seddon was beginning to think that she had somehow stepped into a parallel universe.

When Giles finished his introduction, the applause he received was surprisingly warm. Though the denizens of Fethering had resented his disparagement of their village, they were basically all well-brought-up middle-class people. And

Bonita Green was, after all, one of their own. It wouldn't do
to appear stand-offish towards her son. Also, the wine and
very good nibbles catered by the Crown and Anchor were free.
Common politeness in Fethering dictated that the mouths of
gift horses were never to be examined too closely.

Giles Green raised his hands to quell the applause. 'Anyway,
you haven't come here this evening to listen to me. I
know you'd much rather hear from the creative genius whose
stimulating and challenging work is all around us here at the
Cornelian Gallery – Denzil Willoughby!'

Though Giles was smartly dressed in one of his City suits,
the artist looked, to Carole Seddon's eyes, extremely scruffy.
Maybe it went against the creed of his calling, but she thought
he could have made a bit of an effort.

Denzil Willoughby was probably fortyish, the same kind of
age as Giles Green, though it was hard to tell. He wore a large
knitted woollen hat, which even Carole knew would be described
as Rastafarian. From the back of it hung down some strands
of beige dreadlocks, looking like greasy string from an abandoned parcel. Now, Carole Seddon had never been a great fan
of dreadlocks, but if the style was worn by people of Afro-
Caribbean background, then fine, that was part of their cultural
heritage. Dreadlocks, however, on white Englishmen looked
to her ridiculous, ugly and unhygienic. She thanked the Lord
that her son had never gone through a rebellious phase during
which he had sported dreadlocks. Though when she came to
think about it, she realized that Stephen had never gone through
a rebellious phase sporting anything.

Completing his 'artist look', Denzil Willoughby wore a
plaid work shirt over a sludge-coloured T-shirt, frayed jeans
and scuffed cowboy boots whose disproportionately long toes
curled upwards. He spoke in a kind of slack drawl, which did
not completely disguise his public-school-educated accent.

'I'm not going to say much,' he said, 'because most talk
about art is crap, and particularly when the person talking about
it is the artist. Any statements that need to be made are made
by my work. If you look at my work and get it, that's cool.
If you don't get it, tough shit. Whatever you do, don't ask me
to explain it to you. The world out there's a shit-hole, and art

can't duck that. I don't duck it. I confront it, and my art is the expression of that confrontation. And if people don't like my work, I'm not bothered. It's just what I do.'

He paused and reached into the top pocket of his shirt to produce a crumpled pack of cigarettes and a green plastic lighter. Before the horrified eyes of Fethering, he proceeded, in a leisurely fashion, to light up.

'I'm sorry,' Bonita Green could not help herself from saying, 'but I'm afraid this is a non-smoking venue.'

'Sure,' said Denzil Willoughby, taking a long drag from his cigarette. 'Everywhere's a non-smoking venue these days.'

'But that means,' the gallery-owner insisted, 'that you shouldn't smoke in here.'

'No,' countered the dreadlocked one. 'It means that ordinary people shouldn't smoke in here. One of the important things that anyone with any knowledge of the art world will tell you is that there are no rules for artists.'

'Yes, there are!' The voice that took issue with him was full of fury and alcohol. 'Calling yourself an artist doesn't mean you can evade all human responsibilities.'

The voice was Fennel Whittaker's. Jude looked across anxiously at the girl as she swayed closer to Denzil Willoughby. Carole saw the quick worried look exchanged between Fennel's parents, and the expression of pure fury on the face of her sister Chervil.

'There's no responsibility in telling someone you love them, is there?' the drunken girl went on. 'We've all done that in our time, haven't we? We splash the word "love" around like it was water, don't we? On tap, easily available, doesn't cost anything. Doesn't do anyone any harm. We've all told people we loved them when we didn't, thought we loved people, then found out we were wrong. We've all—'

'Shut up, Fen!' It was Chervil, who had suddenly interposed herself between her sister and the bemused artist.

'No, I won't shut up!'

Like the tongue of a snake, Fennel's hand leapt out and slapped hard across Chervil's face. The younger sister recoiled, started to weep hysterically and backed off into the safety of Giles Green's arms.

This was the signal for Ned and Sheena Whittaker, no longer able to pretend they had nothing to do with her, to move towards their daughter. Jude also went to offer comfort, but Fennel burst free of their restraining hands to continue her tirade. And, though she was undoubtedly very drunk, there was nothing maudlin or pathetic about her. She was in fact magnificent in her anger.

'You used me, Denzil! Pretended you cared about me, pretended you rated my painting, when the only thing that mattered to you was my money. And when I stopped handing that out, you dumped me. By text!

'Well, don't worry. I'll get my revenge on you! The sensitive bloody artist, too caught up in his own creativity to get involved in real life . . . that's how you've always presented yourself, haven't you? Avoid emotional entanglements, so that you can concentrate on your art – huh? Well, you can't avoid everything. People are real! Life's real! Death's real! And anyone who causes the death of another person is responsible for that death. Guilt doesn't go away. Oh, sometimes the guilty person doesn't get branded as guilty in a court of law, but they still know what they've done. And the guilt for causing someone's death will never be forgotten. It will eat away at the perpetrator.' She looked round the gallery dramatically, as if challenging everyone present. 'You may think you have a secret and it's safe inside you. But no, that secret is corrosive and ultimately it will destroy you. The person who has destroyed someone's life will have to live with that fact forever. He or she will never get away with it, never get off scot-free. As they have ruined a life, so will their own life be ruined!'

Having delivered this almost Old Testament curse, the girl moved very close to the artist and spat the next words out at him.

'You know what you are, Denzil Willoughby? You're just like your art – full of shit!'

And, with that parting shot, Fennel Whittaker picked up an almost full bottle of red wine and stormed out of the Cornelian Gallery.

EIGHT

No one could completely ignore what had happened, but the outburst did not put an end to the Private View. The speeches by Giles Green and Denzil Willoughby had been a kind of natural break in the proceedings, and as soon as Fennel was out of the gallery, Zosia and her staff moved into assiduous glass-filling and canapé-offering mode.

There were some murmured comments among the Fethering invitees, but few of them had met the Whittaker family before. The general opinion was that they'd just witnessed the effects of too much alcohol. And, although it would have been embarrassing had the incident involved anyone they knew, the moment of confrontation had actually been quite exciting. Some of the locals, unsure what to expect from the art world, even thought that the scene had perhaps been part of the exhibition. Since the Tate Gallery's purchase in the 1970s of 'a pile of bricks', Fethering folk affected a sophistication incapable of being surprised by anything that went under the name of 'modern art'. After all, you never knew.

Denzil Willoughby himself seemed the least fazed of anyone there. In spite of what Fennel had said about guilt, he appeared to be immune to it. As soon as she had left, he had turned back to a group of younger people whom no one from Fethering recognized, but whom they had already marked down, from their flamboyant manners and clothing, as the 'art college crowd'. On their fringes, trying to look part of the group, lingered Gray Czesky, with his dumpy *hausfrau* wife, Helga, in tow.

Carole Seddon accepted a top-up of her glass from one of Zosia's helpers. She was glad they were serving the Chilean Chardonnay that she particularly liked from the Crown and Anchor's wine list. And it was refreshing not to have to worry about driving. Only a three-minute walk from the Cornelian Gallery back to High Tor.

'Good evening.'

She turned and was surprised to see that the words had come from Spider. Given the framer's shyness, she hadn't expected him to be at the Private View. In fact, she thought he had only just put in an appearance. Surely she would have spotted his bulk and distinctive hairstyle if he'd been there earlier. Perhaps he'd been lurking in his workshop.

'Hello,' she said.

'I recognized you. You came to get that photo framed.'

'Yes. Of course I remember . . . Spider, wasn't it?'

'That's right. Spider.'

'I'm Carole.'

'Carole. Right.'

There was a silence. The conversational sally seemed to have exhausted him. From across the room Ned Whittaker saw Spider and gave him a wave of recognition.

'You know the Whittakers?' asked Carole.

'Yes, I've been over Butterwyke House. Delivered some stuff they'd wanted framing. Posters of Eastern geezers.'

'Buddhas,' said Carole, remembering the pictures she and Jude had seen inside the yurt Chervil had shown to them the previous Saturday.

'I don't know about that,' said Spider.

'Did you deliver them to Butterwyke House?'

'No. To some place in the grounds with lots of, like, huts.'

'Yurts.'

'I beg your pardon?'

'The place is called Walden.'

'I don't know about that,' said Spider again. 'They gave me a full guided tour of the whole place, but I didn't take it all in.'

Once more their conversation was becalmed. Carole racked her brains for something to say, finally coming up with, 'Did you do any of the framing for this evening?'

It took him a moment or two to understand her question. 'Oh, you mean, like, for the exhibition?'

'Yes.'

'No. I frame pictures, prints, photographs. I wouldn't touch garbage like this.'

Carole grinned. 'I'm afraid I agree. Denzil Willoughby isn't my cup of tea either.'

'It's rubbish, that's what it is, just rubbish.' He leant forward, overwhelming her by his proximity. 'If Giles brings in more rubbish like this,' he went on earnestly, 'the Cornelian Gallery will be, like, closed within three months. And what's going to happen to Bonita then?'

What's going to happen to you then? Would it be easy to find another job as a picture-framer? Carole's thoughts were instinctive, but she didn't voice them.

'I think Giles bullies her,' Spider confided. 'She can't stand up to him. Bonita never wanted this exhibition, but Giles bullied her into having it. Then he insisted on it being on a Friday, and Friday's, like, Bonita's day off, her special day when she goes to London. She never misses that, but Giles just doesn't listen to her. He needs someone to tell him to, like, stop meddling in his mother's affairs.'

'That someone being you maybe?'

'I might at that,' Spider replied, and then looked almost embarrassed at having said so much. Big speeches didn't come naturally to him.

At that moment Ted Crisp lumbered up to join them. Carole introduced the two men, who to her surprise seemed instantly to get on and start talking. Or, that is to say, Ted started telling his stock of old jokes and Spider seemed more than happy to listen to them. Carole Seddon would never understand masculine conversation. She slipped away unnoticed into the throng.

In the confusion at the end of Fennel Whittaker's tirade, no one had noticed that Jude had been one of the few people who left the Cornelian Gallery. Outside the warmth held the promise of summer evenings not too far ahead.

While the other departing guests went on their way, Jude lingered, looking along the line of shops for Fennel. But in vain. There was no sign of the girl. For a moment Jude was about to go round the back of the parade, suspecting that Fennel might have taken her sorrows down to the beach. But then she noticed some movement from inside a Mini parked along the road.

She moved towards it. In the passenger seat sat Fennel Whittaker, the bottle of red wine tipped up, pouring its contents into her mouth. When Jude tapped on the driver's side window, the girl appeared not to hear her. She tried the door handle, but it was locked.

That sound made Fennel Whittaker look towards her visitor. After a moment's hesitation, she clicked a button which released the central locking. Jude opened the door and slipped into the driver's seat.

'Didn't realize it was you, Jude. Thought it was my parents. Haven't got the energy to have another boring heart-to-heart with them.'

Though the girl was undoubtedly very drunk, she was still in control. Her words were not slurred, just a bit faster and louder than normal.

'So you had a relationship with Denzil Willoughby?' asked Jude.

'Yes. Dreadful word that, isn't it, "relationship"? Sounds like a purely business arrangement. Some bank managers these days are called "Relationship Managers". Did you know that? I think the word should be kept for people like them, to refer to professional dealings, not to cover all the messy business of living with someone and having sex and making plans and being disappointed. There ought to be another word for that.'

'Was your . . . whatever this new word is . . . with Denzil Willoughby particularly messy?'

'I don't think *particularly* messy. They all are, aren't they? At least all of mine have been. What about you, Jude? Have you had a lot of messy ones?'

'My fair share, I'd say.'

'Well, I think I've had more than my fair share.' Fennel Whittaker let out a bitter laugh. 'Though I don't think "fairness" really comes into it. And to be *fair* to the men who've had *relationships* with me, I don't think it can have been easy for them. Never knowing from one minute to the next what person, what version of me, was going to come through the door.'

'I've had depressive friends,' said Jude gently, 'who've said that the comfort of having an ongoing relationship is that you've got someone who knows you're the same person, whatever mood you're in.'

'Well, your friends have been luckier than I have!' Fennel's anger was less as she went on. 'Men are always making jokes about women's moodiness, uncomfortable jokes about menstrual cycles, but in my experience the women I know have been models of consistency compared to the men. Mind you, any man who takes me on gets a bellyful of moodiness.' A wistfulness crept into her tone. 'That's why I got so excited when I met Denzil. At first he seemed to understand my personality, even see virtues in it. He said that all great artists are volatile, that the volatility is an essential ingredient in the art. He was very understanding.'

'From what I saw of him this evening he didn't seem very understanding.'

'No, Jude. I'm afraid tonight you saw the real Denzil Willoughby – totally selfish. But I was fooled by him for quite a long time. And he can be surprisingly gentle at times. Oh, I know, you always read in the paper about these women who let men suck them dry financially and, generally speaking, you think, "Stupid bitch, why did she let herself be taken for a ride like that?" I've been through it, though. I know how credulous you can be when you think the person conning you is offering *lurve*.' Her jokey emphasis on the word didn't disguise the pain she was feeling. 'But now,' she said, 'I feel better for denouncing the bastard in public.' And she took a celebratory swig from her bottle.

'Good,' said Jude. 'Promise me one thing, Fennel.'

'What?'

'That you won't attempt to drive home in this state.'

'But I'm perfectly capable of driving home,' Fennel replied with the unshakeable confidence of the very drunk. 'If anything, my faculties are sharper than usual. I feel very in control.'

'How you feel and how you actually are may be two very different things.'

'Oh, come on, Jude. You're the last person I would have thought of as a party-pooper.'

'Well, if that's what you want to call it, on this occasion that's the role I'm going to take. It would be a terrible waste if you wrapped this Mini round a tree somewhere between here and Chichester.'

There was a silence as Fennel digested this thought. Then
she said, 'Yes, it would be a terrible waste.'

'So you're not at the moment feeling suicidal?'

'God, no. Oh, I know I have done at times, but I'm putting
that behind me. Now I've expiated the curse of the extremely
unlovely Denzil Willoughby, I very much want to continue
living.'

This positive manner was good in one way, but it also
sounded alarm bells for Jude. She had treated a lot of bipolar
clients, and she knew the dangers of the low that could follow
an ecstatic high.

'Are you taking your medication?' she asked.

'Yes. I'm being a good girl. And I know it says on the
packet you should try not to drink while you're on it, but what
the hell? Do you know anyone who takes seriously that thing
about "avoiding alcohol" when you're on medication – even
antibiotics?'

Jude was forced to admit she knew very few people who
ticked that particular box. 'I think we should get you home,'
she said.

'How?' asked Fennel. 'You say you're not going to allow
me to drive. I don't want to get a lift with my parents – and
all the sanctimonious ticking-off that will involve. Or with
Chervil, come to that . . . though I doubt if she'll be coming
home. No doubt spending the night here with *lover-boy*.' She
infused the word with an infinity of contempt.

'I'll drive you home,' said Jude.

'I didn't know you could drive.'

'Why shouldn't I be able to?'

'Well, you haven't got a car.'

'I haven't got a swimming pool, but that doesn't mean I
can't swim.'

Carole had noticed Jude's absence fairly soon after she'd left.
Her first instinct, to hurry out after her, she curbed. How
embarrassing it would be, she thought, if she left the Cornelian
Gallery and found Jude outside with some man draped around
her. Carole knew that her neighbour's sex life had been much
more varied and adventurous than her own, but in her mind

she did sometimes overestimate Jude's powers as a man-
magnet. Still, having witnessed a New Year's Eve party that
had led to a one-night stand, she wouldn't put anything past
her.

It wasn't as if Jude was dependent on Carole for transport
that evening, as had sometimes been the case. They were both
within a short walk of their homes. And they weren't joined
at the hip, for heaven's sake, Carole told herself. They were
both grown-up women, capable of making their own decisions
and deciding the right moment to leave a Private View. But
she couldn't stop feeling that Jude's departing without telling
her was a slight – a slight slight perhaps, but still a slight.

'We meet again.'

She turned at the sound of a hesitant voice and saw that
Ned and Sheena Whittaker had joined her. 'Yes. Nice to see
you.'

Ned raised his glass. 'Very acceptable red wine. An
Argentinian Malbec. In fact we drink quite a lot of this at
home.'

'The Crown and Anchor has a very good wine list.'

He looked puzzled so Carole elucidated. 'This is being
catered by the Crown and Anchor pub, here in Fethering.'

'Ah.'

'How's the glamping going?'

'We don't officially open till tomorrow evening,' replied
Sheena. 'First guests are supposed to be arriving about four,
I think.' She giggled nervously. 'Thank goodness Chervil's in
charge. I'd be sweating cobs if it was me.'

'You'd do it fine, love,' said her husband. But his reassurance sounded automatic, not convinced that she would.

Carole, whose antennae were very sensitive to deficiencies
in the self-esteem department, was once again struck by the
Whittakers' insecurity. All that money and they never seemed
quite at ease, always pretending to be people they weren't.

'Anyway,' Ned went on, 'Walden's Chervil's baby, so you
don't have to worry.'

'Yes, but suppose she was away one night and you weren't
there either and someone from the site came up to the big
house wanting me to sort something out for them . . .?'

'It won't happen, love,' he said, with a new harshness in his voice, and Carole realized that this was the type of argument they had had time and time again in the course of their marriage. She wondered what level of resentment Ned felt for his wife's pussy-footedness.

'Anyway, Carole,' Ned went on, 'it wasn't Chervil I wanted to talk about. I wanted to apologize for her sister's behaviour.'

'Oh, I didn't really notice it,' Carole responded fatuously.

'The fact is . . .' A look was exchanged between husband and wife. Sheena was clearly urging Ned to stop, but he still proceeded. 'The fact is that Fennel does have some mental health issues . . .'

'I had heard that, yes.'

'. . . and when she has too much to drink, she does things . . . well, you've seen what she does.'

'Yes. Sounded like it was something she wanted to get off her chest.'

'Mm.'

'Had she been with Denzil Willoughby for a long time?' Normally, Carole wouldn't have asked such a question while its subject was still in the room, but the hubbub of conversation was so loud that she didn't worry about being overheard.

'We didn't know she had been,' replied Sheena, rather bleakly.

'Fennel tends to play things rather close to her chest,' Ned added. 'Particularly when it comes to her love life.'

'We kind of knew there was someone in her life, and from things she said, we thought it might be someone in the art world. But no names.'

'Does she live with you down here?'

The Whittakers exchanged another look before Ned replied, 'Not all the time. Mostly she lives in a flat we've got in Pimlico, but . . .'

He ran out of words and his wife filled the gap for him. 'There are times when she needs to be with us. Not that we are particularly happy about that.'

'Nor's she, to be fair, Sheena.'

'No, I suppose she isn't,' his wife conceded.

'It's just –' Ned shrugged – 'a difficult situation.'

'Is she under proper medical supervision?' asked Carole. The question, with its implication that there also existed *im*proper medical supervision from people like healers, was not one she would have asked had Jude been present.

Above his glasses Ned Whittaker's brows were raised heavenwards. 'We've tried everything with Fennel. Paid for the best treatment there is available, right from the moment when she first . . . became ill. Everything seems to work for a while, but then . . .'

This time a look from his wife seemed to stop him from saying more. Carole wished she could read the couple's private semaphore. She got the feeling the Whittakers didn't see eye to eye over the treatment for their daughter's condition. Maybe one of them sincerely believed that Fennel could get better and the other was less optimistic. But Carole couldn't work out which of them took which position.

Further conversation was prevented by a sudden burst of shouting from the other side of the gallery.

'How dare you say that! My artistic vision is at least as valid as yours is!'

The shouter was, perhaps inevitably, Gray Czesky. Carole should have remembered from their previous encounters how susceptible the painter was to the booze. From the security of his expensive seafront house in Smalting and the enduring safety-net of his wife's private income, Gray Czesky loved presenting the image of the volatile, unconventional artist. Some local people might accept his work at his own evaluation of it, but clearly Denzil Willoughby had different views.

'How can you call that art?' he cried, pointing with derision at the framed watercolour of Fethering Beach that Czesky was holding. 'A photograph'd be better than that. It's just a representation of something you see in front of you. You haven't added anything to what a photographer would produce, just made a considerably less accurate picture of some bloody beach!'

There was an indrawing of breath from the locals. Though they had *carte blanche* to moan about the oily fragments of plastic that piled up there, the dog messes and illegal barbecues, they didn't like outsiders criticizing Fethering Beach.

'There is no bloody artistic vision there,' Denzil Willoughby continued.

'Of course there is!' Both men were now very drunk and squaring up to each other, as if about to start throwing punches. 'What you see when you look at a Gray Czesky watercolour may look like an innocuous, innocent image, but there's a lot of subtext there. There's violence, there's political dissent in there, if you only have the perception to see it.'

'Crap!' Denzil Willoughby countered. 'I've got more political dissent in the fingernail of my little finger than you have in your entire bloody *oeuvre*!'

The denizens of Fethering watched these exchanges with the concentration they would apply to a Wimbledon final. Maybe this really was what happened at every Private View. They felt excited to be part of the action.

'So that's what you think, is it?' Gray Czesky spat out the words.

'Yes, that's what I bloody think. And if you want to make something of it—'

'Oh, for Christ's sake, will you all shut up!'

The words were spoken in a shriek, and it took a moment before the spectators could believe that they had issued from the lips of Bonita Green. They turned in amazement towards the diminutive figure of the gallery-owner as she went on, 'This entire evening has been ruined! Probably the Cornelian Gallery has been ruined by all this shouting and insults and accusations.'

She moved towards the back of the shop with considerable dignity. 'I am going upstairs to my flat. And when I come down here tomorrow morning, Giles, I am relying on you to have all the rubbish in here cleared out.'

'Just a minute,' said Denzil, cheated for the moment of one fight but eager to find another. 'When you use the word "rubbish", do you—'

'Yes, Mr Willoughby,' said Bonita Green rather magnificently as she left the room, 'I do include your work.'

NINE

'I think we should go glamping,' Fennel Whittaker announced, as Jude brought the Mini to a neat halt on the gravel in front of Butterwyke House.

'I think we should get you to bed,' said Jude, trying not to sound too much like a nanny.

'Fine, but why not to bed in a yurt?'

'Well . . .'

'Go on. I want to.' It was the urgent pleading of a small child.

'But Walden opens tomorrow.' Jude looked at the girl shrewdly. 'This isn't a plan to mess up Chervil's big day, is it?'

'No, of course it isn't. I wouldn't do anything like that. I've got nothing against Chervil.'

'You seemed to have back at the Private View.'

'What? When I . . .' Her hand shot up to her mouth in consternation. 'Oh my God! Did I actually slap her?'

'Yes, you did. Surely you remember?'

'It's all a bit of a haze. I was so determined to be articulate in what I wanted to say to Denzil that I didn't notice much else that was going on.'

'You had also had far too much to drink,' said Jude severely.

'Yes, you're right. I had,' agreed Fennel, for a moment a contrite schoolgirl. But the mood didn't last for long. Waving the nearly empty bottle she had brought from the Cornelian Gallery, she cried, 'And now I need some more!' She opened the passenger door and tottered out on to the gravel. 'I'll just go and raid Daddy's wine cellar . . . and then . . . I'll go and sleep in a yurt!'

Jude was for a moment uncertain what to do. She knew that, in her current mood, Fennel would not take kindly to being coerced into bed. But she also knew the fragility of the girl's temperament. The high Fennel was on was a big one

and when she came down from it she was going to have a
nasty hangover, both alcoholic and emotional.

Jude decided the best thing she could do was to stay with
the girl, try to be there to help when the mood changed, as it
inevitably would. And if that meant spending a night in a yurt
. . . well, she'd never spent a night in a yurt before and Jude
was always up for new experiences. She hadn't got transport
back to Fethering, anyway.

She took out her mobile to tell Carole what she was doing,
but was prevented by the return from the house of a meandering
Fennel, clutching a wine bottle in either hand. It was the same
Argentinian Malbec that they'd been drinking at the Private
View. Jude got out of the Mini to greet her.

'Forward!' cried Fennel in the manner of a valiant crusader.
'To the yurts!'

Carole got back to High Tor, her mind buzzing with everything
that had happened at the Cornelian Gallery. She was very glad
she had finally agreed to go to the Private View. She wouldn't
have missed it for the world.

But while Gulliver welcomed her return with his usual
display of undiscriminating affection, there was still something
that nagged at Carole. Where was Jude? Landline and mobile
were checked, but there was no message or text.

Carole felt sure it was a man. Quite when her neighbour
had had the opportunity to meet a man at the Private View
and to go through the minimum conversation required before
an agreement to sleep together, Carole didn't know. But that
remained her strongest suspicion.

She remembered how bad she had felt the other time when
Jude had gone off on a one-night stand, that awful teenage
sensation of having been abandoned by a best friend. Carole
went to bed that night with a mix of emotions, half disapproval, half envy.

Jude woke with a head as fuzzy as the sheets of felt that
covered the lattice framework of the yurt. She was still dressed
in yesterday's clothes, but she'd slept deeply and her surround-
ings were surprisingly comfortable. The thread count of the

bedding was luxuriously high and all the other fittings were straight from the top drawer. Since glamping seemed to bear no relationship to the sodden indignities of real camping, Jude thought she could quite get used to the idea.

As consciousness returned, she began to piece together the events of the previous night. She remembered arriving in the yurt with Fennel. She remembered checking whether they should be using the place, with Walden about to open the following day, and the reassurance that only two of the bigger yurts had been booked for the first weekend. 'And staff'll come in and clean the place out,' Fennel had said. 'Always plenty of staff to do everything at Butterwyke House.'

'But don't you think you should tell Chervil you're here?'

'Oh, if you insist,' Fennel had said grudgingly, and dashed off a text to her sister.

Jude also recollected that they had drunk a lot. Out of the corner of her eye, she could see one empty bottle and she wouldn't have been surprised to discover they'd drunk the other one too. Or maybe there had been more. She did have a vague recollection of Fennel having left the yurt at some point in the night. Had that been to get more booze from the house? No, it had been to fetch her latest artwork, the watercolours she'd done in the previous few days. And Jude remembered looking at the pictures, thinking how good they were and how much more serene than the agonized images of earlier in the week.

She also had a recollection of the girl getting a text on her mobile, though quite when that had been she couldn't be sure.

But through the woolliness of her head, what Jude did remember from her night was how well they had got on together, more like two contemporaries than a pair of women with nearly thirty years between them. And she also recalled how positive Fennel Whittaker had sounded. Yes, she was very drunk, but in a strange way she'd been in control, rational, optimistic about her future. Bawling out Denzil Willoughby in public may not have pleased the guests at the Private View, but it seemed at least to have given Fennel some kind of expiation.

Jude looked across to the other bed, hoping that the girl was safely sleeping off the effects of her prodigious alcohol consumption.

With a shadow of foreboding, she saw that Fennel wasn't there. Not in the bed, not in the yurt.

Increasingly anxious, Jude slipped on her shoes and hurried outside. She noticed dew on the grass, it was still quite early. Not of course that the glampers of Walden would actually have to step on grass and risk getting their feet wet. Paved pathways linked the yurts.

The door to the one designated as gym and spa was half open. Jude hurried across.

The sight that met her was appalling. Fennel Whittaker was slumped in a chair beside a small table on which stood a half-empty bottle of wine and a Sabatier kitchen knife. On the floor lay her most recent watercolours.

The blood had almost stopped dripping from the girl's slashed wrists. But it seemed to be everywhere else, splashed and spreading across the white tiles.

TEN

S trange how quickly a hangover can vanish. There seemed to be so much happening that Jude didn't have time to notice her headache. First she'd had the awful task of rousing the owners of Butterwyke House and telling them that their daughter was dead.

She remembered particularly Sheena Whittaker's response, simultaneously bursting into tears and saying, with something that sounded almost like relief, 'At least we don't have to worry about it happening any more. The worst has happened.'

It was a strange reaction, one that Jude would try to analyse when she had more leisure. But the immediate demands on her time included taking Ned to the scene of his daughter's death, knowing that he'd witnessed something similar before in the Pimlico flat. He seemed physically to shrink with the impact of what he saw. Jude knew quite a lot about the bond between fathers and their first-born daughters, and she knew that the wound that had just been inflicted on Ned Whittaker would never fully heal.

Then there was the calling of the police, the half-hearted drinking of coffee until they arrived, followed by the complete official takeover of the situation. As the one who had found the body, Jude was given some fairly basic interrogation about the details of her discovery. She was asked for her contact details and told that there was likely to be further questioning. But, for the time being, she was free to go home. To her surprise she saw that it was still not yet nine o'clock.

Jude had rung for a cab and, while she waited in the stricken hallway of Butterwyke House, she heard the sound of a car drawing up on the gravel outside. Chervil, presumably snatched from the arms of Giles Green by a telephone summons from her parents, burst in through the doors, seeing Jude and saying, 'Isn't this bloody typical? Are there any lengths Fennel wouldn't go to, to spoil one of my projects?'

Another question to be pondered on when Jude had more leisure. Which she didn't have in the half-hour cab ride back to Fethering. She was still in shock and the only question in her mind was whether she could have done anything to save the life of Fennel Whittaker.

To Jude's mind, guilt, like regret, was a completely wasted emotion. Looking backwards and wishing the past undone made for a pointless expenditure of emotional energy. But on this occasion, surprised to find herself sobbing in the back of the cab, Jude did feel some level of responsibility for what had happened.

'Presumably you inspected the crime scene before you went back to Butterwyke House?' Carole's tone turned her words into one of those expressions remembered from school Latin: a question expecting the answer yes.

And she got what she expected. 'I had a quick look round, yes. But I was in shock and pretty bleary.'

'I'm not surprised, given the amount of alcohol you say you'd consumed.' This tart reproof showed that, in spite of Jude's explanation, Carole hadn't quite forgiven her lack of communication.

Jude was about to launch into a defence of empathetic drinking. She knew that the previous evening trying to stop Fennel having more wine would not have worked. Matching the girl glass for glass had increased the closeness between them.

But a look at Carole's face told her that articulating such thoughts would be a waste of breath, so instead she said, 'It looked like a classic suicide set-up. Alcohol, there were pills on the table too, and the kitchen knife, which had clearly been used to cut the wrists.'

'Suicide note?' Jude nodded wearily. 'I don't suppose you read it?'

'I did.'

'What, you opened the envelope? The police aren't going to be very pleased when they—'

'It wasn't in an envelope. Just lying there on the table. I didn't have to touch it to read it.'

'What did it say?'

'I can't remember the exact wording, but the usual stuff . . . "can't go on . . . no talent as an artist . . . everything too painful . . . hate myself . . . simpler for everyone if I . . . " You know.' Once again Jude was surprised by tears in her eyes.

'Did it read convincingly to you?' asked Carole gently.

'Oh yes. That's the kind of thing people write in suicide notes. It always sounds terribly banal in retrospect, but . . .' Jude reached under layers of garments to produce a handkerchief on which she blew her nose loudly.

'So it sounds like it really was a suicide.'

Reluctantly, Jude nodded her head. 'Except . . . when we talked that evening . . . yesterday evening – God, it was only yesterday evening – Fennel sounded so positive about everything.'

'So positive about everything *you can remember*,' said Carole sniffily. The lack of a phone message still rankled. 'Come on, concentrate, Jude. Was there anything else you saw at the scene of the crime that you think might be relevant?'

'That's the second time you've used the expression "scene of the crime". Are you suggesting that it wasn't suicide?'

'I'm keeping an open mind on that.' Though whether Carole Seddon's mind, cluttered as it was by a tangle of prejudices, could ever be described as 'open' was an interesting topic for discussion. 'Anyway, suicide was a crime in this country right up until 1961. And a lot of people still think it is. But don't let's get sidetracked. I'm asking you if you saw anything odd at the scene of the crime.'

Jude gave another firm wipe to her nose and put away the handkerchief. 'Well, the was one thing, but it's more "a dog in the night-time".'

'Something you were expecting that wasn't there?' asked Carole, instantly picking up the Sherlockian reference.

'Yes.'

'So what was it?'

'Fennel's mobile phone. She certainly had it with her during the evening. I even have a vague recollection of her holding it when she went out of the yurt. But there was no sign of it at the . . . all right, I'll use your expression . . . at "the scene of the crime".'

ELEVEN

The phone call from the police to Woodside Cottage came the following morning, the Sunday. The woman's voice said that it was in relation to the death of Fennel Whittaker and asked whether it would be convenient for a Detective Inspector Hodgkinson to visit Jude and discuss a few details with her. The request was put in the form of a question that was very definitely not expecting the answer no.

Detective Inspector Hodgkinson, who arrived just before noon, turned out to be female. She was a tall woman, a large woman actually, though she moved with considerable grace. She was not in uniform, but wore a light green fleece, well-cut jeans and pointy-toed ankle boots. Her manner was easy and her vowels sounded privately educated.

'Call me Carmen,' she said, after accepting the offer of coffee. ('Just black, please.')

Jude made a broad gesture towards the variously swathed

items of furniture in her front room. 'Sit where you want.' And she went off to make the coffee.

By the time Jude returned, Carmen Hodgkinson had a reporter's notebook open on her lap and was consulting some sheets of printed-up emails. 'Just checking what you said to my colleagues yesterday.'

'Ah.' Jude handed across one cup of coffee and sat down opposite the Inspector with the other one, waiting for the interrogation to begin.

The first question was not one she would have predicted in a hundred years. 'Do you ever watch rugby, Jude?'

She admitted that she did. 'I'm not a diehard fan, but come the Six Nations, I'm sometimes found to be glued to my television screen.'

'Me too. I used to play, for my school and at uni.'

Jude let out another cautious 'Ah', not quite sure in which direction the conversation was leading.

'Well, if you've watched a game recently, you'll know that they now have a "TMO" – television match official, video referee, and it frequently happens that the match referee will consult him when a try appears to have been scored, but there's a slight doubt about whether the ball was touched down properly. And the match referee will ask the TMO: "Is there any reason why I shouldn't award this try?" Well, that's really why I'm here today. I'm asking you: "Is there any reason why we should not feel that the death of Fennel Whittaker is as straightforward as it appears to be?" Do you get my drift?'

'I do, yes.'

'It's the old "if it looks like a duck and swims like a duck and quacks like a duck, then it probably is a duck." This looks like a suicide.'

Jude was silent for a moment, as the realization sank in that, for all her folksy roundabout manner, Carmen Hodgkinson was a highly intelligent woman.

'So,' the Inspector nudged, 'do you have any reason to believe that Fennel Whittaker didn't kill herself?'

'Well . . .'

Hodgkinson picked up on the hesitation. 'Right, so you do have some doubts. Can we establish a few background facts first of all? You spent the night in the yurt with Fennel Whittaker. Was that because you were in a relationship with her?'

'"In a relationship"? Are you asking if we were lovers?'

'It seems a reasonable question to me. What you have to remember, Jude, is that you have a lot more information than I do. I heard this morning that I was being assigned to this case. I've read the existing paperwork which, given the fact that the death only occurred yesterday, is pretty minimal. I'm starting really with a *tabula rasa*.'

'A blank slate?'

'Yes. I know nothing about you or the Whittakers. All I do know is that you and Fennel spent last night in a yurt in the grounds of Butterwyke House, a house where she had her own bedroom. So I ask myself why you did that. And I come up with a possible explanation.'

'That I'm lesbian?' said Jude with a smile, imagining how Carole would have reacted to the suggestion if it had been aimed at her.

'Yes. A lot of us are,' said Detective Inspector Hodgkinson calmly.

'Well, no, not in my case. My main relationship with Fennel was a professional one.'

'Of what kind?'

'I'm a healer, alternative therapist, whatever you want to call it.'

Jude anticipated the reaction that statement quite frequently elicited from more conventional members of the public, but it didn't come. Instead Carmen Hodgkinson asked. 'And you were treating Fennel Whittaker?'

'That's right.'

'For depression, bipolar tendencies?'

'Yes.'

'So you knew that she had a history of self-harming and suicide attempts?'

'Of course.'

'Hm.' Detective Inspector Hodgkinson wrote something down. Though she couldn't read the words, Jude noticed that the handwriting was very neat, almost calligraphic in its precision. 'What kind of treatments do you use, Jude? Acupuncture?'

'No. I'm not qualified to do that.'

'I've found acupuncture very effective . . . for quite a lot of complaints . . . both physical and mental.'

Jude had not been expecting this kind of openness from a police officer. She said, 'I have no doubts about its efficacy. I keep telling myself I should get trained in it, but never get round to it.'

'So what kind of therapies are you trained for?'

It was a shrewd question, posed without heavy intonation, but still a probing one. Anyone could call themselves an alternative therapist, and the Inspector was assessing where Jude fitted in on the scale between serious professional and complete charlatan.

'I did a massage therapy training, so I do use massage a lot. But the healing is really a matter of channelling energy.'

Carmen Hodgkinson nodded and asked, still without scepticism, 'Like reiki?'

'I suppose it does have some elements in common, but it's not reiki. Anyway, I'm not trained in reiki, nor have I ever claimed to be.'

'I see. So the healing power comes from within you?'

Jude found herself uncharacteristically embarrassed by the question. 'I suppose it does, yes.'

'I used to be a complete cynic about that kind of thing, but I have seen healing work. On humans and animals. I think it was the animals that convinced me. I mean, you can fool a human being with a load of blarney and mumbo-jumbo, but you're never going to get away with that with a police Alsatian, are you?'

'No.'

'Right,' said Carmen Hodgkinson, suddenly businesslike. 'Let's put you back in your TMO role. Is there any reason why you think that Fennel Whittaker did not commit suicide?'

'My main reason is that she seemed so together on Friday evening, so positive.'

The Detective Inspector consulted one of the printouts on her lap before echoing, '"Together"? From what I've heard about how Fennel Whittaker behaved at the Cornelian Gallery Private View, "together" would not be the first word that came to mind.'

'No, I agree. She was drunk and she did make a big scene.

But the scene she made did have a therapeutic effect on her. She got a lot of stuff off her chest.'

'Stuff like having a go at her former boyfriend Denzil Willoughby?'

'Yes. Have you spoken to him yet?'

For the first time the glaze of police officialdom came over Carmen Hodgkinson's face. 'I'm sure he will be interviewed at the appropriate time,' she replied, in automaton mode. Then, reverting to her more relaxed manner, she continued, 'You also used the word "positive", Jude. You said that Fennel Whittaker seemed "positive".'

'Yes. She said for her to die "would be a terrible waste". She actually said that she wanted to go on living.'

'You mean she was making plans for the future?' Jude nodded. 'Moving into a more manic than depressive phase on her bipolar scale?'

'That's how it felt, yes. Though "manic" is not really the right word. Fennel seemed very in control.'

'In spite of having consumed at least two bottles of wine?'

'In spite of that.'

'Hm.' The Detective Inspector was silent for a moment. 'Presumably, having had dealings with a lot of bipolar patients, you are aware that the period of emergence from a depressive period can be a very dangerous one.'

'I know that.'

'At the really low point the sufferers may have suicidal intentions, but they are too lethargic to be capable of taking any action about anything. As the mood lifts, however, the thought is formed: I'm not going to put myself at risk of that kind of misery again. Now, while I'm actually capable of action, I'm going to do what I've been wanting to do for the past weeks. I'm going to top myself, and I'm going to plan it in such a way that there is no possibility of failure.'

'I am aware that that can happen.'

'And wouldn't you say that Fennel Whittaker fitted that archetype rather well? She had made suicide attempts before . . . As you say, she was emerging from a bad bout of depression. Might not that be the moment for her to put into practice a sequence of carefully-planned actions?'

'"Carefully-planned"? I don't quite get that.'

'We haven't got all the information yet, but the way things look . . . the kitchen at Butterwyke House had been locked by Ned Whittaker on Friday evening, so—'

'Why?'

'Why did he lock the kitchen?'

'Yes.'

'Apparently there was something wrong with the back door lock. He wanted to ensure that anyone who broke in would get no further into the house than the kitchen.'

'Was he expecting someone to break in?'

'They have had problems with burglaries before. The Whittakers have quite a lot of stuff.'

'That's certainly true.'

'Anyway, with the kitchen being locked, it means that Fennel couldn't get in there when she came back after the Private View. Which means that, if the Sabatier knife that was used came from the Butterwyke House kitchen, she must have planted it there for use when required.'

'Do you know that the knife *did* come from the Butterwyke House kitchen?'

'That's being investigated.'

'But—'

'What's more,' Carmen Hodgkinson continued implacably, 'though we haven't had the results of the lab tests back yet, we are pretty certain that the contents of one of the wine bottles left at the scene of her death had been laced with liquid paracetamol. Sounds like some pretty detailed planning had gone into Fennel's death.'

'But was it she herself who had done that planning?'

The Detective Inspector pursed her lips. 'I see. Conspiracy theories? "The murder that was made to look like a suicide".'

'It has happened.' Jude knew as she said the words how feeble they sounded.

'Yes, it has happened, but not very often. And more often in the world of crime fiction than in the real world.'

'Hm.' Jude tapped her plump chin thoughtfully. 'Inspector Hodgkinson, do you mind if I ask you how you got into this kind of work?'

'Why? Do you want me to show you my ID? Are you suggesting I'm impersonating a police officer?'

'No. Far from it. It's just that you're not the kind of person I would have imagined in this role.'

There was a silence, then a slow smile broke across the policewoman's features. 'I think I'll take that as a compliment. Are you suggesting that you expected a police officer to come clumping in in hobnail boots?'

'Well, maybe a bit.'

'All right. I did my first degree in Psychology and Social Anthropology at St Andrews. I then went to Edinburgh to do an MSc in Criminology and Criminal Justice. That led to seven years in HM Prisons. Then into the police force, where I've worked as a psychologist for eleven years. Enough information?'

'Yes, thank you,' said Jude, feeling uncharacteristically cowed.

Detective Inspector Hodgkinson looked at her watch. 'Now, as I'm sure you know, time is money in police work, as it is in most other areas of life. And it's going to become even more precious with all the new government cuts that are coming in. What this means is that at any given time we have to make hard decisions about where our resources are channelled. Getting together the paperwork for a suicide for the Coroner's Court is boring but straightforward. Investigating the possibility that an apparent suicide was in fact a murder would take a huge amount of police time and is therefore not something we would wish to embark on, unless we had cast-iron evidence for our suspicions. So, Jude, I come back to a variation on my original question. The TMO question. Do you have any cast-iron evidence to support the thesis that Fennel Whittaker was murdered?'

'Not evidence as such.'

'But . . .?'

'But I do think it's odd that her mobile phone seems to have disappeared.'

'On what do you base the assumption that it has disappeared?'

'I didn't see it in the yurt when I found her body.'

'No, but that was hardly the moment when you were going to be at your most observant, Jude. You were probably in shock. You knew you were about to face the unpleasant task of telling the girl's parents what had happened to their daughter. Fennel could have dropped the phone anywhere.'

'Yes, but . . .'

Detective Inspector Hodgkinson suddenly gave Jude a narrow look. 'You're not implying, are you, that you made a detailed examination of the yurt where the girl died?'

Jude was quick with her denial. Whatever the truth, she knew the police wouldn't take kindly to the activities of amateur detectives.

The Inspector looked down at her printouts. 'There's no mention in this lot of a mobile having been found.' She made a note. 'I'll check it out. And you're sure the girl had it with her when you were drinking in the other yurt?'

'Certain. And I do have a vague recollection of her receiving a text on it.'

'What time would this have been?'

Jude spread her hands wide in apology. 'Sorry. As I say, it was all a bit blurry.'

'Hm.' Detective Inspector Hodgkinson made another note. 'So, apart from the absence of the mobile, back to the same question. Do you have any evidence that might suggest Fennel Whittaker's death was anything other than what it appears to be – in other words, suicide?'

Jude was forced to admit that she didn't. Just a gut instinct. And though what she'd seen of Carmen Hodgkinson suggested that the Inspector might be more sympathetic to gut instincts than the average member of the police force, she didn't think that sympathy would be sufficient for the initiation of a full-scale murder enquiry.

TWELVE

ost weekends now Carole Seddon heard from the family in Fulham. A weekly call from Stephen was far greater frequency of communication than she had been used to, but then so much in their relationship had changed. His marriage to Gaby, introducing someone who hadn't grown up in the claustrophobia of Carole's own marriage to David, had started the thaw, and its progress had been greatly speeded up by the arrival of Lily. Whereas conversations between mother and son had always been rather stilted, with Stephen talking about his work (which Carole never fully understood) and both of them trying to avoid any mention of David, there now always seemed to be something to say. Lily was developing at such a rate that every week there was some new achievement to report, some physical action, a new word or, increasingly, new sentences.

But that Sunday evening the Fulham call came not from Carole's son but her daughter-in-law.

'About the week after the end of May Bank Holiday . . .'

'What about the week after the end of May Bank Holiday, Gaby?' asked Carole, trying to work out what date that would be. One of the effects of retirement from the Home Office, she found, was a profound vagueness about the dates of public holidays. Now they no longer represented days off work, they seemed infinitely less important than they had.

'I'm talking about the one at the end of May, not the one at the beginning. Well, Stephen's got to be in Frankfurt that week for work.'

'Oh, really?'

'Yes, his bosses never seem to be aware of public holidays.' Carole almost heard that as a criticism of herself. 'So he's flying out on the Bank Holiday Monday and doesn't get back till the Sunday after. And I was thinking: what a perfect opportunity for me to take Lily for a little jaunt to the South Coast.'

'That'd be lovely. You'd be most welcome here, of course, Gaby. Just let me get my diary and check the dates.'

'No, don't worry, Carole. I wasn't suggesting that we should impose ourselves on you at High Tor.'

'Oh?' Being Carole, she couldn't take this statement at face value; she had to read something into it. Gaby and Lily had come to stay in Fethering the previous summer when Carole had rented a beach hut at Smalting for the occasion, and that seemed to have worked all right. But was Gaby now intimating that the visit hadn't been as much of a success as Carole had considered it? Was she finding some inadequacy in their accommodation at High Tor?

Even as she had the thought, though, Carole did also feel a degree of relief. Much as she loved Gaby and Lily, she did find the presence of other people in her house a considerable strain. Any people. The long habit of living on her own meant that she always had to make an effort with other people present, she couldn't be unaware of them and just carry on with her life. In fact, she'd always had the instinct for privacy. She hadn't even felt relaxed with her husband in the house. Maybe that was one of the many factors that had led to their divorce.

'The point is,' Gaby explained, 'that when I had this idea I was with a friend, who's got a little boy roughly Lily's age. And her husband's going to be away the same time as Stephen, so we made this plan for the four of us to come down together, and I know you haven't really got room for all of us in High Tor.'

'Well . . .' said Carole, relief flooding through her. 'I could move things around and make space for you.' She knew she didn't sound convincing.

'No, no, I wouldn't hear of it,' Gaby bubbled on. 'But if we were staying nearby, then we could not get in each other's way . . . you know, meet up with you some days, other days just do our own thing . . .'

'It does sound rather a good idea,' Carole conceded. Yes, wonderful. Gaby and Lily near enough for her to see them, but without the obligation of feeling responsible for their well-being every minute. 'So where were you thinking of staying?'

'Well, that's the point,' said Gaby. 'We don't know. But we thought, with you down there, you know, able to apply a little local knowledge to the problem, well, you might be able to recommend somewhere.'

Carole was hit by a brainwave. 'Gaby,' she said, 'what would you think of the idea of staying in a yurt?'

Of course Walden had its own website. Any project the Whittakers got involved in was organized to a very high spec.

There were beautiful professionally taken photographs of the glamping site, even a video tour of the interiors of the yurts. Chervil's 'Deeply Felt' pun was much in evidence. And there was, of course, a 'Contact Us' page.

Carole no longer really thought about it, but using her laptop had in some ways changed her attitude to communication. Whereas she would have regarded telephoning someone at the weekend on a matter of business as a major social gaffe, emailing seemed perfectly legitimate. So she had no qualms about making contact through the Walden website.

Her emailed enquiry about prices and availability arose partly from her search for accommodation for Gaby and Lily, but she wasn't convinced that Walden would be the right place for them. She felt sure it would be very expensive, for a start. Though, when she came to think of it, her son and daughter-in-law never seemed to lack for money. She had no idea what Stephen earned doing whatever it was he did with money and computers, but she thought his pay packet must be substantial. There certainly hadn't been any talk of Gaby needing to return to her job as a theatrical agent in the immediate future.

But of course Carole's email to Walden had another purpose. It was a legitimate way of making contact with the Whittakers. Jude had brought Carole up to date on her conversation with Carmen Hodgkinson and, despite the Inspector's conclusion, they both still thought there was something strange about the death of Fennel Whittaker. Something that required further investigation.

She was surprised to get a call back only moments after she had sent her email. The voice at the other end of the phone was unmistakably that of Chervil Whittaker. 'Hello, is that Carole Seddon?'

'Yes.'

The girl identified herself. 'Have we met? Your name sounds familiar.'

'We did meet. I came to Butterwyke House with my friend Jude last Saturday. You showed us round Walden.'

'Oh yes, of course, I'm so sorry. I should have remembered.'

'Don't worry about it.'

'Well, I'm glad you were sufficiently impressed by the site to be making further enquiries. Your email said you were thinking of the week after the Bank Holiday at the end of May . . .'

Chervil was all businesswoman, keen to make a booking. She wasn't about to mention that there had been a death at Walden.

But Carole decided that she would. 'Look, I heard about what happened to your sister. I just wanted to say that I'm very sorry.'

'Thank you.' The words were deliberately bleached of emotion. 'Now at Walden we have yurts of various sizes. How many people are you looking to accommodate?'

'It's not for me, actually. It's for my daughter-in-law and I'm really just checking prices.'

'Well, at the end of May you should really be into our High Summer rates, but I'd be prepared to make a deal for you on . . .'

Chervil Whittaker went through a very detailed list of prices and terms of business and concluded by saying that she would also put the information in an email. 'But I'd advise you to move quickly. That Bank Holiday week is already getting quite booked up.'

'I'll get back to my daughter-in-law this evening,' Carole lied. The next day would be quite soon enough.

'Anyway, I'll give you my mobile number,' said Chervil. 'Quicker to get me direct than through the website.'

Carole made a note of the number before saying, 'Presumably you had to delay Walden's official opening.'

'I'm sorry?'

'I thought you were opening this weekend and obviously with what happened to your sister . . .'

'This weekend was only going to be a dry run with some friends testing out the facilities,' said Chervil Whittaker, in direct contravention to what she had told Carole and Jude when they visited Walden. 'My plan was always to have the official launch next weekend.' And she said it with such conviction that most people would have believed her.

'Presumably the site will be fully accessible then . . .?' asked Carole.

'Of course it will be. I'm sorry, what do you mean?'

'I was just meaning that by next weekend the police will presumably have finished their investigations at Walden.'

'They've indicated that they will have done, yes. And, incidentally, for obvious reasons we're trying to keep the news of my sister's suicide out of the papers. So if the subject does come up, I'd be grateful if you could keep quiet about what you know.'

Good luck, thought Carole, if you think you can keep that sort of thing quiet in a place like Fethering. But then again the Whittakers weren't very well known in the village. It was possible that very few local people did actually know what had happened. Whether the media blackout could be continued once the inquest had opened was another matter. But then again the inquest might not happen for a few months and memories could be very short.

'My sister,' Chervil Whittaker continued with some asperity, 'may have done her best to upstage the opening of my project, but I can assure you I am not going to let her succeed. Walden will open next weekend and none of the visitors will ever know that a selfish suicide had taken place there.'

The girl's words were unequivocal. She still saw Fennel's death as another in a series of attention-seeking actions. And in her voice was a note of satisfaction from the knowledge that it would be the last one.

If, thought Carole, Fennel's death had been murder, then the person with least motive for committing it would be her sister Chervil. Public knowledge of a crime at her precious Walden would be the last thing she wanted.

THIRTEEN

The call came through to Woodside Cottage on the dot of nine thirty on the Monday morning. Jude, who had been going through some yoga exercises, answered and found a very distraught-sounding Ned Whittaker at the end of the line.

Would it be all right if he came to see her? He wanted to
talk about Fennel's state of mind in the weeks running up
to her death. He respected Jude's strictures about client confidentiality, but surely the situation was different once the client
in question was dead?

Jude had a couple of people booked in for healing sessions
in the afternoon, but she told Ned she was free all morning
and he was welcome to come to Woodside Cottage as soon
as he liked. He must have left Butterwyke House almost
immediately, because within twenty-five minutes there was a
knock at her front door.

Ned Whittaker still looked boyish, but there was a greyness
about his face which seemed to contradict that impression.
Behind the rimless glasses his eyes were red and hollow. He
didn't look as if he'd had any sleep since the news of his
daughter's death.

There was a jumpiness about him too, he was more uneasy
than ever. 'I'm sorry to trouble you, Jude,' he said, 'but I feel
I have to find out everything I can, try to make some sense
of what's happened.'

'Yes, I fully understand. Would you like some coffee?'

'Thank you. Black. I seem to have lived on black coffee
for the last few days.'

'I'm not surprised.' As she settled him on one of the draped
armchairs in her sitting room, Jude could not help being
reminded that it was a week to the day since Fennel had been
there. The recollection brought a pang of loss to her and a
determination, like Ned's, to find out the truth about what had
happened to the girl.

When she placed his coffee on the table between them, Ned
Whittaker tried to take a sip, but his hand was shaking so
much that he put the mug back down. 'Jude, I know Fennel
was coming to see you . . .'

'There was no secret about it.'

'No, I didn't mean that. And it was depression she was
seeing you about?'

'Yes. Though the depression was just one manifestation of
a great number of symptoms. When I treat a client, I treat the
whole client.'

He nodded. 'When we last met . . . well, that is to say not when we met at Butterwyke House after . . .' He couldn't shape the words. 'When we met at the Private View, I told you that over the years we'd tried all kinds of treatments for Fennel. Most of them started promisingly, but then . . . If it was medication, she'd forget to take it – or perhaps deliberately not take it. What I'm saying is that we had tried everything.'

'I'm sure you did all that anyone could have done. You shouldn't be blaming yourself, Ned.'

He smiled grimly. 'Easy enough to say, Jude, but when your oldest child, a girl you've adored for . . . when she . . . it's inevitable that I blame myself. I keep trying to work out where I went wrong, what I did that precipitated . . . what happened.'

'That's a natural human reaction. But what you have to remind yourself, Ned, is that Fennel was suffering from a very serious illness – the fact that it was a mental illness doesn't make it any less real than heart disease or cancer. As I say, you did everything any parent could have done – more than most would have done – to help her cope with that illness. But sadly all your efforts failed.'

Jude was not ready, at this stage, to express any doubts she harboured about the authenticity of Fennel's suicide. Though the idea of murder might have energized Ned Whittaker, reduced his feeling of guilt, maybe even given him a quest to identify the perpetrator, it would have been irresponsible of Jude to set that particular hare running.

'Where do you stand,' he asked, 'on the causes of depression? Do you think it's kind of genetic?'

'I think it can be. Some medical authorities divide depression into two categories: reactive and endogenous. Reactive depression is triggered by some life event; the break-up of a relationship, the death of a loved one. Endogenous depression doesn't seem to have such a readily identifiable cause. The sufferer is just born with it.'

'And that's what Fennel had?'

'Definitely.' Jude posed her next sentence with some delicacy. 'It is frequently thought that endogenous depression is hereditary.'

Ned Whittaker looked at her blankly for a moment, then caught on. 'Ah, you're asking if I've ever suffered from depression . . .?'

'Yes.'

'I'd say the answer is a definite no. I've felt terrible at times – God, I can't imagine ever feeling worse than I do at the moment – but I don't think it's depression. Fennel used to tell me how she felt at times, and I've read descriptions of depression, both in medical works and novels . . . I mean, Holden Caulfield in *The Catcher in the Rye* is reckoned to be a good description of a depressive, but I've never had feelings like that. When things go wrong for me, I don't get mad, I want to get even.'

'Which is perhaps why you're feeling so bad at the moment. Because there's no one you can get even with?'

Ned Whittaker nodded thoughtfully. 'You could be right, Jude.'

'Anyway, that's your side of the family. You don't have a genetic disposition towards depression.'

Once again he seemed rather slow to pick up the implication of her words, but this time Jude suspected the slowness might be calculated. 'Oh, you mean Sheena. You're asking if there's a predisposition towards depression in her family?'

'Yes.'

He shook his head firmly. 'No, definitely not. With Sheena what you see is what you get. She's very upfront. No murky hidden depths there.'

His answer seemed a little too emphatic, but Jude didn't pick up on it. There'd be time enough to find out more about Sheena Whittaker, and at the moment her main priority was to give Ned any support that she could offer to alleviate his current misery.

In the circumstances, Jude didn't have any inhibitions about divulging what Fennel had confided to her in the course of their sessions. A lot of what she reported – the circling, ingrowing sense of inadequacy – was familiar to the girl's father. But he hadn't realized how much guilt Fennel had felt; guilt for taking up too much of her parents' attention, guilt for ruining their lives.

At the end of Jude's long narrative, Ned Whittaker still looked shrunken and feeble in his chair, but he did seem calmer. 'So do you reckon – in spite of the fact that Fennel's depression was endogenous – there was some big shock that prompted her into actually taking action? You know, as opposed to talking about it, as she had done for years?'

Jude repeated Detective Inspector Hodgkinson's observation about depressives frequently committing suicide at the moment when their mood was improving and he seemed to take that on board.

'What about the scene she threw at the Cornelian Gallery, though?' asked Ned. 'Do you reckon that was what triggered it?'

'I suppose it's possible.' But Jude then told him how positive the outburst seemed to have made Fennel, almost as if the denunciation of Denzil Willoughby was something essential to her, a task that had to be ticked off a list.

'But maybe,' suggested Ned, 'that was also part of her preparations for the suicide . . . you know, she wanted all the loose ends of her life neatly tied up?'

Jude conceded that that was a possibility. 'What I really want to know, though, Ned, is what happened the first time . . . you know, in the flat in Pimlico . . .?'

He went even paler and trembled. He still hadn't touched the mug of coffee, which must have long since gone cold. 'That was terrible. I'd always known that Fennel had problems. I suppose I put a lot of it down to growing up, though . . . you know, the difficulties of adolescence, of coming to terms with leaving childhood and becoming an adult. I suppose I kidded myself that it was just a phase she was going through. But what happened in the flat in Pimlico . . . that told me how serious the illness Fennel was suffering from was. It was a horrible shock.'

'Was there something that precipitated it that time? Some emotional trauma?'

'I don't know. I'm pretty certain once again there was a man involved. And not a very suitable man. I'm afraid Fennel has – used to have, I should say – a rather *kamikaze* track record with relationships. According to Chervil, while she was at St Martin's her sister had been seeing some fellow art student, who messed her around a lot. I'm afraid both my girls have to be careful when it comes to men. Once it's discovered how well off Sheena and I are, they tend to attract a lot of spongers.'

'Is that true of Chervil too?'

'It has happened.'

'And what about her current beau, Giles Green?'

'Sheena and I have only met him a couple of times. He seems pleasant enough. Quite a bit older than Chervil, which may not be a bad thing.'

'And you don't think he's after her money?'

'Why?' Ned Whittaker was instantly alert. 'Do you know something about him?'

'No. Very little. I'd maybe met him once or twice in the gallery, and then at the Private View. All I know is that he's recently lost a rather lucrative job in the City.'

'Hm . . .' The millionaire looked exhausted, as if he couldn't cope with anything else. His grief over the loss of one daughter was such that he couldn't begin worrying about the love life of the other.

'You haven't heard, I suppose,' said Jude, changing direction, 'whether the police have found Fennel's mobile yet?'

He shook his head wearily. 'No. If they have, they haven't told me. Why, is it significant?'

'It might be. It'd offer a record of the calls she'd made and received on Friday evening. I mean, I know she sent a text to Chervil, and I'm pretty sure she received one later in the evening. Knowing the contents of that one could be important.'

'You mean it might contain something that'd pushed her over the edge?'

'Possible.'

'Hm.'

'Ned, presumably you saw the note that Fennel had left in the yurt?' He nodded. 'You didn't notice anything strange about it?'

He was silent for a moment, as if thrown by the question. Then he replied bitterly, 'Well, I suppose I thought it was strange that my beautiful daughter would want to kill herself.'

'No, I meant strange about the actual note. For instance, there's no question that Fennel wrote it?'

'Who else might have written it? Chervil?' The tone in his voice was almost one of petulance now. Apparently the thought had never crossed Ned Whittaker's mind that his daughter might have been murdered. And Jude felt glad she'd refrained from planting it there.

'No. I meant the writing, the phrasing – did that read like Fennel's?'

'Yes.'

'Was it similar to the note she left the last time . . . the time Chervil found her in the flat in Pimlico?'

Ned Whittaker looked her straight in the eyes and replied, 'On the previous occasion Fennel didn't leave a note.'

'Ah. Right.'

He took off his glasses and rubbed his eyes even pinker. 'I've thought about her so much over the last few days. Wishing things could have been different, wishing I could have done something . . . you know. I wish there was someone I could blame apart from myself.'

'I suppose you could blame Fennel.'

'Yes, at times I've felt furious with her. Furious at her selfishness. She knew how much pain it would cause me, and yet she just went ahead and did it.'

'Hm.' Jude tried to keep all intonation out of the monosyllable.

'At times I've always wished that Fennel had been murdered.'

'Oh?' This was a new tack, which took Jude by surprise. 'What makes you say that?'

'Well, then I would have someone to blame, wouldn't I? The bastard who did it. And I could turn some of my hatred away from myself.'

'Perhaps.' Since he'd raised the subject, Jude went on, 'You've no reason to believe Fennel was murdered, have you?'

'No logical reason, no. Just, as I say, it might make me feel better about myself.'

'Hm.'

'Why, is there gossip about Fethering that she might have been murdered?'

'No. Very few people in Fethering even know she's dead yet. There's been nothing in the press.'

'And that's the way it's going to stay,' said Ned Whittaker with considerable vehemence. 'One thing I've learnt over the years is how to keep the press out of my life. I've got quite good at that, from harsh experience.' After a silence, he continued in a softer tone, 'Do you imagine, when people know about her death, that some people will think it was murder?'

Jude shrugged. 'Being the kind of village it is, Fethering's a hotbed of gossip and half-baked conspiracy theories. I'm sure someone who's watched too many episodes of *Midsomer Murders* will already be putting the final touches to their crackpot solution.'

Ned Whittaker sighed. 'And in the meantime, Fennel's dead.'

He looked so abject that she couldn't help saying, 'I know this is hell for you, but it will get better.'

'How?' he asked in a dull voice. 'She's not going to come back to life, is she?'

'No. If you'd like, I could give you a massage, relax you a bit.'

'Thanks, Jude, but no. I don't think anything's ever going to relax me again.'

'How's Sheena? Presumably she's taking this pretty badly too.'

He let out a bitter bark of laughter. 'You'd think so, wouldn't you? I can't believe the way she's reacting. You're married to someone for nearly thirty years, you think you know them inside out, then something like this happens and you realize you don't know them at all. Sheena's main emotion at the moment seems to be relief. She says we've had the threat of Fennel doing something like this hanging over us for so long that now it's finally happened, at last we can get on with our own lives.'

There was an infinity of pain in Ned Whittaker's hollow eyes as he looked at Jude and said, 'Sheena seems almost to be pleased that Fennel's dead.'

FOURTEEN

That Monday morning, Carole Seddon's Labrador, Gulliver, was in bad odour. Literally. As usual, he and his mistress had left High Tor at seven for their customary early morning walk, but as soon as they'd reached Fethering Beach the dog had found a particularly noxious pile of tar-covered seaweed in which he had immediately rolled. And the manner in which he rolled in it suggested that his actions were entirely deliberate, almost as if he were cocking a snook at his owner's obsessive standards of hygiene. This was most unlike his usual equable demeanour, and earned him a severe reprimand.

Some dog-owners might have completed their walk before embarking on the decontamination process, but not Carole Seddon. A chastened Gulliver was immediately dragged back to High Tor where an elaborate cleansing routine began. Carole had a book which told her the methods for removing various clogging agents from dog's coats: ice cubes for gum, a sewer's seam ripper for burrs, soapy water for emulsion paint and, for oil-based paint and tar, vegetable oil.

Cowed by his mistress's disapproval, Gulliver submitted without argument to his ritual humiliation. He was made to stand on a rubber sheet on the kitchen floor, as maize oil was rubbed into the tarry knots of his coat. The dissolving lumps of blackness were then wiped off with kitchen roll and smaller droplets combed out. Finally Gulliver was bathed from top to toe with his usual Groomers shampoo, meticulously dried, combed and brushed. The whole process took a surprisingly long time but at the end – thanks in part to the maize oil – his pale biscuit-coloured coat had an unrivalled glossy sheen.

But his docile endurance of these attentions did not seem to have improved the mood of Gulliver's owner. Carole Seddon's morning routine had been thrown out and she knew from experience that the day ahead might never recover from such disruption. The rubber sheet had not collected all of the dropped hairs and other mess, which necessitated a complete cleaning of the kitchen floor. Then Carole realized she was hungry and assembled a boiled egg and toast for her breakfast. This again annoyed her. She didn't like having breakfast before her walk on Fethering Beach; she liked having it after.

The result of all this delay was that Carole Seddon and Gulliver didn't make their second attempt at leaving High Tor until nearly half-past nine. To emphasize the fact that he still hadn't been fully forgiven, she kept the dog on the lead for the outward part of the walk, but she relented and let him run free along the beach on the way back. Gulliver rewarded her by behaving immaculately. He seemed consciously to avoid the messiest piles of weed revealed by the low tide, and even to the rich gift of a large rotting fish he gave no more than a cursory sniff. He was working hard to curry the reinstated favour of his mistress.

And he did look so beautiful, with the May sunshine catching lights in his gleaming coat, that by the time they had reached the parade of shops that backed on to the beach, Gulliver had been completely forgiven.

As Carole stopped to reattach his lead, she noticed that there was a large removal van outside the Cornelian Gallery. Was it possible that Bonita Green was moving out? Fortunately the route back to High Tor went directly past the gallery, so Carole was able to observe without appearing to snoop.

As she got closer it was clear that what was being removed into the van was not Bonita Green's goods and chattels, but Denzil Willoughby's artworks. The invitations to the Private View had made it clear that the exhibition was scheduled to continue for the next four weeks. Clearly the change of plan which Bonita Green had announced at the Private View was being put into practice. She'd told her son she wanted Denzil Willoughby's exhibits out on the Saturday and two days later she was getting her wish.

By serendipity, just as Carole and Gulliver were passing the gallery door, Bonita came out to supervise the loading of the final pieces. Now that they'd been properly introduced, she merited much more than a 'Fethering nod', and Carole was by her standards almost effusive as she greeted Bonita and thanked her for the Private View.

The gallery-owner harrumphed. 'Not a huge success, so far as I was concerned.' She gestured to the van. 'As you see, there goes the last contact between Denzil Willoughby and the Cornelian Gallery.'

'Mm, I suppose the scene there did rather put a damper on the evening . . . I mean, with all those accusations flying back and forth.'

'What accusations?' the gallery-owner asked sharply.

'What Fennel Whittaker said.'

'Oh, of course. Yes.' The removals van started up and moved slowly on the road towards London. 'Good riddance!' said Bonita Green with some venom. Then a shrewd look came into her black-rimmed brown eyes. 'I'm dying for a cup of coffee. You wouldn't care to join me, would you, Carole?'

There were two places for coffee in Fethering – it was reckoned too small to have succumbed to the invasion of a Starbucks or a Costa – but Bonita did not lead the way toward the Seaview Café on the beach. Instead she moved instinctively towards Polly's Cake Shop, only a few doors along from the Cornelian Gallery, and the manner of her greeting there left no doubt that she was an extremely regular customer.

The waitress knew Bonita's order would be a large Americano without milk, and Carole asked for 'just an ordinary filter coffee, black'. Bonita, confessing that she hadn't had any breakfast, also ordered a *pain au chocolat*. Carole, who had long nurtured an atavistic taboo against eating between meals, said that she had had breakfast.

'Did you know that girl well, Bonita?' she asked, 'the one who threw the scene on Friday?'

'No. First time I'd met her. She's the sister of Giles's current girlfriend.' The way she said the last two words did not suggest she was a great enthusiast of Chervil Whittaker, nor indeed that she expected the relationship to last very long. Carole also noticed her use of the present tense when referring to Fennel. So perhaps she didn't yet know about the girl's death. If that were the case, Carole had no intentions of being the person who told her the news.

'Could you make head or tail of what the girl actually said?' asked Bonita.

'Not really. Clearly she had had a relationship with the artist, Denzil Willoughby, and it had ended badly.'

'Yes. I pieced that much together.'

Carole was wary of admitting she knew more about Fennel and her family background. She'd bide her time until she found out how much Bonita Green knew. After all, it was the gallery-owner who had initiated their meeting. She was the one who'd suggested coffee, so maybe she had some agenda of her own. Carole was content to play a waiting game.

'I think,' Bonita went on, 'that Denzil is one of those artists who regards mistreating women as part of the job description.'

'He certainly gave that impression.'

'No lack of them around in the art world,' said the gallery-owner with a harshness that could have been born of personal experience. 'Though it's rather a pity in Denzil's case because when I first knew him, he was quite a sweet boy.'

'I didn't realize you'd known him a long time.'

'My husband and I knew his parents. Denzil and my son Giles have been friends since school. They were at Lancing together.' Now Carole understood the all-purpose accent Denzil Willoughby had used to disguise his upper-class vowels. 'Thick as thieves, they were. Shared everything. Even girlfriends, I think, at one stage. And when they went their separate ways, Giles to Leeds to read Economics and Management, Denzil to St Martin's – that's St Martin's College of Art – they still stayed in touch.'

'Even at school, though,' Bonita went on, 'Denzil did have an amazing talent for art.'

'What, you mean proper art?' Carole couldn't help asking. 'Painting things that looked like things?'

The other woman smiled. 'What a perfect definition. There were teachers I had when I was at the Slade who would have appreciated that description of "proper art", Carole. But oh yes, Denzil could do it all. Still could, I'm sure, be producing conventional landscapes and portraits – and very good ones too – if he hadn't been sidetracked by the siren call of "conceptual art".'

Carole's surprise must have shown, because Bonita went on, with a little smile, 'I see. You thought that Denzil stuck photographs of black teenagers on guns because he wasn't capable of doing the "proper" stuff.'

'I had rather assumed that, yes.'

'Maybe he's found there's more money in his new kind of work.'

'Do you mean people would actually pay the prices that he was asking for that rubbish?'

Bonita Green pursed her lips in mock-affront. 'Ooh, be wary of using that word when you're discussing art, Carole. One day's "rubbish" can so easily become the next day's record-breaker at auction. Look at what's happened to Andy Warhol's prices since he died.'

'But come on, you can't have rated Denzil Willoughby's stuff that highly. You've just cut short his exhibition and taken it all out of your gallery.'

'Yes, I have. But my reasons for that were probably based more on emotion and business sense than on artistic judgement.'

'Oh?' said Carole, waiting to be told more.

'Look, as you'd probably gathered, mounting an exhibition of Denzil Willoughby's work in the Cornelian Gallery was not my idea. It was my son Giles's initiative, and I had misgivings about it right from the start. But Giles had lost his job, he wanted to have some input into the business, and I thought I should give him the chance. He kept telling me I was far too conservative in the way I ran the gallery, and of course he was right. So I thought, let Giles have his head, what harm can it do?

'Sadly, as I realized the moment the Private View started, the answer to that question was that it could do quite a lot of harm. Harm to my business . . . and harm to my relationship with my son.' The emotion prompted by that second thought stopped her short.

'I'm very sorry,' said Carole, hoping that the flood of confidence had not been permanently stemmed.

Bonita Green was silent for a little longer, but then mercifully continued. 'Giles and I had rather a major row on Saturday. I'm afraid it had been brewing for some time.'

'Was it disagreement over the Denzil Willoughby exhibition? You said you wanted him to get it out of the gallery.'

'That was part of the problem, yes. And Giles insisting that we had the Private View on a Friday, when he knows that Friday's my day off. And then he said it'd be fine for me not to be there during the day on Friday, but of course things got out of hand and I had to change my plans and . . . Anyway, all kinds of resentments came to the surface on Saturday. He had a terrible hangover which didn't improve his mood – I think he'd been drinking with Denzil most of the night – and . . . Anyway, some things were said that probably shouldn't have been said.

'Finally I told him I was going to send Denzil's work back where it came from, and Giles said, if that was the case, then he was going to move out. I can't pretend to be sorry that he's moved out. That flat over the gallery is pretty cramped for two of us. But I hope the row hasn't done permanent damage to our relationship. Giles is really all I've got now.'

'I thought I'd heard from someone that you had two children.'

'Yes, I have a daughter. But she's a lot older than him. And I never see her.' The subject was dismissed with flat, unemotional efficiency.

'And their father . . .?' asked Carole tentatively.

That question was given the same short shrift. 'My husband died when we were on a holiday in Greece. He drowned. It's a very long time ago. The children were very small.' Whether or not she still felt any pain over her loss, she was certainly not about to show it to a virtual stranger.

'So you brought them up on your own?'

'Yes.' Again no volunteering of further information. That was all Carole was going to get.

Time for a change of subject. 'You say Giles has moved out. Where's he gone to? Back to his wife?' Carole wasn't expecting an answer in the affirmative, but she saw another way of finding out a little more about the Green family.

'Oh, I wish he had. I'm sure he will eventually. Nikki's right for him, in a way that none of his replacements for her have been. This latest, *Chervil* –' she loaded the name with contempt – 'he'll be bored with her pretty soon.'

'I couldn't help noticing on Friday,' Carole observed, 'that Nikki seemed completely at her ease, unworried by the fact that Chervil was all over her husband.'

'Well, that's just a mark of what a very sensible girl she is. Nikki knows that Giles will come back to her eventually, so she's not going to get jealous of some little *chit* like that.'

It was an unusual word for Bonita to use, an echo of an earlier age.

'Presumably you know,' said Carole, 'that the Whittakers are extremely wealthy?'

'I had heard that. So what?'

'Well, just that . . . if Giles is without a job . . . maybe part of Chervil's appeal might lie in . . .?'

'Oh, I see what you mean. Only after her money. In the same way that her sister accused Denzil of being. Hm . . . I don't think Giles's mind works like that, but I suppose it might be possible.'

'Does Denzil have a private income?'

'What on earth makes you think that?'

'Well, he was at Lancing and—'

'Carole, not everyone who goes to public school has a private income.'

'No, but—'

'As a matter of fact, Denzil Willoughby's parents do have money. His father's very well-heeled, but I think he may well have got bored with bankrolling his son.'

'So Denzil Willoughby might well have been after Fennel Whittaker for her money?'

'Possible. As I say, I haven't really seen much of him since he was a schoolboy. He was a nice enough lad then . . . but people change.'

'Where does he live? Where are his masterpieces being taken back to?'

'He's apparently got a large warehouse in Brixton which he uses as a studio, or "workshop", I think he prefers to call it. I think Giles said he lives there too.'

'And you don't know any more about his relationship with Fennel Whittaker, do you, Bonita?'

'I was unaware that he had a relationship with Fennel

Whittaker. First thing I knew about it was when she suddenly lashed out at him on Friday.' Carole felt again the shrewd beam of the brown eyes. 'Why, do you know any more?' A shake of the head from Carole. 'Did you know what the girl was talking about when she spoke of "someone who causes the death of another person"?'

'No idea. I assumed it had some private meaning for Denzil Willoughby. Reviving something they had argued about before maybe?' What Carole didn't say was that the words could, in retrospect, be understood as a suicide threat. Fennel could have been saying that her former lover would have been the cause of her killing herself. If indeed she had killed herself.

Bonita Green seemed somehow relieved by the answer. But there remained an anxiety about her. Maybe she was still feeling bad about the row with her son.

'Do you know where Giles has gone?' asked Carole, with uncharacteristic gentleness. 'Back to London?'

'No. I assume he's shacked up with the girlfriend. She's living with her parents at the moment, I gather. Somewhere near Chichester.'

'Butterwyke House.'

'Oh, do you know them?'

'I've met them. Butterwyke House is an enormous pile. They'd certainly have room for Giles there.'

Bonita Green's shrug demonstrated how little interest she had in the Whittakers.

'Do you think,' asked Carole, fishing tentatively, 'that Friday's events will really have done harm to the Cornelian Gallery?'

'In the short term, yes. I know my business strategy there has not been very adventurous, but I have built up quite a loyal client base. A few of them might have been put off by the scene.'

'I don't think you need to worry about that. Although they may look embarrassed, people in Fethering love dramas like that. Gives them something to talk about for weeks. Then they'll revisit the Cornelian Gallery as they would the scene of a fatal car crash.'

A tired grin crossed Bonita Green's face. 'You may be right. Actually, having had Denzil Willoughby's works on display may have done more permanent damage than the row.'

'I wouldn't worry too much about that. The speed with which you've got rid of them will commend itself to your loyal customers.'

'I hope so. It's quite important, actually, because I've been thinking of selling up for some time.'

'Selling up the Cornelian Gallery?'

'Yes. I'm not getting any younger.' Her words made Carole think for the first time how old Bonita Green must be. The dark hair and make-up was an efficient disguise, but the woman underneath it was probably nearer seventy than sixty. Quite a lot nearer seventy.

'But obviously I want to sell the gallery as a going concern. Anyone interested is going to check out the turnover figures, so I don't want any blips.' She sighed. 'I should never have listened to Giles. I knew from the start that putting on a Denzil Willoughby exhibition was a bad idea, but I let myself be persuaded. Mothers can be very blinkered when it comes to dealing with their sons.'

'Yes,' said Carole, wondering whether 'blinkered' had ever been the right word to describe her dealings with Stephen.

'Still,' Bonita Green went on, 'I'm going to survive this setback. The Cornelian Gallery is my baby and when I come to sell it, I will ensure that all my hard work has been properly rewarded. And no one – family or not family – is going to prevent that from happening.'

Carole was surprised by the ferocious determination in Bonita Green's tone. Beneath her faintly ridiculous dated appearance there was a core of steel.

FIFTEEN

On the Tuesday morning, Jude had a phone call from Chervil Whittaker. No mention was made of Fennel's death. 'I just wondered if you'd thought any more about my idea?'

'Which idea?'

'Of you doing some healing sessions at Walden?'

'Well, I still don't want a permanent commitment of the kind you were talking about . . . you know, with a financial retainer.'

'No, OK, that's cool. But I'd just like to list you as an available service . . . you know, for the right people and obviously according to your availability.'

'Well . . .'

'I mean, at Walden we're now offering acupuncture, reiki and hot stone massage.'

'You've found people to do those?'

'Yes, been doing a bit of local research. And I'd love to add your "Total Healing" service to the list.'

'I wouldn't really want it to be called that.'

'Why not?'

'Somehow "Total Healing" sounds too all-embracing. If I read that in a brochure, it'd set alarm bells ringing for me.'

'What kind of alarm bells?'

'I'd suspect charlatanism.'

'Ah. If I just called it "Healing" . . .?'

Jude was torn. She didn't like the idea of her services being offered as an optional extra for holidaymakers with more money than sense. On the other hand she did want to find out the truth about Fennel Whittaker's death and having an ongoing link with Butterwyke House might prove very useful to the cause of her investigation . . .

'I'd be happier with that,' she said.

'Great.' Chervil took the words as full assent to her proposition. 'I wonder . . . would you be free this Saturday?'

'Possibly. What for?'

'We're having the official launch of Walden.'

'The one postponed from last weekend?'

But the girl wasn't going to go down that route. She seemed to be deliberately avoiding any mention of her sister's death. 'It's really only in the last couple of days that I've decided to make the launch more public. I'm inviting the local papers along, and some of the trade press. You know, holiday magazines, catering journals, that kind of thing.'

'Isn't it going to be rather short notice for them to come this Saturday?'

There was a confident canniness in Chervil Whittaker's voice as she said, 'It might be for some events, but I happen to know that the press have been desperate to get into Butterwyke House for some time.'

Of course. Though Ned and Sheena Whittaker were familiar figures on the charity entertainment circuit of West Sussex, they were notoriously jealous of their privacy when it came to their home. Their daughter knew the publicity value of what she'd be offering the local press.

'Also, I think I might be able to organize a few celebrities at the launch.'

'Really?'

'Oh yes. So would you be able to make it to Walden this Saturday?'

'I'm sure I could.'

'I wonder . . . You live in Fethering, don't you?'

'That's right.'

'Look, I'm coming over there shortly with my boyfriend.'

'Giles.'

'Oh yes, of course, you've met him. I forgot. Anyway, he's got to pick up some stuff from his mother's flat.'

'I heard he was moving out of there.'

'Mm. Anyway, we'll be over in, I suppose, about half an hour. Wondered if we could just meet for a chat about your involvement in the Walden project?'

'Fine,' said Jude instantly. She wasn't going to turn down an investigative gift like that.

'What, shall we come to your place?'

'Why don't we meet for a drink in the Crown and Anchor?'

Jude got to the pub before her visitors and was served by the landlord himself. And, as was so often the case, Ted Crisp had a joke for her. 'How do you recognize a dyslexic Yorkshireman?' he asked.

'I don't know,' she replied dutifully. 'How do you recognize a dyslexic Yorkshireman?'

'He's the one wearing a cat flap!'

Jude quite liked the joke, but didn't laugh at it as loudly as Ted himself did. 'Again, how much the stand-up circuit must miss you,' she said.

'Ooh, incidentally, you must come to this. Week tomorrow.' He shoved a printed flyer across the bar to her. The space was dominated by an image of Elvis Presley in his sequinned romper-suit phase. The text read: 'FOR ONE NIGHT ONLY – ELVIS COMES TO THE CROWN AND ANCHOR! RECAPTURE YOUR YOUTH, THRILL TO THE HITS! LET ELVIS LOVE YOU TENDER. 8.00 p.m. TICKETS: £5.'

'What on earth's this?' asked Jude.

'Like it says – Elvis.'

'The real one?'

'Of course.'

'Oh yes? And he'll be arriving with Lord Lucan, both of them riding on Shergar?'

'Uncanny, Jude. How did you know that?'

'Instinct. Unless, of course, you prefer to give me the real explanation . . .?'

'That bloke Spider.'

'The one who does the framing at the Cornelian Gallery?'

'The very same. I got talking to him at that Private View. Turns out he does the full Elvis impersonation schtick.'

'That would at least explain his haircut.'

'Yeah. Anyway, I said I'd give him a night in the function room. See what he's like. You'll come?'

'Sure.'

'And bring Carole.'

Jude looked dubious. 'I'm not sure that Elvis would be exactly Carole's sort of thing.'

'Bring Carole,' Ted Crisp repeated forcibly.

'OK,' said Jude with a grin, and took her large Chilean Chardonnay across to one of the alcove tables.

Chervil Whittaker and Giles Green appeared only moments later. Both were wearing pinstriped City suits, hers with the understated perfection of cut for which the best designers charge a small fortune. His was more conventional, but pretty expensive too. Having checked Jude had a drink, Giles got fizzy mineral waters with ice for both of them. Clearly this was going to be a business meeting.

'I just wanted to run this text by you,' said Chervil, handing across a rough of a flyer for Walden. As with the website which Carole had shown her, the quality of the printing and detail was very slick, set over professional photographs of the glamping site. And the 'Deeply Felt' pun featured again. 'It's there, under "Therapeutic Services".'

Jude read the indicated paragraph. 'An expert healer may also be booked by arrangement for one-hour sessions. She has wide experience in dealing with a variety of conditions, both physical and mental.'

She didn't like what it said; she was still alienated by the thought of her skills being sold off in convenient chunks like carpet tiles. But she did want to keep Chervil Whittaker onside in the cause of investigation. So the only objection she made was to the description of 'one-hour sessions'.

'You mean the healing takes longer?' asked Chervil.

'It can do.'

'How long?'

Jude puffed out her cheeks and spread her hands helplessly wide. 'How long is a piece of string? I'm afraid I can't predict the duration of a healing session. Sometimes it just works and only takes ten minutes. Other times it doesn't work at all. The energy's just not flowing.'

'Well, suppose,' said Chervil, 'that I just cut the "one-hour" and say: "An expert healer may also be booked by arrange- ment for individual sessions"?'

Jude still didn't feel quite comfortable with the wording – or indeed the whole concept – but she didn't raise any further objections.

'Good,' said Giles. 'We can get these printed this afternoon and email the text to the press list.'

He spoke with authority, and Jude wondered whether he was now muscling in on his girlfriend's business, just as he had with his mother's. If that were the case, Chervil didn't seem to resent the intrusion.

'I'll talk to Gale Mostyn,' he continued.

'Fine,' said Chervil.

'Sorry, who's she?' asked Jude. 'Gale Mostyn.'

'It's not a she,' replied Giles. 'It's a PR company.'

'One of the best in the country,' said Chervil. 'Mum and Dad have used them for yonks.'

'And are they organizing the launch on Saturday?'

'Giles and I are actually organizing it, but Gale Mostyn will have quite a lot of input. A couple of their people will be attending.'

'Ah,' said Jude, and then went on. 'I couldn't help noticing, Giles, as I went past the Cornelian Gallery, that the Denzil Willoughby artwork was no longer on display.'

'No,' he agreed airily. 'I'm afraid there was – as so often happens in the art world – a slight difference of opinion between artist and gallery-owner. Denzil had a bit of a row with my mother, I'm afraid, and so he decided to withdraw from the exhibition.'

That wasn't the way things had happened according to what Bonita had told Carole, but Jude didn't argue with the facts. 'And have you had a row with her too?'

Giles looked at Jude in puzzlement. 'What do you mean?'

'Well, I heard you'd moved out of her flat.'

He grimaced. 'Not much escapes the gossips of Fethering, does it? There was a social network here long before Facebook and Twitter were invented. Anyway, with regard to my moving, that was always part of the plan. I was only camping with Mother on a temporary basis . . . until I moved in with Chervil.'

'Which he has now done,' said the girlfriend with considerable satisfaction. 'We're sharing one of the guest flats at Butterwyke House.'

'Not one of the yurts at Walden?'

Chervil grinned. 'No, I think there's a strong argument for us not living over the shop.' She spoke as if the glamping site was already an established business, and one in which she and Giles were equal partners. 'Besides,' she continued bullishly, 'we're hoping to have all the yurts full of paying customers. I've a feeling we're going to get a lot of coverage for the launch on Saturday. Gale Mostyn are bloody good at securing column inches. They'll see to it that Walden gets maximum publicity.'

'But presumably,' suggested Jude, 'only the right sort of publicity.'

'What do you mean by that?'

'I'm sorry, but I can't help observing that you haven't mentioned your sister.'

'Why should I?'

'Well, it was only a few days ago that—'

'Listen, Jude, the fact that I don't mention Fennel doesn't necessarily mean I didn't care about her. I'll find time for my grief, just as my parents will for theirs.'

'Your father's in a pretty bad state. He came to see me yesterday.'

'I know. He said. But look, Walden is a business proposition. I've given up a high-paying job in the City to bring my skills to bear on it.'

'What were you actually doing in the City?'

'Oh, you know,' replied Chervil with a shrug. 'Kind of PR.'

Jude got the impression that perhaps Chervil Whittaker's previous career hadn't been as successful as previously implied. Maybe her parents hadn't been so much taking advantage of her skills as bailing her out with the Walden project.

'Anyway,' the girl went on, 'I'm going to make this thing work, and I'm not going to let anything – even my sister's suicide – stop me from realizing that dream.

'I'm very sorry for Fennel, sorry for the illness that she suffered from, and sorry that she couldn't see any other way out of that illness than taking her own life. But I'm not going to let thoughts of her stand in my way. For too long I've had to worry about her, worry what effect anything I did would have on Fennel's –' she put the next two words in quotation marks formed by her fingers – '"fragile psyche". Well, I've had enough of that. From now on I don't have to worry at all what she thinks; and let me tell you, it's a bloody relief. Getting on with my own life from now on will be a lot easier without Fennel around!'

Chervil seemed almost shocked by the vehemence of her own words. In the ensuing silence, Jude heard from the bar the voice of Ted Crisp asking yet another customer, 'How do you recognize a dyslexic Yorkshireman . . .?'

Then she said to Chervil, 'Presumably, if you're having the opening on Saturday, the police have finished any searches that they have been making at Walden?'

'Yes, they've cleared the site.'

Which, Jude reckoned, must mean that they were concluding their investigations; that they had categorized Fennel Whittaker's death as the straightforward suicide it appeared to be.

'Oh, and incidentally, Jude . . .'

'Yes.'

'At the launch on Saturday, no mention of what Fennel did. We don't want that spoiling all the positive publicity we're going to get for Walden.'

'You mean you're hoping to keep Fennel's death out of the press?'

'We are not hoping to, Jude. We are definitely going to keep Fennel's death out of the press.'

'You'll be lucky in a place like—'

Chervil Whittaker smoothly rode over her words. 'We are going to keep it out of the press. Gale Mostyn are very good at that sort of thing, you know.'

SIXTEEN

'So they're just trying to airbrush Fennel's death out of history, are they?' asked Carole.

'Seems that way,' said Jude.

'But can they? I'd have thought, given the amount of gossip there is around an area like this, the news'll get out, won't it?'

'They can't stop people talking, no, but they can keep the story out of the media.'

'By using the Gale Mostyn company?'

'Certainly. Privacy may come expensive, but it can usually be bought. Think of all those footballers taking out super-injunctions to keep the press away from their mistresses.'

'Huh. And we're supposed to be living in a society that prides itself on the rights of free speech.' Carole turned a beady eye on her neighbour. 'You don't seem too worried about it, Jude.'

'No, I'm not really. Having talked to Ned on Monday and seen the state he's in, I'm in no hurry to make things worse for him. He can do without having reporters camping on his front doorstep.'

'I can see that, but, on the other hand, if Fennel Whittaker was actually murdered . . .'

Jude screwed up her face wryly. 'And what are we basing that supposition on?'

Carole was affronted. 'We're basing it on what you told me. You said that Fennel was so positive on the night she's supposed to have killed herself that she couldn't possibly have done it.'

'Yes . . .' Jude looked uncharacteristically dubious. 'But now I'm beginning to wonder about that. I told you what Detective Inspector Hodgkinson said about depressives often doing it when their mood begins to lift.'

'You did.'

'The trouble is, Fennel would fit that profile exactly. She'd been through a really bad depression. Bawling Denzil Willoughby out had lifted her out of it. In a more positive mood she says to herself, well, I'm never going to go through that again, she laces a bottle of wine with liquid paracetamol, she secretes a knife from the kitchen, she . . .' Jude's open-handed gesture showed that she didn't need to complete the sentence.

'Is that really what you think?'

'Well . . .'

'Jude, are you saying you really think Fennel Whittaker committed suicide?' A silence. 'Or do you think she was murdered?'

There was another silence before Jude conceded, 'I think she was murdered.'

'And what do you base that conclusion on?'

Jude replied apologetically, 'Instinct.'

'Well, that's good enough for me.'

The following day, the Wednesday, Carole was surprised to get an email from Chervil Whittaker, inviting her to attend the launch of Walden. 'Since you've expressed interest in making a booking, we thought you might like to have a look at the facilities on offer.'

Of course, she was delighted and had no hesitation in accepting. Jude was going to be there and Carole would much rather share the occasion than rely on a report from her neighbour. And any opportunity to snoop round the environs of Butterwyke House could only be helpful in their ongoing investigation.

But the invitation still sounded a strange chord with her. After all, she had already had 'a look at the facilities on offer.' Chervil Whittaker herself had shown Carole and Jude round the weekend before last. Surely the girl would have remembered that. She had registered that they'd already met when they'd spoken on the telephone about the potential Walden booking.

Carole got the uneasy feeling that, however much she was keen to snoop on Chervil Whittaker, the girl was at least as keen to snoop on her.

SEVENTEEN

The weather couldn't have been better for the press launch of Walden on the Saturday. A perfect West Sussex early-May day, not a cloud in the sky, the Downs rolling opulently to the north, and the other way the glint of the English Channel. Maybe perfect weather was just another luxury service laid on by Gale Mostyn.

They certainly seemed to have arranged everything else with exemplary efficiency. Their greatest achievement – given how loath local reporters usually are to attend any function, least of all at a weekend – was the number of press representatives they had managed to drum up. There were some very young ones, presumably working on local papers, who looked tentative and nervous, perhaps wondering how much longer there would be any local papers for them to work on.

But there were also some older, hard-bitten-looking journalists from the nationals, with matching older, hard-bitten-looking photographers.

It was soon obvious to Carole and Jude that the press hadn't just come to look at yurts, however well appointed they might be. They had come for the famous faces.

Clearly Gale Mostyn had pulled out all the stops for the launch. A few of the famous faces were familiar to Carole, though she couldn't put names to them. Jude recognized more and, chatting to other people (how was it she always started so easily chatting to other people, Carole wondered plaintively for the millionth time), managed to get the identities of the others. Though Walden hadn't justified the appearance of any A-list celebrities, those who had turned up were definitely towards the beginning of the alphabet and would deserve inclusion in most of the national gossip columns.

They included, Carole was informed, a lingerie model who had just dumped a Premiership footballer after tabloid 'love rat' allegations, a singer predicted to go Top Hundred on iTunes within the next week, a stand-up comic who had recently become the voice of a smoothie-maker in a new ad campaign, and a girl from Rochdale whose dance act with her Siamese cat was tipped to win a major television talent show. It may not have been the Great and Good of West Sussex, but then the Great and Good of West Sussex wouldn't even have got the local newspapers to turn out at a weekend. Gale Mostyn had, however, produced a guest list to set contemporary journalists slavering.

And there was one person there whom even Carole Seddon recognized. Sam Torino. Well over six foot tall, leggy, long black hair, hazel eyes with glints of green in them. Canadian by birth, international model, former lover of a good few of rock's royalty, she was present with the three children born of her three most famous liaisons. She and they were dressed in the kind of casual wear which looked wonderful on them, but which would never look the same on ordinary people who bought the identical garments.

Sam Torino was a woman with a Teflon reputation. Affairs, marriages and divorces came and went, but her serenity seemed

undiminished. In spite of her jet-set lifestyle, she had a core
of domestic ordinariness which earned her the respect of the
wives whose husbands fancied her, both in her adopted British
home and in the States, where she still frequently flew for her
most lucrative fashion shoots. To have got Sam Torino to
Chervil Whittaker's launch, Gale Mostyn must have had
considerable muscle.

And it soon became clear that she wasn't just there for the
Saturday. She and her family were tasting the Walden experience to the full, staying overnight in one of the yurts, and
going to be photographed over breakfast the following
morning. The column inches for Butterwyke House's new
venture would be gratifyingly long. Carole and Jude wondered
whether Sam Torino had been lined up for the previous
weekend and then agreed to the postponement following
Fennel's death. Somehow they thought not. They got the
impression Chervil and Giles had been telling the truth and
the initiative for the launch had been conceived within the
last few days.

The one person who wasn't present that afternoon was Ned
Whittaker. His wife Sheena was there, more relaxed than
Carole and Jude had seen her before, drinking and chatting
cheerfully with anyone and everyone. Carole thought her
husband's absence was odd. Jude, who knew the depth of
Ned's grief over his daughter's death, was less surprised. To
both of them Sheena's apparent insouciance seemed in the
circumstances bizarre.

The whole of the Walden site was *en fête* for the occasion.
Bunting hung from the trees and, rather incongruously, a
maypole stood one side of the central area, with a bonfire on
the other. The yurts themselves were garlanded with coloured
cloth and their doorways hung with bright curtains. Every
viewpoint offered a photo opportunity.

And the assembled *paparazzi* were not wasting those opportunities. Smartly-suited girls from Gale Mostyn, looking
impossibly cool in the warm sunshine, choreographed the
photographs, lining up the assembled celebrities in one setting
after another, all the time working in close consultation with
Chervil Whittaker and Giles Green. Meanwhile black-trousered

waitresses moved among the guests with trays of champagne, Pimm's and fruit juices.

Sam Torino and her family had their own minder who organized the photos they were required for. Dressed in an oatmeal-coloured linen suit with an open-necked blue shirt, he was introduced to Carole and Jude as Nigel Mostyn. Clearly Sam Torino's stature required the personal attentions of one of Gale Mostyn's partners.

A lifetime's modelling had given her grace and patience. She made no fuss as the photographers posed and reposed her; and the less-experienced ones from the local papers seemed to need a lot of reposing. If any of her children showed signs of boredom or restlessness, she reprimanded them in a manner that was old-fashioned almost to the point of being schoolmarmish.

To her surprise, Carole was having a rather good time. Because she would later be driving her Renault back to Fethering, she had determined at the beginning of the afternoon to restrict herself to one drink, but the first Pimm's weakened her resolve and she allowed her glass to be refilled from the ever-circulating jug. Despite inevitable misgivings before the event, she enjoyed having no responsibility. She could just melt into the background and observe what was going on, hoping – though with small expectation of fulfilment – to pick up some small clue that might help her solve the mystery of Fennel Whittaker's death.

For Jude the situation was different. She had been invited to the launch in her professional capacity and, as the various minor celebrities were photographed with various alternative therapists, she felt a growing sense of awkwardness. The lingerie model who had just dumped a Premiership footballer after tabloid 'love rat' allegations was led into the treatment room to be shot revealing a lot of flesh while she underwent a mock-up of a hot stone massage. The stand-up comic who had recently become the voice of a smoothie-maker in a new ad campaign was posed by an acupuncture chart with needles stuck in his nose. Jude felt uncharacteristically ill at ease.

The moment came. Chervil approached her, together with

one of the smoothly suited Gale Mostyn girls. 'I wonder, Jude, whether you'd be up to a photograph with Shaylene?'

'Shaylene?'

'She's the girl from Rochdale who's got this fantastic dance act with her Siamese cat.'

'And what do you want me to be doing with her?'

Chervil Whittaker looked nonplussed. 'Well, healing, obviously.'

'Healing isn't a very photogenic subject, I'm afraid.'

'Well, can you be sort of waving your hands around or something? I was hoping Shaylene would be able to bring Gin Seng with her.'

'Gin Seng is nothing to do with the kind of healing I do.'

'Gin Seng is the name of her cat. But since they've got famous, Gin Seng's insurers have got very strict about how much he can travel around with Shaylene.'

'I'm sorry, Chervil,' said Jude firmly, 'but I'm afraid I can't be photographed healing. It wouldn't be real, unless I was actually doing the healing. And if I was doing it, I certainly wouldn't be being photographed.'

Carole, standing nearby, was mildly surprised. Her neighbour was usually up for most things. But now Jude was showing the kind of reticence that would have been more characteristic of Carole herself.

'Oh,' said Chervil, puzzled by not getting her own way.

Rescue for Jude came in an unexpected form. 'You can't photograph someone healing,' announced a warm Canadian voice.

It was Sam Torino who had overheard their conversation as she passed from one photo opportunity to another.

'What do you mean?' asked Chervil.

'It trivializes the whole thing,' said Sam Torino, putting into words exactly what Jude had been feeling.

Chervil Whittaker backed down immediately and moved off to get the singer predicted to go Top Hundred on iTunes within the next week to take up some positions with the Hatha yoga instructor.

'Thank you for that,' said Jude to her rescuer.

Sam Torino shrugged. 'No problem. So many people just

don't *get* healing. They think it's some kind of conjuring trick.'

'Have you had some yourself?'

'Yes, a good few times.' The famous hazel eyes looked into Jude's brown ones. 'I get the feeling you're a good healer.'

The line needed no explanation; their contact was instinctive. 'Thank you,' said Jude.

'I have a problem,' Sam Torino confided. 'Would you be able to take a look at it?'

'For the cameras?'

'Of course not. For me. Would you mind staying a bit when all this hoopla's over?

Jude agreed.

Wandering round Walden, taking everything in and feeling atypically mellow after her third glass of Pimm's, Carole found herself with Sheena Whittaker and suddenly realized that she hadn't expressed condolences to the bereaved mother. She made up for lost time, stammering out appropriate platitudes.

But she was surprised to be cut short in her sentiments. 'We don't need to talk about that today,' said Sheena quite sharply.

'I'm sorry. I just thought—'

'Fennel was headstrong. She always went her own way. And she was always drawing attention to herself too. I know this is not something that a mother should say about her daughter, but in many ways my life will be simpler without Fennel in it.'

Carole Seddon was profoundly shocked. For two reasons. First, because Jude hadn't told her what Ned had said about his wife's reaction to their daughter's death. And, second, because of the transformation in Sheena Whittaker's manner. Gone was the tentative insecurity Carole had noted on their previous meeting. It was as if the absence of Fennel had literally lifted a burden from her mother's shoulders.

So marked was the change that, for a moment, Carole even wondered whether Sheena Whittaker might have had a hand in arranging the outcome which was clearly such a relief to her. It was not impossible.

EIGHTEEN

'Are you sure this is all right? There isn't something else you should be doing?'

'It's fine and dandy, Jude,' said Sam Torino. 'They got their pound of flesh. I've done all they asked me to. I've earned a little "Me Time".'

'What about the kids?'

'They're fine. They're toasting marshmallows over the bonfire with Katya.'

'Katya?'

'One of their nannies.'

'Oh. Right. You said you had a problem . . .?'

They were in one of the side rooms of the treatment yurt with the door firmly closed. Even though everything had been meticulously cleaned and the white tiles gleamed, Jude could not quite remove from her memory the image of the space spattered with Fennel Whittaker's blood.

Sam Torino, incapable of looking less than elegant in any posture, draped her long limbs across the treatment couch. 'It's a back thing. I always swore I'd never turn into one of those old women who had *backs*, and Lordy, Lordy, it's caught up with me. Maybe growing old is just a process of becoming all the things one swore one'd never be.'

'You're not old,' said Jude.

'I am too.'

'You still look stunning.'

'Maybe. But if you knew how much longer it takes me to look stunning these days . . .' She laughed grimly. 'As I say, it's a back thing.'

'Caused by any particular injury?'

'I don't think the last divorce helped.'

'But no physical injury?'

'Not that I know of. Mind you, I grew up in the School of

Hard Knocks. So it could be any one of those knocks that started the thing off.'

'How long have you had the pain?'

'Since the last divorce.'

'Really?'

Sam Torino nodded. Close to, Jude could see the fine tracery of lines around her eyes. The model had been right. She'd always be beautiful, but time was beginning to fray away at her perfect outline.

'Lie down on the couch and let's have a look.'

'Sure.' Sam swivelled round to lie on her back. 'Do you want me to take anything off?' After a lifetime of backstage changing at catwalk shows, she had no coyness about removing her clothes.

'Just the shoes for the time being.'

Sam Torino slipped off what looked like Converse Hi Top trainers (though a discerning *fashionista* would have recognized them as being by a far more exclusive designer). Like all her clothes, they appeared to have been put on the first time that day.

'Could you just lie down on your front?' Sam obeyed. 'Just get comfortable. From what you said, you've used healers before.'

'Sure. I'll try anything. Anything that helps.'

'And did the healing help?'

'Sometimes.'

'When you said you'd had the pain since your last divorce, was that a joke?'

'No, I had the pain before the divorce, but then I divorced him.' She stopped herself. 'Sorry, I suffer from Reactive Wisecrack Syndrome. When I'm nervous I make dreadful jokes.'

'Are you nervous now? You don't look it.'

'One thing you learn with a career like mine . . . Whatever you're feeling, don't look it.'

'Well, you're succeeding. Nobody would know you're nervous.'

'I am too.'

'So why are you nervous now?'

'Because if you're anything like a decent healer – and I get the feeling you are – then you aren't just going to be checking out my body, you're going to be looking inside my soul. And I've got a lot of clutter down there in my soul, and some of it's clutter I'm ashamed of.'

Jude nodded. What Sam Torino was saying to her didn't seem strange at all. With an inward smile, she thanked the Lord that Carole wasn't in the yurt with them at that moment.

'OK, Sam, just relax. I'm just going to check where the pain is.' Jude ran her hands expertly along the contours of the woman's body. No contact was actually made with the designer clothes, her fingers hovered a couple of inches above the famous contours. They kept being drawn back to one source of heat.

'That's where the pain is, isn't it?' pronounced Jude, lightly touching a spot just above Sam's right buttock.

'Hey, you're good,' said the model. 'Got it in one. Any idea how to get rid of the sonofabitch?'

'I can try.' Jude focused her energy on to the troublesome area. 'So you say this started at the time of the divorce?'

'In the run-up to it, yeah.'

'You know why, don't you?'

'Do I? You tell me.'

'It's because you're Sam Torino. Everyone who meets you gets the full Sam Torino experience, regardless of whether you're feeling very Sam Torino or not.'

'Meaning?'

'You know what I mean. You never give yourself a break, Sam.'

'I do too. I programme gym visits and spa days into my schedules. If I listed the number of vacations I take it'd embarrass me.'

'That's not what I'm talking about. When you're in the gym, when you're on vacation, you're surrounded by other people. Other people who admire you, who're impressed with the way you manage all the demands of your life. They expect you to give them the full-on Sam Torino treatment every moment of the day. And you oblige them.'

There was a long silence. Still not touching the woman's

body, the knuckles of Jude's hands were whitening with the intensity she was channelling into it. Then, in a long drawl, Sam Torino said, 'Yes, Jude. You're good.' Then, after a moment, she asked, 'Can you take away the pain?'

'I think I can for the time being. If you want it to stay away, you'll have to make some changes.'

'Like what?'

'For your condition I would prescribe solitude.'

'How d'ya mean?'

'Just as important as your gym and spa visits, you need time on your own. You should programme that into your schedule. Time to think.'

'Are you talking meditation? Because I've done classes in that and—'

'Classes, no. Classes are with other people. They still have expectations of you. You want to be alone when the only person who has expectations of you is you.'

'I have very high expectations of myself.'

'Of course you do. And that's good. All I'm asking is that you carve out for yourself half an hour a day to think about those expectations. Are they realistic? Would it really matter that much if you let your guard slip for a moment? Why not allow a little imperfection into your life? You're a human being. All human beings have flaws.'

There was an even longer silence while Sam Torino took this in. Then she said, 'Do you know how much you're asking?'

'I know exactly how much I'm asking.'

'Hm.' More silence. 'I'll give it a go. More "Me Time".'

'Don't think of it as "Me Time". Think of it as "Nothing Time". Just time when you stop feeling the pressure to be Sam Torino. See where it takes you.'

'OK.' She flexed her long legs. 'The pain's easing, you know.'

'Yes. A little bit longer and it'll be gone . . . for the time being.'

'And whether or not I keep it away is up to me, huh?'

'Sure is,' said Jude, dropping into a parody Canadian accent.

'Right.' Sam Torino looked around the interior of the treatment yurt. 'Funny, this place doesn't have any ghosts . . . considering what happened here so recently.'

Jude was shocked. 'I didn't know you knew about that.'

'Ned told me.'

'You know Ned?'

'Sure.'

'Can I ask how?'

'No problem. There are a lot of events which people with a certain level of income get involved in. Charity fund-raisers, that kind of stuff. I can't remember the first one I met him at, but we kind of got on and stayed in touch.'

'So is that why you're here for the Walden launch?'

'Sure.'

'I thought Gale Mostyn had organized your participation.'

Sam Torino let out a haughty laugh. 'Gale Mostyn are not big players. I have my own personal PR company. Sure, Gale Mostyn can organize a line-up of reality TV hopefuls, but they don't have access to the A-list.' Somehow her words didn't sound arrogant. She was just describing the realities of celebrity life. 'And, incidentally . . .' She reached into her back trouser pocket and produced a neat card case. 'If you ever need to contact me, use this mobile number. If you try going through my PR people, they won't let you near me.'

'Thank you,' said Jude, pocketing the card she'd been given. 'So, Sam, I assume you heard from Ned about what happened to Fennel?'

'Sure. I also heard that you were the one who found the body.'

'Yes.' Jude had a sudden thought. 'Was that why you wanted to talk to me?'

'Sorry?'

'Is that why you asked me to stay behind after the launch?'

Sam Torino looked puzzled. 'Hell, no. I asked you to stay behind because you're a healer. Because you're doing wonders for the pain in my hip.'

'Oh, good.'

'Why would I want to talk to you about Fennel?'

'I don't know. Sorry, I wasn't thinking straight.'

'Ned's in a terrible state about it.'

'I know.'

'He always was besotted with that girl. Fathers and first daughters, you know . . .'

'Whereas Sheena . . .?'

'Hell, who knows what goes on in a mind like hers?' Sam Torino clearly had less time for Fennel's mother than she had for her father.

'Did you know Fennel?'

'I met her a couple of times. Ned brought her along to a few charity things. I think the idea was to promote her career as an artist . . . you know, get her some wealthy contacts who might commission stuff from her. I don't think it paid off. Ned can sometimes be a bit naive in the workings of the celebrity circus.'

'How did Fennel strike you when you met her?'

Sam Torino shrugged. 'Pretty. Nice kid. If I hadn't heard from Ned about her mental problems I'd never have guessed there was anything wrong.'

'Has he talked to you much about her illness?'

'Not a lot. He told me when she made the first attempt.'

'You already knew him then?'

'Sure.'

'Did he give you much detail about what happened?'

'No, he just told me that she'd done it. Up until then, like I said, I wouldn't have known there was anything wrong with her. But from that time on I could see how much it got to him. Worrying about Fennel was a constant anxiety to him, and a constant drain on his energy.'

'Did Ned tell you about her death before today?'

'Sure. He called me the weekend it happened. He was in a hell of a state.'

'Yes. I saw him soon after.'

A new shrewdness came into Sam Torino's eyes. 'He was also worried about local gossip.'

'Oh?'

'Even the suggestion that some people thought it wasn't suicide at all. That Fennel was murdered.'

'When something like that happens in an area like this,' Jude responded breezily, 'you're bound get a lot of crackpot theories doing the rounds.'

'Ned said there were a couple of things you thought were odd when you found Fennel's body.'

'Well, really only the fact that there was no sign of her mobile.'

'Hm.' The famous eyes were turned searchingly on to Jude. 'So does that mean you're one of the people who thinks it might have been murder?'

Jude was torn. Part of her wanted to admit the truth, in the hope perhaps of getting more information out of Sam Torino. But she knew the dangers of spreading suspicions and allegations. She also got the feeling that anything she said would get straight back to Ned Whittaker. And she didn't want to do anything that might add to his misery.

So all she came up with by way of reply was: 'I suppose I just didn't want to think it was suicide, so I considered all of the other options.'

'And are you still considering them?'

'Maybe a bit.'

Sam Torino nodded slowly. 'But the police took the suicide at face value?'

'Oh yes. Sam, don't you worry about what I'm thinking. I've allowed myself to get rather emotionally involved.'

Another slow, thoughtful nod.

'No, really, I'm sure it was suicide,' Jude lied. 'When Ned talked to you, did he have any idea what might have tipped Fennel over the edge?'

'No. But she'd been ill for a long time. And I can't think getting involved with that little shit Denzil Willoughby can have helped.'

'You know Denzil?'

'Sure.'

'Why, have you bought stuff from him?'

Sam Torino's fine nose wrinkled with disgust at the suggestion. 'Hell, no. If I buy art, I go for the real McCoy. If I want a Damien Hirst, I get a Damien Hirst. Not Denzil Willoughby's kind of imitative rubbish.'

'So how did you meet Denzil?'

'Through his father.'

'Oh?'

'Addison Willoughby. You heard of him?'

'I've heard the name.'

'Founded one of the biggest advertising companies in the world. Another of the super-rich mafia.'

'Whom you have met at charity events?'

'Exactly. He brought Denzil along to a few, maybe trying to do the same service as Ned was for Fennel.'

'Was that when the two of them met?'

'I don't know about that. They may have known each other before. All I know is that when I heard from Ned they were an item, I thought: "Uh-oh, that's going to mean trouble."'

'Why did you think that?'

'Denzil Willoughby once had a thing with a girlfriend of mine. She didn't enjoy the relationship one bit.'

'Why? Because he's so up himself?'

'No, she could have coped with that. She's a model, she's used to dealing with egos. You wouldn't believe how many dickheads hang around the catwalks. No, with Denzil Willoughby, it was the physical violence she couldn't put up with.'

'Really?'

'Yes, that boy's got a sadistic – not to say murderous – streak in him.'

'Has he ever been charged with anything?'

'Girlfriends have tried, but they've all been bought off. By Addison.' Sam Torino grinned cynically. 'Amazing how flexible the law becomes for those who can afford it.'

NINETEEN

Of course, the Whittakers had a driver. And of course he looked as unlike a uniformed chauffeur as it was possible to be. The laid-back style of Butterwyke House was carried through in all its domestic staff. Though they were undoubtedly servants, they dressed and were treated more like members of the family. Ned and Sheena still weren't quite at ease with their huge wealth.

The driver's name was Kier. In his early thirties, casually dressed in a crisp white T-shirt, well-ironed jeans and neat moccasins. Chervil had arranged before Jude started her session with Sam Torino that he would drive her back to Woodside Cottage and he was hanging around Walden when she appeared from the treatment yurt. But Kier didn't look as though he were waiting in a professional capacity. That wouldn't have been cool. He somehow managed to make it appear as if he just happened to be there, and yes, he'd be happy to take Jude home.

He drove a very new-looking Toyota Prius. Of course, the Whittakers would run green cars. Though their contribution to saving the planet might have been a little diminished by the size of their fleet of Toyota Priuses.

Jude was pleased to have the opportunity to question someone with perhaps a different view of recent events at Butterwyke House. And though, as ever, she was emotionally drained by her healing efforts, she quickly got on to the subject of Fennel Whittaker's death.

Kier, she found, was more than ready to talk about it. In fact, from the fervency of his words, she got the impression that he might have held a candle for the dead girl for some time. He certainly didn't have much time for Denzil Willoughby.

'I used to drive the two of them around a bit. Ned's very generous with my services.' He didn't sound as though he were entirely happy with that state of affairs. 'And of course when it came to Fennel . . . well, he could never refuse her anything.'

'No. I saw him earlier in the week. He was terribly cut up about what happened to her.'

'I don't think he'll ever recover,' said Kier, as if stating an unarguable fact. 'I think she could have got better. There seem to be lots of new treatments, drugs, talking therapies . . . It's probably the best time ever to suffer from depression, in terms of getting the condition cured.'

'Is it something about which you know a lot?' It was the polite way of asking whether Kier himself suffered from depression.

'No. Not really. I've got most of what I know from talking to Fennel. She was up with all the latest treatments. She was absolutely determined to get better, somehow. That's why I was so devastated when I heard that she'd actually done it.'

This was good news to Jude. It meant that she wasn't the

only person who had found positivity in the girl's mindset. 'And you think she did actually do it?' she asked gently.

The slowness of Kier's response showed that the idea of murder had never entered his head. 'How d'you mean?'

'Well, I'd seen her a couple of times in the weeks before her death and, like you, I thought she seemed quite up, certainly not on the verge of topping herself. So, if she didn't commit suicide . . .'

'Well, it sure as hell wasn't an accident.' Kier was again slow – or perhaps unwilling – to make the logical connection. 'Are you suggesting that she might have been murdered?' he asked at last.

Jude shrugged. 'As Sherlock Holmes put it, "Once you eliminate the impossible, whatever remains, no matter how improbable, must be the truth."'

'Yes, I've read some of those stories,' said the driver thoughtfully, still trying to come to terms with the new idea. 'I think I'd rather believe that Fennel was murdered . . . you know, as opposed to killing herself.'

'If that were true, we'd be back to the old question: "Who Done It?'

Kier nodded slowly. 'Yes, we would.'

'Any thoughts?' asked Jude. 'Anyone you'd cast in the role of murderer?' He remained silent. 'You probably know as much as anyone about what goes on at Butterwyke House.'

'Yes, I see quite a lot.'

'And you probably know how the different family members get on together . . .' Jude knew she was pushing her luck. The Butterwyke House staff she'd met all seemed extremely loyal and might be reluctant to confide anything to their employers' discredit.

But Kier seemed to be too caught up in the ramifications of the new idea to feel such scruples. 'Well, Chervil and Fennel always had a fairly volatile relationship, but I think basically they were OK with each other. I mean, I think Chervil resented Fennel's illness . . .'

'That's the impression I got.'

'At times she almost seemed to suggest her sister was putting it on . . . you know, just to draw attention to herself.'

'And do you believe that?'

'No,' he replied vehemently. 'I've seen the states Fennel used to get into . . . you know, when I was driving her around. No, the illness was genuine. I even . . .' He stopped himself.

'You even . . . what?' asked Jude softly.

He paused, as if deliberating whether to tell her or not. Then he said, 'I drove her back to Butterwyke from the Pimlico flat . . . you know. Well, perhaps you don't know . . . when—'

'I did know about her previous suicide attempt, yes.'

'We were all very shocked by that. Ned in particular. He was in a terrible state. I mean, up until then we knew Fennel had problems, but we'd never have guessed they were that serious . . . you know, that she'd go as far as to . . .'

'You say you drove her back to Butterwyke House. Was she not hospitalized after the attempt?'

'No. Chervil found her in the flat and managed to wake her up. Got her to sick up most of the pills, bandaged the cuts and filled her full of black coffee. Then she called Ned. I drove him up to London. God, the red lights we shot through that day, I was lucky not to be booked twenty times. And when we got to the flat, Ned checked Fennel out and reckoned she'd be OK to be taken back to Butterwyke and treated there. He didn't want the publicity, both from Fennel's point of view and his own. And he knew if the press got a sniff of what'd happened, it'd be over the front pages like a rash. Besides, down here he's got a doctor who he knows is very discreet.'

'Did Chervil drive back with you that day?'

'No, just Ned and Fennel. He was cradling her in the back of the car, like she was a baby, and he was crying all the way there.'

'Any idea where Chervil went?'

'I think she sorted out someone to clean up the flat.'

'Again someone discreet?'

'You betcha. Ned and Sheena have got quite good at preserving their privacy over the years. They've needed to. You know how obsessed the papers are with people who've got money. Anyway, Ned and Sheena know the right people to pay to ensure that they are left alone.'

'And tell me, Kier, did you actually see Fennel's . . . you know, where she made the attempt?'

'I saw the bathroom. There was blood all over the place. But Chervil had tied torn-up towels round her sister's arms and got her lying down on the bed by the time Ned and I got there.'

'And you didn't see a suicide note?'

'No. Chervil said there wasn't one.'

'Right.' Jude suppressed a yawn. The session with Sam Torino had really taken it out of her. 'So . . . back to the Who Done It question . . .'

'Well, it seems hard to imagine that anyone . . . certainly nobody in the family.'

'Are you sure about that?'

'Look, you've seen the state Ned's in. Nobody would bring that on himself.'

'No, probably not. What about Sheena?' Again Jude worried whether she was pushing too hard. 'She doesn't seem to be making any secret of the fact that she's relieved by her daughter's death.'

'Yes, she's a strange one, Sheena. I shouldn't say this, but I think she did rather resent Fennel's hold over Ned. Still, harbouring those kind of feelings . . . well, it's a long way away from murdering someone.'

'Yes. But it's interesting to weigh up the possibilities.'

'I suppose so. Gives something to focus the mind on. But just a minute, if there was any thought of murder, surely the police would have been on to it?'

Jude was forced to admit that, so far as she could tell, the police had taken the suicide at face value. As it got further away in her recollection, the encounter she had had with Detective Inspector Hodgkinson seemed to have become more and more patronizing.

'Well, the police know what they're doing,' said Kier, perfectly reasonably. 'And they've released Fennel's body, so they must have finished any forensic examination they might be doing. The funeral's going to be on Wednesday week.' This was new information to Jude. 'Just family and very close friends.'

'Where?'

'There's a chapel in the grounds of Butterwyke. It's being held there.'

Typical, thought Jude. Whoever had built the house back in

the eighteenth century must have had the same desire for
privacy as the Whittakers. Everything sewn up and sanitized
within the boundaries of the estate.

'Kier, indulge me for a minute. Just imagine that Fennel's
death wasn't suicide . . .'

'That she was murdered?'

'Yes. If that were the case, would you have anyone in the
frame as a suspect?'

'There's an obvious one.' The driver answered that question
readily enough. 'I heard their conversations in the back of this
car when I was driving them about. He treated her like shit.'
The resentment was back in his voice.

'Sorry? Who are we talking about?'

'That sleazebag Denzil Willoughby.'

'I suppose we could try and get a contact for him through
Bonita Green,' said Jude somewhat lethargically. She still felt
drained by her healing session with Sam Torino. 'Though I
don't know whether the number of her flat is in the book. The
Cornelian Gallery will be, but it'll be closed now, and actually,
I seem to recall she doesn't open on Sundays, so we won't
be able to get her tomorrow either.'

'Oh, really,' said Carole, uncharacteristically perky. 'Come
into the twenty-first century, Jude. There's no problem these
days with finding a contact for anyone.'

'If you're talking about Facebook and Twitter, I'm—'

'I'm not talking about them. You don't have to go to those
kinds of lengths. Google will be quite sufficient. You can find
virtually everyone, and certainly anyone who's trying to present
some kind of public profile like Denzil Willoughby. Come on,
bring your wine glass with you and we'll check it out on my
laptop upstairs.'

'Carole, I thought the point of having a laptop was that it's
mobile.'

'Sorry?'

'You can use it anywhere. On the train, in a coffee shop,
upstairs, downstairs.'

Carole Seddon's face took on a bleak, old-fashioned look.
'I prefer to use mine in the computer room,' she said.

Jude sighed wearily, picked up her glass of Chilean Chardonnay and followed her neighbour out of the kitchen.

The 'computer room' was in fact Carole's spare bedroom, very rarely used for its primary function. She almost never had people to stay, except of course for Stephen's family, and even them she found something of a strain. A guilty feeling of relief came into her mind at the thought that Gaby and Lily would be staying elsewhere on their visit at the end of the month. Which reminded her, she must ring Fulham and report back on Walden. She didn't really think it would be suitable for them. Fine for the Sam Torinos of this world, but maybe a bit too posh for Gaby . . . though of course she's be far too discreet to say that to her daughter-in-law's face.

She brought the laptop out of hibernation and googled Denzil Willoughby. There were, to her, a surprising number of references. Maybe his self-estimation was not so disproportionate to his fame as she had thought.

Carole homed in on the artist's own website, whose home page contained, in her view, far too many four-letter words. As he had amply demonstrated at the Private View, his target audience was not genteel retired ladies in Fethering.

Links directed browsers to other parts of the website. There was a rather aggressive biography which certainly didn't mention the shaming fact that he had been a public schoolboy at Lancing College. There were lists of galleries where he had exhibited, though interestingly the Cornelian Gallery was not among them. Whether this was because he thought Fethering too insignificant to mention, or whether he had removed the reference in a fit of pique after the early closing of his exhibition, it was impossible to know.

The website contained pages of photographs of Denzil Willoughby's work. Guns were evidently a fairly recent preoccupation. Previous collections of work he'd done around the themes of famine, AIDS, tsunamis and the Rwandan genocide. Yet again, Carole Seddon didn't see anything that she would have given houseroom to.

But the artworks were very definitely for sale. Though the website didn't quote prices, there were links to Denzil Willoughby's agent and a couple of galleries with whom he had deals to sell his work. And if he ever sold anything at the prices that had been quoted at the Cornelian Gallery Private View, then he could make quite a good living.

Another link on the website was entitled 'Artist at Work'. When the two women got into it, all they could see was what appeared to be a dark interior of a huge room.

'What's he selling there?' asked Carole cynically. 'Space? Darkness? Air? No doubt, because the Great Denzil Willoughby had the *concept* of marketing such stuff, he can charge what he likes for it.'

'I don't think that is one of his artworks,' said Jude. 'I think it's his workshop.'

'Oh?'

'And I think there's a webcam on it permanently, so that members of the public can go online and watch the "Artist at Work".'

'What, watch him sticking photographs of black teenagers on to fibreglass guns?'

'If that happens to be the creation of the moment, yes.'

'What incredible arrogance! To assume that anyone would be interested in his work in progress. Artists used to work on their own and not show their work until they'd finished it.'

'That's not true of all artists, Carole. A lot of them used to treat their studios as a kind of salon, through which all and sundry could pass at will.'

'Yes, but they were at least real artists.'

'They "painted things that looked like things"?'

'Exactly,' replied Carole, unaware that she was being sent up.

'Anyway,' Jude went on, 'I'm pretty sure that's what's happening. When Denzil Willoughby's there in the workshop, the lights are on and we can watch the genius at work. But presumably neither the genius nor his assistants are working on a Saturday evening.'

'Assistants?' Carole repeated incredulously. 'Why does he have assistants?'

'Oh, to do the work for him. You don't think he actually stuck those photographs on the gun himself, do you?'

'Well, he must have done. If he's claiming that it's his work of art, the least he must've done is to make the thing.'

'No, Carole,' said Jude, an amused grin on her tired face. 'He just had the *concept* of doing it.'

As she knew she would, her neighbour just said, 'Huh.'

Carole went back to the home page of the website, where Jude saw something else of interest. There were two tabs labelled 'Virtual Visitors' and 'Real Visitors'. The first one took them back to the webcam shot of the darkened studio. But the second tab took them to a page on which there was an image of the back of a postcard, artfully scrawled with the words:

'Want to see the artist at work in the flesh? Every Monday between eleven o'clock and four Denzil Willoughby's studio is open to any motherfucker who wants to have a look.' This was followed by instructions as to how to get to the studio.

'Well,' said Jude, 'if we want to talk to Denzil Willoughby, we know what we have to do, don't we?'

'Oh, but we couldn't,' said Carole.

'Couldn't we?' said Jude.

In the gossip column of Carole's *Sunday Times* the following morning there was a photograph of Sam Torino at Walden. It was a measure of her celebrity that space had been made for her in a paper most of whose feature content had been put to bed by the Friday evening.

It was a great advertisement for Chervil Whittaker's glamping site.

And, needless to say, there was no mention of her sister's recent death.

TWENTY

Denzil Willoughby's workshop, they discovered, was in Brixton. This immediately set alarm bells ringing for Carole. Though she didn't read the *Daily Mail*, faithful to her *Times* and its crossword, her mind could sometimes run on distressingly *Daily Mail* lines. So for her the word 'Brixton' was shorthand for race riots . . . and all that that entailed. The fact that the riots had happened over thirty years ago did not have any effect on her knee-jerk reaction.

Looking at the A–Z when working out their optimum route to the workshop, Carole was struck by how near Brixton was to what she regarded as 'nice' suburbs. Wandsworth was very near, Battersea not far away, and even the adjacent Clapham was apparently now a suitable location for the aspiring middle classes. Carole Seddon's deep-frozen attitudes demonstrated how rarely she actually went to London. How rarely, in fact, she left Fethering.

Needless to say, the remainder of her weekend had been spent in paroxysms of indecision as to whether she and Jude should actually go to Denzil Willoughby's studio. Carole ran through a more or less exact repeat of the feeling she had had running up to the Private View. And an invitation on a website was even less specific than one handed over in a gallery. At least in the first instance she had known Bonita Green and the venue was local. Turning up at an artist's workshop unannounced represented a very different level of intrusion.

And Jude's reassuring words hadn't totally convinced her. 'Come on, we want to talk to the guy. We don't have any other obvious way of contacting him. And the invitation for anyone to drop into his workshop couldn't be clearer. After all, Carole, what's the worst that can happen?'

That question, so casually thrown around by people less paranoid than herself, always caused Carole Seddon great anguish. Though meant to be rhetorical, it was an enquiry which never failed to set her imagination racing. She could always supply a long list of worst things that could happen.

Of course, as with the Private View, something deep inside her psyche knew that ultimately she would end up going to Denzil Willoughby's workshop. So on the Monday morning, having taken Gulliver for his customary romp on Fethering Beach, Carole checked on the website to see whether anything had changed on the 'Artist at Work' link. The only difference was the amount of daylight, which now left no doubt that what the webcam showed was the workshop interior. It lit up what, to Carole's mind, was an amazing amount of junk, none of which could ever be included in her definition of 'art'. But the warehouse space was still uninhabited.

Carole closed down her laptop and joined Jude on the first cheap train from Fethering Station to Victoria. From there they would get the Victoria Line to its southernmost outpost of Brixton.

On the journey they didn't talk much. Carole hid behind the screen of her *Times*, while Jude just looked out of the window. She did sometimes read – usually books from the Mind, Body and Spirit section at which her neighbour would be guaranteed to harrumph noisily – but that particular morning she was content just to let her thoughts flow. Carole wished she ever felt sufficiently relaxed just to let her thoughts flow.

Once she'd read all *The Times*'s news and features, she addressed her mind to the crossword, but felt awkward doing it with someone she knew beside her. Carole Seddon was very anal about her crossword solving, and the knowledge that even as close a friend as Jude was present put her off. The fact that her neighbour was totally uninterested in the clues or her answers did not fully remove the feeling that she was under surveillance. As a result, her concentration suffered and she was slow to make the necessary verbal connections.

When they emerged from Brixton Station, Carole was surprised to find herself in what felt like just another upmarket London suburb. True, there were more dark faces on the street than she was used to, but then she did come from the backwater of Fethering, where even the convenience stores had yet to be taken over by Asians. And some of the vegetables on display outside the Brixton shops were a little more exotic than what she'd find in the local Allinstore. But otherwise, not for the first time, Carole Seddon felt slightly embarrassed by her unthinking readiness to accept stereotypical attitudes.

The address they'd found on Denzil Willoughby's website was at the end of a street of small houses built for railway workers but now gentrified to a very desirable standard. Their destination was an old warehouse, which had also been expensively converted. Curtained windows on the upper storey suggested that a loft apartment had been carved out of the space, though whether or not Denzil Willoughby lived up there Carole and Jude didn't know.

The warehouse had high double doors, presumably to let in wagons or heavy machinery for its original owners and life-size guns plastered with photographs for its current incumbent. Into one of these doors was set a smaller door which opened at Jude's touch. There was no sign of a knocker or bell, so she just led the way in. Carole was happy to follow, aware that she might not have been so bold had she been on her own.

They found themselves in a space high enough to garage three or four double-decker buses. A spiral staircase led to the floor above, and two doors at the back led off perhaps to offices or other utilities. In reality the level of clutter inside the workshop was even more chaotic than it had appeared on the webcam. Carole was vaguely aware of the concept of *objets trouvés*, art made from everyday articles dignified with unlikely titles, but she could not for the life of her imagine how some of the detritus collected in Denzil Willoughby's workshop would ever make it into a gallery.

Among the objects on display were a rusty tractor and an assortment of car engines. A decommissioned red telephone box with its glass replaced by kitchen foil stood next to an antiquated milking machine. A broken neon sign reading 'Kebab' was propped against a collection of blue plastic barrels which had contained pesticide. Three collecting boxes moulded in the shape of small blind boys with white sticks loitered in the company of some mangy cuddly toys. Two Belisha beacons leant against a wall with an assortment of golf clubs, fishing rods and ice-hockey sticks. Superannuated cigarette machines were piled up next to a set of giant plaster frogs.

Near the door were some artefacts Carole and Jude recognized – the photograph-covered gun and the framed pieces which had recently been returned from the Cornelian Gallery. They had been piled up higgledy-piggledy, almost as if the artist had lost interest in them.

In the centre of the warehouse was what appeared to be a fully functional fork-lift truck, though whether that was there to move about the other junk or destined to form part of an artwork in its own right neither Carole nor Jude could guess.

As they took in the warehouse's bizarre contents, they realized that the space was no longer uninhabited. On the floor at one end lay a life-size painted wooden crucifix into which a shaven-headed young man was banging galvanized nails. Laid out on the floor the other end was a giant poster of President Obama over which a young woman was laying a painstaking trelliswork formed by strips of Christmas Sellotape. There was no sign of Denzil Willoughby.

Neither of what were presumably his assistants took any notice of the new arrivals, but continued with the work of realizing their master's 'concepts'. Carole couldn't somehow see a direct line in what she was witnessing back to the studios of the Old Masters, where eager helpers were allowed to do limbs and draperies while the boss took over to do the clever stuff like the faces.

She cleared her throat to draw attention to their presence, but neither of the assistants looked up from their toil. Then Jude announced, 'Good morning. We've taken up the invitation on the website to come and have a look at the "Artist at Work".'

'That's cool,' said the girl, her eyes still fixed one her parallel lines of Santa-decorated tape.

Carole moved across to the young man with the crucifix. 'And what are you doing here?' she asked.

'I'm banging nails into the bloody thing,' he replied, as it talking to someone educationally subnormal.

'Yes, but why?'

'What do you mean, "why"?'

'Why are you doing it?'

'Well, because Denzil told me to.' Again he sounded as though he couldn't believe the stupidity of her question.

'And because Denzil's told you to do it, does that make it art?'

'I don't know, do I?' said the young man. 'If you want to call it art, fine.'

'I definitely don't want to call it art.'

'Still fine.'

'Does Denzil think it's art?'

'Denzil doesn't care. He does what he does. He's not

bothered by definitions. If people want to call it art, he's not about to contradict them.'

'And if people want to buy it?'

'He won't try and put them off,' said the young man, banging a galvanized nail into the wound where the soldier had pierced Christ's side.

'Is Denzil around?' Jude asked the girl.

'He may be,' she replied gnomically.

'Are you expecting him?'

'Usually. Sometimes.' An answer which wasn't a lot more helpful than the previous one. The girl, Jude noticed, was slight and dressed in black, perhaps rather like Bonita Green might have looked when she was twenty. And though she wore no make-up and seemed to have made no effort with her appearance, the assistant breathed an undeniable sexuality. Jude wondered whether Denzil Willoughby claimed the same *droit de seigneur* over his female assistants that artists are traditionally reputed to exercise over their models.

Since the person they had come to visit wasn't there, Jude could see no reason not to try and get some information out of his staff, so she asked, 'Did you know that Denzil had recently had an exhibition in Fethering.'

'Where?'

'Fethering. The Cornelian Gallery.'

'Oh, I heard the name of the gallery, yes. Didn't know where it was.'

'Except, of course, the exhibition didn't run its full course.'

'So?'

As interrogations went, this one hadn't got off to a very good start. And it didn't get any further, because at that moment Denzil Willoughby's feet in their toe-curled cowboy boots appeared at the top of the spiral staircase, quickly followed by the rest of his body as he descended. His dreadlocks looked more than ever like knotted string, and he was dressed in jeans and T-shirt. He stopped halfway down as he saw Carole and Jude. 'Good God,' he exclaimed. 'Ladies of Fethering.'

Carole was surprised that he'd even registered their presence at the Private View.

'Good morning,' said Jude.

'And to what do I owe this pleasure?' The sneer was still there, but the mock-formality took his voice back to its public school origins.

'We saw on your website that anyone is free to come and watch the "Artist at Work".'

As Denzil Willoughby reached ground level, he gestured around his workshop. 'Well, here you see it. The "Artist at Work".'

'We haven't yet seen much evidence of you doing anything,' Carole observed tartly.

He looked at her pityingly. 'You just don't get it, do you, Carole?' Again she was surprised that he knew her name. 'You still think art is one guy sitting there with his pots of paint and brushes, "painting things that look like things".'

That was even more of a shock, Denzil quoting her own lines back at her. It raised the possibility that he had been talking about them to someone else, a possibility that was both intriguing and mildly disturbing.

'God, my brain's not working yet,' the artist announced to the workshop at large. 'I need coffee.'

The girl immediately rose from her Obama poster and walked towards one of the doors at the back of the warehouse. In the alternative world of Denzil Willoughby, it seemed, male chauvinism still ruled. The other assistant hadn't looked up from his re-crucifixion of Christ.

'Make a *cafetière*,' Denzil called after the girl. 'My visitors may want some too. And bring it out on to the terrace.'

No 'pleases', no blandishments of that kind. He crossed towards the other door at the back, gesturing Carole and Jude to follow him.

They found themselves in a surprisingly well-tended yard, whose red-brick walls were animated by colourful pot plants and hanging baskets. A wrought-iron spiral staircase led to the upper storey. White-painted Victorian cast-iron chairs stood around an equally white circular cast-iron pub table with Britannia designs on the legs.

Denzil indicated that they should sit down, and he joined them. Beneath his customary sneering manner, Jude could detect tension. And his next words explained the reason for that tension. 'Presumably,' he said, 'you've come to talk about Fennel Whittaker's death.'

TWENTY-ONE

'What makes you think that?' said Carole.

'Because Giles Green had told me all about you,' Denzil Willoughby replied.

'Oh. I wasn't aware he knew anything about us.'

'He's heard it from his mother. Apparently Bonita knows everything that goes on in Fethering.'

'So what has Giles told you about us?' asked Jude.

'That you're nosey, like most people down there.'

Jude spread her hands wide in a gesture of mock-innocence. 'So little happens in a place like Fethering. The only growth industry in a village is gossip.'

Denzil Willoughby smiled, acknowledging her humour, but it was an uneasy smile. Both Carole and Jude sensed that he was at least as keen to find out things from them as they were from him. Or maybe he just wanted to find out how much they knew. Either way, from the point of view of their investigation his behaviour was very encouraging. It suggested that Denzil Willoughby had something to hide.

They were interrupted by the appearance of the girl with the tray of coffee. This too was produced with unexpected elegance, green, gold-rimmed *bistro*-style cups and saucers beside the *cafetière*. It was another detail at odds with the shabbiness of the adjacent workshop.

Denzil said no word of thanks to the girl, and she was silent too. He waited till she had gone before politely asking his guests how they would like their coffee and pouring it. Then he sat back and looked at the two women. 'Giles heard from his mother that your particular style of nosiness takes the form of imagining murders and attempting to investigate them.'

Instinctively they both remained silent, waiting to see where his questioning would lead next. Appearing even more uncomfortable, Denzil took an iPhone out of the back pocket of his jeans and checked its display. Whatever he was expecting to see wasn't there. For the rest of their conversation he continued fiddling with the phone.

'According to Bonita – via Giles – there's been talk in Fethering that Fennel's death wasn't the suicide that it appeared to be. That in fact it was murder.'

Still they let him squirm.

'And apparently gossiping tongues have even suggested that because Fennel bawled me out at the Private View down there, my name's in the frame as her murderer.'

'Well, it's a thought, isn't it?' said Jude with what her neighbour considered to be inappropriate levity.

'It may be a thought, but it's not true,' protested Denzil Willoughby.

'I'm sure it's not,' said Jude with a reassuring smile. 'So maybe you could tell us why it's not true?

'For starters I don't think Fennel was murdered. If you knew her history of depression, you'd—'

'I do know her history of depression,' Jude interposed. 'I had been treating her for it.'

'Oh? Are you a doctor?'

'No, I'm a healer.'

The expression on Denzil Willoughby's face suggested to Carole that, unlikely though it might seem, there could be at least one subject on which she and the artist might agree.

'So,' Denzil went on, 'you'll know that Fennel had made a previous suicide attempt. She was all messed up in her head. She talked a lot about topping herself. It was only a matter of time before it happened.'

'And if it was suicide, would you feel any guilt?' asked Carole, at her most magisterial.

'Guilt? Why should I feel guilt?' He genuinely did not seem to understand.

'From all accounts, during your relationship you didn't treat her that well.'

'Look, hell, I can't do anything about it if women fall in love with me,' said Denzil Willoughby. 'I try to reciprocate, but I admit it isn't the highest priority in my life. I'm an artist.'

At that point both Carole and Jude would quite happily have knocked the young man's block off, but they both realized it wasn't the moment and restrained themselves.

'At the Private View,' said Carole beadily, 'Fennel accused you of only being interested in her money.'

'That wasn't true.'

'But you didn't mind accepting money from her?'

'Look, her parents are loaded. If she wanted to give some of it to me, surely that was her decision.'

'So long as it *was* her decision,' said Carole, still in inquisitorial mode. 'So long as you didn't pressure her.'

'Look, I'm an artist,' said Denzil Willoughby, again prompting block-knocking-off urges in both his listeners. 'My art's the most important thing in my life. That has to be funded; that's the main priority. Where the money comes from to fund it isn't important.'

'Are you saying you'd do anything to get money?' asked Carole.

'Pretty much, yes.'

'I thought your father was also loaded,' said Jude, causing her friend to look at her in some surprise. The secrets of Jude's healing sessions remained sacrosanct. Except for mentioning to Carole the rumour of Denzil Willoughby's violence to women, she hadn't reported any other details of her conversation with Sam Torino in the treatment yurt at Walden. 'He's a big shot in advertising, isn't he?'

'Yes, he's loaded all right,' Denzil admitted. 'Just he doesn't always feel like sharing his goodies with his son. He's never forgiven me, you see, for becoming an artist. My Dad – the great Addison Willoughby – he did all his training at the Slade and everything, and then prostituted his talents for the rest of his life in an ad agency. How commercial can you get? He's jealous as hell of what I've done, jealous of me not having made any compromises in my life, and that jealousy is quite frequently expressed in a tightening of the purse strings.'

Carole decided to set out on another tack. 'Since you've cast us as the snoopers of Fethering, we'd be failing in our duty if we didn't interrogate you about Fennel's death.'

Denzil Willoughby shrugged. 'You can interrogate away to

your heart's content. You'll find I have nothing to tell you on the subject. I didn't see Fennel after she stormed out of the Private View having given me that right royal bollocking.'

'You didn't see her again on the Friday night?'

'Of course I bloody didn't.'

'So where were you? Did you stay in Bonita Green's flat?'

'No way. It's tiny. Cramped enough with her and Giles there. Not that I wanted to stay there, anyway. Bonita's not really my type of person.'

'Oh?'

'Another of those who's frittered away her talents. She trained at the Slade, like my Dad, and like him, she never tried being a proper artist. Just set up that mimsy-pimsy gallery to sell Toulouse-Lautrec fridge magnets to people who wouldn't recognize a work of art if it came up and bit them on the shin.'

'She did have two small children to bring up on her own,' Jude interceded on Bonita Green's behalf.

'So what? A true artist wouldn't let considerations like that get in the way of their work.'

'Right.' Carole picked up her interrogation. 'So where did you go after the Private View?'

'Back to the hotel they'd booked me into. Place called the Dauncey. Fairly primitive, but probably as state of the art as hotels get in a backwater like Fethering.' Carole curbed the instinct to defend her home village against the allegation. 'I spent the whole night there.'

'Do you have someone who can vouch for that?' asked Carole.

He smiled at her infuriatingly. 'My, oh my. You've completed the full Amateur Sleuths' Correspondence Course and passed with distinction. Know all the questions about alibis, don't you?'

'I asked if anyone could vouch for the fact that you'd spent all of Friday night at the Dauncey Hotel,' Carole continued implacably.

'So you did. And the answer, I am glad to tell you, is yes.'

'Was it someone you'd picked up at the Private View?'

He smiled lazily. 'I'm glad my reputation as a babe magnet has spread as far as Fethering. But no, on this occasion I wasn't working my magic for some fortunate and grateful woman. I was with someone of my own gender.'

'Oh?'

The disapproval in Carole's tone clearly communicated itself, because with another lazy smile, he said, 'No, not that. I know you expect artists to be capable of any depravity, but to my chagrin I've never fancied boys. Sure I'm missing a lot, but there you go . . . No, I actually spent the night drinking with my old mucker Giles.'

'Giles Green?'

'I didn't notice any other Gileses around at the Private View.'

'So the two of you were drinking all night in the bar of the Dauncey Hotel?'

'Not the bar, no. The hotel manager had rather old-fashioned ideas about licensing hours; he seemed to believe that no one in Fethering ever wanted a drink after nine in the evening. So Giles and I bought a couple of bottles of Scotch and retired with them to my room to drink the night away.'

'And in the course of that night,' asked Jude, 'did you talk about Fennel Whittaker?'

'We may have done. My recollections of the occasion are necessarily somewhat hazy.'

'But you probably did?'

'Probably. Giles and I have always tended to talk about women. We've known each other for a long time.'

'From your time at Lancing,' said Carole.

'Ooh, you have been doing your research.'

'And has there been rivalry between you when it comes to women?'

'A bit. Benign rivalry, I'd say.'

'Never come to conflict?'

'Good God, no. The woman hasn't been born who's worth spoiling a male friendship for.' This was said with a challenging smile. Denzil Willoughby was fully aware of the effect his words were having. It was almost as if he were trying to goad his two visitors into some reaction, but they were determined not to give him the satisfaction.

'So that night after the Private View,' asked Carole, 'did you talk about Giles's relationship with Chervil Whittaker?'

'It probably came up.' He grinned complacently. 'Though there wasn't really much he could tell me there.'

Jude was quicker to pick up the implication than Carole. 'You mean you'd already had a relationship with Chervil yourself?'

'Spot on.'

'Recently?'

'Fairly. It was when I got bored with the younger sister that I moved on to the older one.'

'And Giles picked up with Chervil?'

'Exactly. We've always kind of shared girlfriends.'

'At the same time?'

'Not very often.' He sniggered. 'Wouldn't have worried us, but girls can be funny about that kind of thing.'

'And what about Fennel?' asked Jude.

'What about Fennel?'

'Was she another girlfriend you shared? Did Giles have a relationship with her as well as you?'

Denzil Willoughby was silent, assessing his reply. Though there was an insolent pleasure in his manner, enjoying telling his visitors what a bad boy he was, an undercurrent of anxiety remained. The iPhone still moved restlessly around between his hands. Both women got the impression he was deliberately extending the conversation, that he still hadn't got from them what he wanted to know.

He made his decision. 'Yes, Giles had a bit of a fling with Fennel.'

'Before you did?'

'Yes.'

'While he was still with his wife?'

'Sure. Giles always thought that he and Nikki had an open marriage.'

'There are a lot of husbands who think that,' said Carole with some bitterness, 'but quite a few of them forget to explain the situation to their wives.'

Denzil Willoughby did another of his infuriating shrugs. 'Having never been married, I wouldn't know,' he said in a voice of assumed piety.

'But this is rather important,' announced Jude. 'Now we

know that Giles also had a relationship with Fennel, the whole situation becomes—'

'It doesn't change anything if you're looking for a murderer,' Denzil pointed out. 'Because if Giles is my alibi for the relevant time, then I'm also his.'

'But surely—'

Carole didn't get beyond the two words, as Denzil suddenly reacted to a beep from his iPhone. Maybe it announced the text he's been expecting all morning, but the news it brought certainly gave him a shock.

With a cry of, 'Oh my God, no!' he leapt to his feet and rushed back into the workshop.

TWENTY-TWO

On the assumption that when he had done whatever the text demanded of him, Denzil Willoughby would return either to pick up the conversation or end their meeting, Carole and Jude stayed out on the terrace. The *cafetière* retained enough warmth for them to refill their cups.

They talked casually, about anything except the death of Fennel Whittaker. Though both women were full of new ideas relating to their investigation, on Denzil Willoughby's home territory they felt somehow under surveillance.

Some twenty minutes passed before the conviction hardened in both of them that he wasn't coming back, so they ventured into the workshop. There nothing seemed to have changed. The young man had found a new area of Christ's carved wooden flesh into which to bang galvanized nails, and the girl was still laying her meticulous lines of Christmas tape over President Obama. There was no sign of Denzil Willoughby.

Neither of the assistants so much as looked up from their work, so Carole and Jude reckoned they were capable of seeing themselves out. They had almost reached the small door to the street when they heard the sound of feet descending the spiral staircase.

This pair of legs was also wearing jeans, but they fitted the more shapely contours of a woman. A few seconds more descent and Carole and Jude found themselves facing Nikki, Giles Green's wife.

She seemed unfazed to see them. 'Ah. Denzil said you'd been here. I thought you might have gone.'

'Good morning. I'm Carole and—'

'We met at the Cornelian Gallery.' There was something strikingly direct about Nikki Green.

'Yes, of course we did. I wasn't sure you'd remember.'

The two assistants on the floor showed no more interest in this exchange than they had in anything else that had happened that morning. Maybe they were under orders to make no response, or just too preoccupied in realizing the 'concepts' vouchsafed to them by the genius who was their employer.

'I'd better explain what's happened,' said Nikki Green as she reached ground level. She looked around the workshop and seemed to dismiss it as a venue. 'Let's go out and get a coffee. There's a Starbucks just down the road.'

Jude saw Carole about to say that they'd actually just had downed the contents of a *cafetière*, but managed to stop her with a look.

The three of them didn't speak until they were sitting in the café with yet more coffee in front of them. Then Nikki Green said, 'Apologies for Denzil not saying goodbye to you. He'd just received some bad news.'

'Oh? We saw he'd just had a text that—'

'Yes. That was it. His mother's just died.'

Jude said she was sorry and Carole came up with the customary elaborate expressions of regret that people in Fethering always produced at the news of the death of someone they'd never met.

'Denzil and Philomena were very close, texting each other every day. More like lovers than mother and son. He'll be pretty cut up about it.'

'Maybe,' suggested Jude, 'that's the explanation for his behaviour to other women. None of them could ever match up to his mother.'

'That's one explanation for it,' said Nikki Green, 'though I favour the view that he behaves like that because he's basically just a little shit.'

'And how well do you know him?' asked Carole in a manner that she couldn't prevent from sounding old-fashioned.

'Ah, yes. Well, a legitimate question, I suppose. Given the fact that I was introduced to you in Fethering as Giles Green's wife and here you find me *in flagrante* with Denzil.'

'Well, hardly *in flagrante*.'

'To all intents and purposes. I did spend the night with him. I'm not pretending otherwise. I don't know the simplest way to explain that. It's all rather complicated.' Nikki Green swept the long highlighted hair back off her forehead. Carole and Jude were again reminded of her likeness to Chervil Whittaker.

'Look,' she said, 'I married Giles because he asked me to. It seemed to matter to him in a way that kind of thing has never mattered to me. Maybe because he lost his own father so young, he always dreamed of some kind of stability. A kind of family life; though not with children, not if I was going to be involved. I made it clear from the start there wouldn't be any of them.'

'Because you couldn't have children?' asked Carole.

'No. Because I didn't want them. So far as I know, I've got no malfunction in my apparatus for the manufacture of sprogs, I've just never fancied them. At the core of my being there's a strong spine of selfishness. I enjoy life. I look after number one, and I'm quite good at being independent.'

'But you still married Giles,' Jude pointed out.

'Yes, and that, as I said, was because he asked me to. I had no idea whether it would last or not. I knew neither of us would be faithful. It's not in our nature.'

'So you fully expected your husband to have affairs?'

'Yes. Just as I fully anticipated having a good few myself. Over the years I've probably seen more action in that respect than Giles has. When he had his job in the City he worked much longer hours than I did. So I had more time to stray.' Nikki Green grinned wolfishly.

'What do you do?' asked Carole.

'I'm an artist's agent.'

'Oh, my daughter-in-law's in a theatrical agency for—'

'No, artists, not *artistes*. I represent people in the visual arts.'

'Painters and people? Like Denzil?' asked Jude.

'Precisely.'

'So you met him first as an artist?'

'Yes. And he introduced me to Giles.'

'From what Denzil was saying this morning, he and Giles had quite a few girlfriends in common.' The old-fashioned quality remained in Carole's voice.

'Yes. So Denzil and I had been having a thing for a while before I hooked up with Giles.'

'An affair that continued?'

'On and off. For someone so self-centred and up himself, Denzil is a surprisingly generous lover. Very good in bed – and I speak as a connoisseur.'

'And would you say the two of you are "an item" now?' asked Carole.

'We never were an item. It's some months since Giles and I have been living together. I have quite a strong sex drive, but I don't want to go through all that rigmarole of online dating and . . . It's better to hook up again with someone you know well. So when Denzil and I are both free . . . like last night . . . we get together.'

Nikki Green spoke with no embarrassment and with absolute certainty about what she wanted from life. Carole could not imagine anyone conducting sexual relationships on such a casual basis. But at the same time a bit of her did find the idea rather appealing. 'So don't you ever feel jealous?' she asked.

Nikki Green grinned. 'Haven't for a long, long time. Maybe all it means is that I've never properly fallen in love. Well, if that's the case, fine by me. Imagine what it would be like actually worrying about what some little shit like Denzil – or Giles, come to that – was up to every minute of the day.' She shook her head and chuckled. 'Give me the quiet life.'

'So,' Carole went on, still intrigued by the woman's attitudes, 'it doesn't worry you when you see Giles with Chervil, like you did at the Private View?'

'Doesn't worry me at all. He can work his way through the entire spice rack, so far as I'm concerned.'

'And what about Giles and Fennel Whittaker?' asked Jude gently.

For the first time here was something that did give Nikki Green pause. 'That one I wasn't so happy about.'

'You were jealous of her?'

An impatient shake of the head. 'I wasn't unhappy from my point of view. But from hers. I knew how vulnerable that girl was. The last thing she needed was Giles and Denzil messing with her head.'

'Did you talk to Giles about it?'

'Yes, but he wasn't listening. It was round the time that his job was on the line. Considering other people's feelings was never high on my husband's list of priorities; back then, he was even more blinkered than usual.'

Carole took up the baton of interrogation. 'Had you met Fennel before the Private View?'

'I'd met her at other private views, arts functions, gallery openings. It's a smallish world, you know.'

'Before your husband started having an affair with her?'

'Yes, and after.' Nikki Green grinned again. 'And I wish you could get that note of shock out of your voice. It really wasn't such a big deal.'

'But at the Private View, when she started bawling Denzil out, did that embarrass you?'

'I was embarrassed for the girl . . . well, no, not embarrassed, sorry for her. She clearly had so much she needed to get off her chest. I wouldn't be surprised if letting it all out made her feel a whole lot better. You know, like lancing a boil.'

'You're right, actually,' said Jude, not expecting such psychological perspicacity. 'That's what she said to me afterwards. She'd planned that public denunciation of Denzil, and letting it all out had been a very positive experience for her. But then within a few hours, she apparently killed herself.'

Nikki shrugged. 'That's mental illness for you. Sad, but you can't do a lot about it, I gather. Just bad luck, like being born ginger.'

'That's how Fennel described it to me,' said Jude.

'There you are then. Just an incredibly bum deal donated to

you by your genes. I've been lucky. I may be a selfish cow, but
at least, thank God, I've never had a negative thought in my life.'

Jude had frequently heard Carole make similar statements
– well, without the 'selfish cow' bit – and she knew how at
odds with the truth they were. And she'd have put money on
the fact that Nikki Green's carapace was equally fragile. But
now wasn't the moment for psychoanalysis.

'I was just wondering,' Jude began casually, 'whether that
diatribe of Fennel's at the Private View was only aimed at Denzil?'

'What do you mean?'

'Well, it was very public, wasn't it? I'd assumed the attack
was aimed where it seemed to be – at Denzil. But at that stage
I didn't know she had also had an affair with Giles.'

'Oh, I see what you mean. Killing two birds with one stone.'
The idea seemed to amuse Nikki Green. 'I suppose it's possible.
If so, bad luck for Fennel, if she thought she was going to
make either of those bastards feel guilty. Giles and Denzil
have two of the thickest skins I have ever encountered.'

Again Jude wondered how true that was. From the intimate
communications of her healing sessions, she knew that
everyone had their vulnerabilities. She also knew that the more
rigidly people tried to deny their fallibility, the more destructive those vulnerabilities could be.

And the genuine distress shown by Denzil Willoughby at
the news of his mother's death suggested that his skin was far
from thick.

'It's a thought, though,' said Carole. 'Fennel Whittaker did
say some pretty odd things that evening.'

'So? She was mentally ill.' Nikki Green said these words
as though they put an end to the conversation.

'She talked about someone "causing the death" of another
person. If that was addressed to Denzil, do you have any idea
what it could have meant?'

'Pretty straightforward, I would imagine. She was intending
to top herself and, when she did, she was saying it would be
his fault.'

'Yes, I suppose she could have meant that.'

'I can't see what else she could have meant.'

'No, maybe not.'

'Would the words have meant anything different,' asked
Jude, 'if they'd been addressed to Giles rather than Denzil?'

Nikki Green looked genuinely puzzled by the question. 'I
can't see how.'

Carole tried another approach. 'Did you represent Fennel
Whittaker as an agent?'

'No. I wouldn't have minded doing so. She was undoubtedly talented. But unreliable. It's difficult to represent an artist
who's liable suddenly to destroy all her best work.'

Jude nodded, recalling what the girl had said about her
violent reactions against her own paintings. Not to mention
the torn-up watercolours by her body in the yurt. 'Going back
to what you were saying about Denzil's mother . . .'

'Yes.'

'He seemed terribly shocked by the news of her death. Had
she been ill?'

'Hard to tell. Philomena was always a terrible
hypochondriac.'

'But did she live with Denzil's father?'

Nikki Green let out a snort of laughter. 'Not for a long time.
Addison Willoughby has always been totally preoccupied with
his work.'

'Like his son?'

'I suppose so, but in a different way. Addison's full of
bitterness.'

'Denzil said that was because he'd never fulfilled himself
as an artist, taken the easy commercial route.'

'Yes, I know he always says that. And there may be a bit
of truth in it. But I don't think Addison's route has been easy.
That's the last word I'd choose. He's worked unbelievably
hard to make a success of the advertising agency.'

'And was it because he was a workaholic that the marriage
didn't work out?' asked Jude.

'Probably that had something to do with it. Philomena has
lived apart from him for years. He's got a big place in the
Boltons. She has – or she had – a nice flat of her own in
Highgate. And she was always telling Denzil how ill she was.
I thought it was just her way of keeping control over him . . .
but now she seems to have been proved right.' The woman

chuckled. 'She'll have to have the Hypochondriac's Epitaph on her tombstone: "I told you I was ill".'

'You don't seem very upset by the news of her death.'

Once again, Nikki Green was completely unembarrassed as she said, 'I'm not. I never liked her. And I think maybe now she's gone, it'll be a good thing for Denzil. Not straight away, of course. He'll be very cut up. But in a few years I think he'll realize that she was an impossible woman to please and he no longer has to expend so much effort trying to please her.'

'Did Denzil talk to you about us?' asked Carole suddenly.

Nikki Green looked astonished at the question. 'No. Why the hell should he? He hardly knows you. He didn't know you were going to appear on his doorstep this morning.'

'Well, he seemed to know about us, even seemed to be expecting us. He'd somehow got the impression from Giles's mother that we were showing too much interest in Fennel Whittaker's death.'

'How do you mean, "too much interest"?'

'Denzil had got the idea we might have thought Fennel's death wasn't suicide at all.'

'Well, if it wasn't, it was a pretty unusual accident.'

'Not an accident. Murder.'

That did stop Nikki Green in her tracks. Her eyes widened as she looked from one woman to the other. 'And is that what you think? That Fennel was murdered?'

'We think it's a possibility,' said Jude.

Nikki didn't ask why they thought that. She was silent while she assessed the idea, mentally testing it for feasibility. Then she asked, 'If you're talking about murder, then that means that you must have cast someone in the role of murderer.'

'We haven't quite got that far,' said Jude. 'We are still kind of considering the possibilities.'

'And Denzil was one of them?'

'He was the person Fennel bawled out at the Private View.'

'Yes, but for someone like Denzil that was just water off a duck's back. It didn't get to him at all. He'd regard it just as an endorsement of his self-image as the Great Lover.'

'There was something else,' said Carole. 'We also heard a

rumour that Denzil had a habit of being violent towards his girlfriends.'

She didn't attribute the rumour to Sam Torino, but it had a strong effect on Nikki Green. For the first time in their conversation she was really angry. 'That is complete nonsense!' she snapped. 'Denzil may be capable of all kinds of mental cruelty – he's totally self-centred – but there's no way he'd ever physically hurt anyone. Now, if you were talking about Giles, that would be a different matter altogether . . .'

On the train back to Fethering, Carole and Jude were as puzzled as each other. 'I was inclined to believe Nikki,' said Jude.

'About Denzil's violence towards women?'

'Yes.'

'Then why would Sam Torino have mentioned it? This friend of hers he was supposed to have beaten up?'

Jude tapped her chin pensively. 'That's what I'm trying to work out.'

'On the other hand, Nikki was pretty categorical about Giles having a tendency towards violence. And with her being married to him, you'd have to believe her on that.'

'Hm . . . I sort of get the feeling that somebody's covering up for someone, but I can't work out who's covering up for who.'

'No,' said Carole thoughtfully. 'And I keep coming back to that mutual alibi of Denzil and Giles for the night of Fennel's death. Is that where the cover-up was?'

That evening Carole Seddon sat in front of her laptop and googled 'Addison Willoughby'. There were plenty of results. His agency's official website chronicled his phenomenal success, building up a small company by skilful acquisitions into one of the world's most successful advertising agencies. Their client list embraced a wide range of global companies.

Images of Addison Willoughby showed him to be a handsome man in his sixties, dressed in expensively casual tieless style.

There appeared to be no reference to his private life. Even

on Wikipedia his wife Philomena was not mentioned. Nor was there anything about his relationship to challenging contemporary artist Denzil Willoughby.

Carole Seddon found that rather odd.

TWENTY-THREE

'I'm afraid my parents always regarded Elvis Presley as rather common,' said Carole Seddon.

'Ah,' said Jude, wondering why somehow she wasn't surprised, and also trying not to smile.

'Anyway, I'm rather too young for him to have been a major influence on my life. I'm more of the Beatles generation.' Though the idea of Carole having been part of the Swinging Sixties was an incongruous one. 'I don't think this evening at the Crown and Anchor really sounds my sort of thing.'

'It may not be your sort of thing, but I think we should be there to support Ted.'

'Ted can manage perfectly well without me. He won't notice whether I'm there or not.'

'That's not the point. I should think there's also a strong chance that Bonita Green will be there. Spider works for her, after all. We might get an opportunity to find out more about Fennel Whittaker.'

That argument clinched it, of course. To Carole Seddon's mind, Elvis Presley would always remain common, but one could even put up with commonness in the cause of an investigation.

There was a surprisingly large turnout in the Crown and Anchor's function room that Wednesday evening. Elvis Presley had a wider fan-base in Fethering than Carole might have imagined. And Spider's performance was certainly unlike anything she had ever seen before.

She wasn't quite sure what she had been expecting, but what impressed her about the framer was his total seriousness.

His routine was like some religious rite, an act of transubstantiation whereby he actually became Elvis Presley. Carole had vaguely anticipated that he might sing, but he didn't. He simply mimed to The King of Rock 'n' Roll's songs. And he did do it brilliantly.

He'd got all the gear too. Carole didn't know it, but Jude recognized that Spider was wearing a perfect facsimile of the white suit with a sunburst motif that Elvis had worn for his final concert at the Market Square Arena in Indianapolis on 26 June 1977. And the set he performed included many of the songs that had been sung on that iconic occasion. 'Jailhouse Rock' was there, 'Hound Dog', 'Teddy Bear, 'I Can't Stop Loving You', along with other classics from the canon: 'My Way', 'Unchained Melody' and 'Love Me Tender'.

But Spider had somehow improved on the original. Though he had the physical bulk of the grotesquely bloated Elvis of his later years, the versions he did of the songs, based on the studio recordings, had a musical purity rarely evident onstage at that time. The effect was strangely disconcerting for *aficionados* of The King, but nonetheless impressive. The Crown and Anchor crowd gave each number an ecstatic reaction and at the end, before his carefully choreographed encores, Spider got a standing ovation.

Clearly every facial tic, every bodily swivel, every hand gesture had been rehearsed in exhaustive detail. Each time the act was performed it would be exactly the same. To Carole and Jude, who had inevitably been preoccupied with such matters, it raised interesting speculations about the nature of art. What Spider did was far from original, and yet it had an integrity of its own. Was a man who duplicated exactly the movements of a long-dead singer any less of an artist than someone who had the idea of sticking photographs of dead black teenagers on to a fibreglass cannon?

The other detail about the evening that surprised them was the involvement of Bonita Green. They had expected her to be there to support her employee, but they didn't think she'd be part of the act. It was Bonita, however, who controlled the pacing of the show. She was in charge of the CD player from which the Elvis numbers were played. She judged how long the applause after each number should be allowed to continue before she started the next track. She was, in fact, a very efficient stage-manager.

Into both Carole and Jude's minds came the question as to how close the relationship between gallery-owner and framer actually was. There was between them during the performance a practised ease, but after the final ovation they still seemed very relaxed in each other's company. Again Spider's manner was protective, almost proprietorial. Perhaps this was simply the result of the two of them working together in the Cornelian Gallery for so long, but both Carole and Jude suspected there might be something more to it.

After Spider had finished his act, a good convivial atmosphere had built up in the Crown and Anchor. Beneath the beard on Ted Crisp's face was something that came very close to a beam. Elvis Presley had brought the punters in and the bar takings by the end of the evening would be very healthy. The landlord was clearly thinking that Spider's routine might become a regular booking.

While Carole queued in the crush at the bar for more Chilean Chardonnay, Jude drifted across to join the congratulatory throng around the star of the evening. Bonita Green, she noticed, sat very close to Spider, almost as if she were acting as his minder.

Among the crowd she was surprised to see Ned Whittaker. She hadn't noticed him earlier in the evening, but presumably he had been there for the duration. It struck her that she hadn't actually seen him since the Monday of the previous week when he'd come to Woodside Cottage seeking explanations for his daughter's death. The millionaire's face was still very drawn and his eyes were surrounded by dark shadows. He didn't look as though he had slept much since the loss of Fennel.

Jude wondered why Ned was there. It was of course entirely possible that he was just a big Elvis Presley fan, but it seemed a strange choice of an evening out for someone so clearly still suffering from recent bereavement.

But he seemed pleased to see her; in fact he positively sought her out. 'Could I have a word, Jude?'

'Sure.'

He looked uneasily around the crowded pub. 'I meant somewhere a bit more private. I've got the car parked outside. It'll
only take a minute if you . . .?'

'Of course.' Jude semaphored across to the bar that she'd be
back shortly. Carole started to semaphore back a supplementary
question, but Jude and Ned Whittaker had already gone.

They sat in another of the Butterwyke House fleet of Prius
hybrids. With the moon nearly full, it was a surprisingly clear
night.

'Fennel's funeral is set for Wednesday week,' Ned announced.

'Yes, I heard that from Kier. I'll try and make it.'

'Don't. It's just going to be family. We'll probably do a
party for her later at Butterwyke, a kind of celebration of her
life.'

'That'd be good. Let me know when.'

'Of course.' There was a silence. Jude felt pretty sure that
the funeral wasn't what he really wanted to talk to her about.
'Listen, Jude, you keep your ear pretty close to the ground
round Fethering, don't you?'

'I hear things, yes. It's a small community.'

'Mm.' Ned still wasn't finding it easy to broach his subject.
Then he leapt in. 'Look, have you heard any people saying
that Fennel was murdered?'

Inexplicably – and uncharacteristically – Jude felt guilty.
She tried to think to whom, apart from Carole, she had confided
her suspicion. Sam Torino, maybe . . . Except really it had
been Sam who had raised the topic, rather than her.

She fell back on a platitude about people gossiping more
than was good for them.

'And what about you, Jude? Has the thought crossed your
mind?'

Again this was awkward. 'Ned, we've had this conversation before. When you came to see me at Woodside
Cottage the Monday after Fennel's death. We went through
the whole thing.'

'Yes, but I just wondered whether your thoughts on the subject
had changed since then . . .?'

'Not a lot, Ned. All I keep coming back to is the fact that when I last saw her, Fennel wasn't behaving in the manner of someone about to kill herself. She positively said to do so would be a waste. And then again there was the matter of her missing mobile. Did you hear any more from the police about that?'

Ned Whittaker shook his head. 'The police seem to have given up on the case. Apparently a suicide verdict suits them very well. Less paperwork, I guess. And they've released Fennel's body for the funeral. So I would assume that means any investigations they're undertaking are at an end. Probably just as well. The last thing I need at the moment is the cops trampling over my family with their insensitive hobnail boots.'

Jude thought back to her encounter with Detective Inspector Hodgkinson. 'Insensitive hobnail boots' was the last attribute she would have applied to that particular member of the police force. And in fact, if she were ever to find proof that Fennel Whittaker had been murdered, she would have had no hesitation in re-contacting Carmen Hodgkinson. Which had to be a first in Jude's dealings with the police.

'Anyway, Jude,' Ned continued awkwardly, I guess why I wanted to talk to you was to ask . . . if you do have any further thoughts about Fennel having been murdered . . . could you keep them to yourself?'

Finally he'd come out with it. That had been the reason why he'd wanted to talk to her on her own, perhaps the only reason why he'd come over to the Crown and Anchor to witness Spider's Elvis Presley act.

'But I haven't been spreading any rumours like that,' Jude protested. 'Who did you hear that from? Was it Sam Torino?'

Ned denied the allegation hotly, but Jude didn't believe him. She couldn't think of any other person he might know with whom she'd shared her suspicions. And she began to wonder even whether Ned had set up Sam Torino deliberately to sound out her views of Fennel's death. She remembered the card the supermodel had given her. A call to that private mobile number at some point might be in order.

'I'm not just saying this on my own behalf,' Ned Whittaker

volunteered. 'I'm speaking for the whole family. We don't want any gossip. Sheena's particularly insistent on that.'

'So is it Sheena who's put you up to this – you know, warning me off?'

That suggestion was denied with equal vehemence, but again Jude got the feeling that she might have stumbled on the truth. Sheena Whittaker remained enigmatic, her only identifiable emotion seeming to be relief at her daughter's death. Jude reckoned she and Carole should try to find out more about the dead girl's mother.

She tried to get more out of Ned Whittaker, but without success. From his point of view, discouraging her from suggesting his daughter might have been murdered was the sole aim of their meeting. Why he was so worried about that happening he did not reveal. But, given the fact that the police had concluded their investigation, he seemed disproportionately anxious about the matter.

Which suggested to Jude that Ned had suspicions that someone he knew might be implicated in his daughter's death. But who that person was, she had no idea.

TWENTY-FOUR

It was typical of Carole Seddon that she hadn't waited in the Crown and Anchor for her neighbour to return from the assignation in the car park. Wearily, Jude reminded herself that anyone who wanted to be friends with the owner of High Tor had to reconcile themselves to a regular amount of bridge-building and fence-mending. There were no two ways about it – Carole Seddon was touchy. She had felt slighted by her friend going off without telling her, and she wanted that slight to be registered, so she'd gone home alone . . . no doubt leaving two untouched glasses of wine in the Crown and Anchor function room. It was just to be hoped that somebody had drunk them, rather than wasting good Chilean Chardonnay.

As a result of this, before she went to bed in Woodside Cottage, Jude found herself going next door on a ruffled-feather-smoothing mission. It was characteristic of Carole that, once they were sitting either side of her kitchen table with glasses of wine, she didn't mention the instance which had caused her touchiness, but listened with interest as her neighbour relayed the conversation she'd had in Ned Whittaker's Prius.

'But, Jude, how does he know we've been discussing the possibility of Fennel's death being murder?'

'That's what I've been trying to work out. As I say, he could have got it from Sam Torino, but then again, if he actually set up Sam Torino to question me, he must have had his suspicions before that.'

'And you think he's protecting someone?'

'I can't find any other explanation for his behaviour. And I've been thinking since I left him that the only two people Ned might really have an interest in protecting are Sheena or Chervil.'

'You mean he thinks one of them killed Fennel?'

'Well, was implicated in her death in some way, yes.'

There was a beady look in Carole Seddon's eyes as she reflected her friend's thoughts. 'Sheena's the one who intrigues me,' she said.

As it turned out, they didn't have to go looking for Sheena Whittaker. Jude had a call from her the following morning, the Thursday. The social unease the woman manifested on public occasions was nowhere evident in her manner. Just talking on the phone she sounded in control. And she was very direct.

'Ned told me about the conversation you had last night.'

'Oh yes?'

'I want to talk to you about it.'

'Fine. Talk away.'

'I'd rather do it face to face.'

It was arranged that Sheena Whittaker would come straight round to Woodside Cottage.

* * *

Sheena was wearing a pink top and jeans, both of which had too much glitter on them. She looked what she was, a chubby East London hairdresser who had got lucky. But though she spent much of her life being paraded as her husband's accessory, there was no doubt that she had a strong will of her own.

'Ned's very upset,' was the first thing she said, after refusing offers of tea or coffee.

'I know. He made clear to me how much Fennel meant to him.'

'Yes. There was something between them that I . . . well, sometimes I have to confess it made me feel rather uncomfortable.'

'Oh?'

'I don't mean any of that child abuse nonsense they keep doing television programmes about. I just mean they had this kind of . . . I don't know what you'd call it . . . a kind of psychic connection.'

'Telepathy?'

'Yes, maybe that's the word. Anyway, I know you probably think that my reaction to Fennel's death has been rather heartless . . .'

'I've never said—'

'But you've thought it. The fact is, I've spent many years dealing with my daughter's depression . . . her fragility, her breakdowns. We've tried every kind of medication, every kind of treatment – including what you were doing for her – and none of it worked. I've felt for a long time that whatever we did, it was just delaying the evil hour, that one day she would . . . do what she did.'

Sheena Whittaker's voice caught on the last few words, the first indication that her narrative was taking any emotional toll on her. She drew the back of her hand firmly across her nose before continuing, 'So I have spent a long time preparing for this moment.'

'I'm sure you have,' said Jude. 'I hope you don't mind my asking you something . . .'

'What?'

'When Ned came to see me the Monday after . . . you know . . .' Somehow to say the words would have felt like an intrusion on Sheena's emotions. 'We talked about Fennel's depression and discussed whether it might be hereditary. And Ned said he'd never actually been depressed, but—'

'He didn't say that I was a depressive, did he?'

'No, but—'

'Thank goodness for that. Because I never have been.'

'You haven't ever—?'

'No!' The expression 'protesting too much' came instinctively into Jude's mind, as Sheena Whittaker went on, 'I am extremely lucky. I have a great lifestyle. I'd be mad to be depressed.'

'Exactly.'

'What do you mean?'

'Depression is a form of madness, so if you say you'd be "mad to be depressed", what you mean is—'

'That's not what I'm talking about.'

'After what happened with Fennel, it'd be no surprise if you—'

'I am not depressed!' Sheena seemed taken aback by her own vehemence. 'Yes, I'm shocked. I've lost my daughter. And though, yes, obviously I feel a terrible sadness, I also can't deny a sense of relief.'

'But Ned doesn't share that feeling?'

'No, he's still just too caught up in his grief. He's too raw. I think maybe in time he may come round.'

Jude pushed the flopping blonde hair up off her forehead. 'And Chervil . . . she doesn't seem to be suffering too badly either.'

'Chervil's a businesswoman. You've only seen her in her professional mode. She wouldn't show her real feelings in such circumstances.'

'No, of course not.' Jude would have given a lot to know what conversations had been shared between Sheena Whittaker and her surviving daughter since Fennel's death. But that was not information she thought she was about to be vouchsafed. And she still hadn't worked out precisely why Sheena had been so insistent on coming to see her.

'I'll tell you why I'm here, Jude.' Ah, so she was maybe about to be given the answer to that question. 'I want to ask you a few details about that night you spent with Fennel in the yurt . . . you know, the night she died.' Again the actual mention of death brought a slight tremor to her voice.

'I'll tell you as much as I can remember. As you know, Fennel and I had both had quite a lot to drink.'

'Yes. When the police talked to me, they said you'd mentioned Fennel having a call on her mobile.'

'A call or a text. I think it was a text, but I was half asleep when it happened.'

'Obviously, in the light of what subsequently happened, the identity of the sender of that text becomes rather important.'

'I couldn't agree with you more.'

'But in their searches of the yurt – in fact of the whole Walden area – the police didn't find any trace of Fennel's mobile.'

'Ah. I didn't know that. The officer who interviewed me – Detective Inspector Hodgkinson – said she'd check it out. But I never heard any more from her.'

'You met Detective Inspector Hodgkinson too, did you?

'She questioned you?'

'Mm. Though she did it in such a subtle way that it didn't feel like questioning.'

'I know what you mean. I thought she was quite bright.'

But clearly Sheena Whittaker hadn't shared that opinion. She shuddered slightly as she said, 'I didn't warm to her. Too clever for her own good, if you ask me. And I think she was probably lesbian.'

Jude shrugged. 'Anyway,' Sheena went on, 'Ned's been worrying a lot about the missing mobile . . . and what it implies.'

'That someone took it?'

'That's one possible explanation, yes.'

'But if someone took it, that would change the way one views the circumstances of Fennel's death.'

'It certainly would. '

'So, Sheena, do you have any suspicions who might have taken it?'

'I certainly do.'

'Right. So who is your suspect?'

'There's only one person it could have been.'
'Who?'
'You, Jude.'

TWENTY-FIVE

'But why did she think you'd taken it?' asked Carole somewhat plaintively.

'I suppose I was on the scene. I had the opportunity.'

'But for what reason did she think you might have taken it?'

'That's what I couldn't get out of her. Because if someone did take the phone, then they were probably trying to cover something up. What might they be trying to cover up? Well, one thing is obviously murder.'

'So did you ask Sheena whether she'd considered the possibility of murder?'

'Yes. And she wouldn't be drawn on that. She's a very stubborn woman. Maybe not stubborn . . . strong-willed perhaps is the word I'm looking for. She comes across as all meek and fluffy, but she has a core of steel. I think she's the dynamo in that marriage.'

'So how were things left between you?'

'Rather as they were with Ned yesterday evening. I was strongly discouraged from suggesting to anyone that Fennel might have been murdered.'

Carole nodded and took a sip of coffee. They were at the kitchen table in High Tor. It was so mild that the Aga had now been switched off for the summer, but out of habit Gulliver still lay beside it, snuffling quietly in his doggy dreams. He had a slight inflammation on one of his paws, not doubt caused by some foreign object on Fethering Beach. An appointment at the vet's had been booked for later that day, but the injury didn't seem to be worrying him.

'So, Jude, do you think Ned and Sheena have the same agenda?'

'In what way?'

'Well, the fact that they both seem so keen to get you – or us – off the case might suggest that they're trying to protect someone. The question is: are they both trying to protect the same person?'

'I see what you mean. Well, Ned had certainly relayed to Sheena the conversation I had with him in the car park last night. That's what brought her round to see me.'

'But he didn't accuse you of taking Fennel's mobile?'

'No. He mentioned it, just said so far as he knew the police hadn't found the thing. It's Sheena who leapt to the conclusion that I'd nicked it.'

Carole was thoughtful as she had another sip of coffee. Then she said slowly, 'You don't think it's herself that Sheena's trying to protect?'

'What, you mean that she killed Fennel and she thinks the mobile might contain some evidence against her? Like the text with which she set up their meeting?'

'Perhaps. What do you reckon?'

Jude pursed her full lips. 'I find it hard to cast Sheena in the role of murderer. I find it hard to cast any mother in the role of the murderer of her own child.'

'It has happened. Read your classical myths.'

'I know, but . . .'

Carole pressed home her advantage. 'And Sheena Whittaker's making no secret of her relief that Fennel's no longer around.'

'Yes, but . . .' Jude moved her head abruptly, as though there were a troublesome thought she wanted to shake out of it. 'For some reason my mind keeps coming back to the first suicide attempt.'

'In the flat in Pimlico . . .'

'Yes. Sheena wasn't involved in that. Well, obviously she was in the sense that it was her daughter who'd made the attempt. But it was Chervil who found Fennel and it was Ned who rushed up to London to sort things out. Why didn't Sheena go?'

Carole shrugged. 'There could be any number of reasons. And Sheena talked about the close relationship Ned always had with Fennel.'

'Yes . . . I almost get this picture of a house divided. Sheena and Chervil on one side, Ned and Fennel on the other. Which is why he's so desolated by Fennel's death, and his wife seems relatively unaffected.'

'And I wonder where Chervil fits into this emotional scale . . .?' Carole mused.

'Well, outwardly, as we saw at the Walden launch, it doesn't seem to have got to her. Mind you, Sheena hinted that there might be strong feelings under the surface, which were being controlled because Chervil was there in her professional capacity.'

There was a silence, broken only by the grunting of Gulliver, pursuing some dream rabbit.

'Thinking back to the Walden launch,' said Carole eventually, 'I was intrigued by what you said about Sam Torino.'

'Oh?'

'The feeling you got that Ned Whittaker might have set her up to sound you out.'

'Well, I haven't got any proof that he did.'

'No, it's an interesting idea. Pity you can't make contact with Sam Torino to follow up on it.'

'Ah,' said Jude perkily. 'But I can.'

In spite of her apparent confidence, Jude had not expected her call to be answered immediately. And it wasn't. The answering message was not in the distinctive Canadian tone of Sam Torino, just an anonymous mechanical voice. Jude left her name and number, by now doubtful that she would ever hear back.

Carole, she could tell, was disappointed. Both of them worried that their investigation was drowning in inertia. Their suspicions about the circumstances of Fennel Whittaker's death seemed increasingly tenuous. They needed some kind of breakthrough, but there was no hint that any might be imminent.

A subdued Jude returned to Woodside Cottage. She had a couple of clients due on that Thursday afternoon, but she didn't feel in the right mood for them. Her mind was too full to find the focus and clarity she needed for healing.

She was contemplating calling them to put off their sessions when her mobile rang.

'Hi, this is Sam Torino.'

'Thank you for calling back.'

'No problem.' But there still seemed to be a slight tension in the voice, almost a wariness.

'How's the back?'

'Fine and dandy at the moment. Can't thank you enough for that, Jude.'

'And are you taking the prescription I gave you?'

'For solitude?' She let out a throaty laugh. 'Hell, I'm trying, but it's hard with a schedule like mine. Why couldn't you have prescribed something easy – like running a marathon every day?'

'Because if you ran a marathon every day, you'd run it surrounded by *paparazzi*. Besides, that prescription wouldn't make you better.'

Sam Torino chuckled again. But it wasn't a completely relaxed chuckle. She was still circling round, waiting to hear the real reason why Jude had contacted her.

Time to own up. 'I wanted to talk to you more about Fennel Whittaker.'

'Uh-huh.' No surprise. Sam had been expecting it. Jude wondered how recently Ned had been in touch with his glamorous friend.

'I was thinking back to what we talked about in the treatment yurt . . .' No response, just an expectant silence. 'You said Ned had been worried there might be local gossip about Fennel having been murdered.'

'I remember.'

'Then maybe you also remember that I asked you at the time whether you'd set up our therapy session specifically to talk about her death.'

'And I said no. Hell, are you suggesting the pain in my back wasn't genuine?'

'No, I'm not suggesting that at all. I could feel that pain. But maybe getting me to do the healing session was convenient because it *did* give you an opportunity to find out what I was thinking about Fennel's death.'

'I don't think I'm following you here. What are you trying to get me to say?'

'I'm not trying to get you to say anything. I promise there's nothing sinister in my getting in touch with you.'

'Good. Because I'm afraid someone in my position does have to be a bit careful. You know, you meet people who seem to be all upfront and then you discover that they're trying to get something out of you. Of course, I don't feel that with you, Jude . . .' But the caution still lurked in Sam Torino's voice.

'The only thing I want to get out of you is an admission that you set up our therapy at Ned Whittaker's request.'

A long silence ensued while the supermodel considered her response. Then slowly she said, 'Well, OK, it was a bit of each. I was talking to Ned at the launch and—'

'Ned wasn't at the launch.'

'No. OK, he wasn't on the Walden site, I agree. I talked to him before the launch up at the house.'

'And he then asked you to set up the healing session with me?'

'It wasn't as overt and calculating as that. Ned was kind of marking my card for the afternoon, telling me who I might expect to meet there . . .'

'I thought Walden was Chervil's project.'

'I guess, but Ned seemed to know all about it. Anyway, he mentioned you and he said you were a healer and I said, "Maybe I should get her to take a look at this bastard back of mine." And he said, "Not a bad idea. Well, if you do talk to Jude, ask her if she thinks there's anything odd about Fennel's death." And I ask him how he means "odd" and he says there's rumours going round she might have been murdered. And so I do as he asks. But it was really just that I wanted to get my back looked at. And I'm sure as hell glad I got you to sort that out.'

There was almost a note of pleading in Sam's voice by the end, so Jude granted her forgiveness. 'Thank you. That's all I wanted to know.'

'Well, you can't just leave it there,' said Sam Torino.

'How do you mean?'

'I've answered your question, but you haven't told me why you needed to ask it. Do you have some reason to believe that Fennel was murdered?'

'More of an instinct than a reason. But what you've told me about Ned does open up other possibilities.'

'How so?'

'If he does think someone killed his daughter, then why hasn't he shared his suspicions with the police? There's only one reason I can think of for him doing that.'

'Which is . . .?'

'That he knows who the killer is, and he wants to protect that person from prosecution.'

'I see what you mean. So we're talking someone very close to him here, are we?'

'We could be. Actually, I've just remembered, Sam . . . there was another thing I wanted to ask you.'

'Ask away.'

'We've established that Ned set you up to question me. Did he also instruct you that, if I did seem to be thinking along the lines of a murder, then you should encourage me to cast Denzil Willoughby in the role of murderer?'

The guilty silence had already answered Jude's question before Sam Torino admitted, 'Yes, he did. Look, I didn't know what the stakes were – I still don't, come to that. Ned was just a friend going through a bad patch – a really bad patch – he'd kind of lost the love of his life when Fennel died. And he asked me to do something for him and I thought, hell, if it's going to make the poor bastard feel better, there can't be much harm in it.'

'Maybe not,' said Jude ruminatively. 'You and Ned . . . you were never more than friends?'

'Hell, no.' She seemed affronted by the idea. 'I never mix friendships and love affairs. Friends are kind of private people you get along with privately. Love affairs are big public commitments.'

'To be splashed all over the tabloids?'

'If I'm one of the people involved, then I'm afraid the answer's yes. It's not something I've particularly sought out, but that's the way it is. My love affairs have become part of my career. So I wouldn't spoil my friendship with someone like Ned by going to bed with him. Apart from which, I've never begun to fancy him. And then again he's absolutely locked into that marriage with Sheena.'

'You think the marriage is secure?'

'God, yes.'

'But there seem to be things about which they disagree.'

'Look, it's a marriage – what the hell do you expect?'

'But like the way they've reacted differently to Fennel's death . . .'

'The reason for that is that Ned always tries to keep the bad stuff away from Sheena. You talk about him trying to protect someone . . . well, the person he's protected right through their marriage is his wife.'

This was a new perspective on the lives of the Whittakers. It stimulated a niggling suspicion about Sheena that Jude had been nursing for some time.

'I mean,' Sam Torino went on, 'look what happened over Fennel's first suicide attempt.'

'Sorry? I don't really know much about what happened then.'

'Chervil found her sister in the Pimlico flat. She immediately rang Ned who went straight up to London, *without even telling his wife what had happened.*'

'I didn't know that.'

'He got Fennel safely back home and had her checked out by a doctor, and it was only then that he told Sheena. He didn't want to worry her until the situation was as stable as it could be.'

'Right.' Jude nodded thoughtfully.

'Ned did his best to keep all the unpleasant details away from Sheena. He didn't even show her the suicide note that Fennel had written.'

'Ah,' said Jude. 'I didn't know there had been a suicide note.'

TWENTY-SIX

As soon as she had finished the call to Sam Torino, Jude hurried round to High Tor to bring Carole up to date with the new development. But there was no reply. Of course, Gulliver was being taken to the vet's about his inflamed foot.

Back at Woodside Cottage she didn't hesitate, but straight away rang Ned Whittaker. The phone was answered by a girl whose laid-back manner did not disguise the fact that she was actually a secretary. As ever, the slightly hippyish atmosphere of Butterwyke House masked rigid efficiency.

Ned came on the line immediately on hearing who was asking for him. His 'Hi, Jude' was spoken with a degree of caution. Presumably Sheena had updated him on their encounter that morning.

As soon as Jude told him that she knew about the suicide note found in the Pimlico flat, he announced that he'd come over to Fethering immediately 'to explain what happened.'

The Prius in which he arrived outside Woodside Cottage soon after was driven by Kier, who had clearly been told to wait in the car. In spite of his T-shirted dress code, the young man was as much a chauffeur as one in a uniform and a peaked cap.

Ned Whittaker looked more stressed than ever. Refusing offers of tea or coffee, he asked immediately, 'How did you find out about the suicide note?'

'Sam Torino.'

He sighed with annoyance. 'I'd forgotten she knew. I should have warned her to keep quiet about it.'

'Tell me what happened in the Pimlico flat after the first suicide attempt,' said Jude calmly.

'You know most of it. The flat's a kind of family bolt-hole in London. There have been times when one or other of the girls were living there full-time . . . you know, when Fennel was at St Martin's . . . or when Chervil was between jobs or houses. We all have keys. Thank God, because otherwise Chervil wouldn't have found Fennel that afternoon and . . . Mind you, Fennel's dead now, which means . . .' Grief threatened to overwhelm him.

'So Chervil just dropped into the flat that afternoon by chance?' asked Jude.

'Yes. And she found Fennel unconscious. She realized

immediately what had happened. The pill bottles and the whisky left her in no doubt.'

'Nor did the suicide note,' Jude prompted.

'No.' Ned sighed again. There was despair in his manner, but also an element of relief. Holding in the information had taken its toll on him. 'I have, incidentally, called Chervil. Told her that you knew about the note and that I was coming to see you. She may appear here at any moment.'

'Fine. So go on. Chervil rang you after she'd found Fennel, you got Kier to drive you up to London . . .'

'How do you know that?'

'He told me.'

'Ah.' Wearily he said, 'Very difficult when you try to keep things quiet, you know. You think you've warned off everyone you should . . . and then you discover there's someone you've forgotten.'

'So when you got to Pimlico, Chervil showed you the suicide note?'

'Yes.'

'Was it straight away that you decided to keep quiet about it?'

'Pretty much. I was terribly shocked, but it looked as if Fennel was going to pull through. The cuts on her wrists were only surface injuries, most of the painkillers had been flushed out of her system and I was starting to think: no one need actually ever know that this has happened. No one outside the family, that is . . . or close friends.'

'Like Sam Torino?'

He nodded.

'So did you take the suicide note with you?'

'No, I left it with Chervil. Told her to destroy it before the people arrived to clean out the flat.'

'And do you think she did destroy it?'

'I assume so.'

'No, you don't, Ned,' said Jude, with a new strength in her voice. 'Because you've seen that suicide note since then, haven't you?' He made no attempt to deny the allegation. 'It was the suicide note that was found near Fennel's body in the yurt at Walden.'

Ned Whittaker looked totally drained. He couldn't summon up the energy to provide any further defence. He just sat slumped in his armchair as Jude went on, 'Which of course does put a whole new interpretation on the circumstances of her death, doesn't it? There was no way Fennel herself left that note, was there?'

'No,' Ned agreed wretchedly.

'Equally, there's no way that Chervil destroyed it, as she said she had.'

Before Jude could pursue this argument to its logical conclusion, she was interrupted by a ring on the doorbell. With no great surprise, she found Chervil Whittaker standing outside.

Ned had followed her to the front door. 'I'd better go,' he said.

'But, Daddy—'

'I'd better go,' he repeated, pushing past his daughter without making any eye contact. And as Ned Whittaker walked along Jude's garden path towards the waiting Prius, his body language reflected deep pain and a sense of betrayal.

TWENTY-SEVEN

Chervil Whittaker walked through into the sitting room of Woodside Cottage in silence and sat herself down in one of the armchairs. She was, as ever, perfectly groomed in designer jeans and polo shirt, but her face had lost its animated sparkle.

Jude took a seat opposite her. 'So . . .?' she said.

'Daddy told me you'd found out about the suicide note.'

'Yes. You didn't destroy it after Fennel's first attempt?'

'No.'

'Can I ask why?'

'You can ask. I'm not sure how coherent an answer I can give you.'

'Oh?'

'Have you got a sister?' Jude shook her head. 'Well then,

you'll just have to take my word for it that relationships between sisters can be quite complex.'

'I know that from my work as a therapist.'

'Yes, of course you would. I'm sure there are all kinds of psychological terms applied to the situation – "sibling rivalry", that kind of thing – but I don't know that they quite cover it. The fact is, within our family I've always felt that I was kind of playing second fiddle to Fennel.'

'Because she was your father's favourite?'

'It's not as simple as that. Daddy loves both of us, in his way, but if there ever was a direct competition for his attention, Fennel would win it.'

'Because she was needy?'

'I guess, yes. You might imagine that someone with power over other people has to be pushy and upfront . . .'

'I wouldn't imagine that, actually. I know how potent vulnerability can be.'

'I'm sorry, of course you'd understand. Presumably you deal with that kind of stuff every day. Anyway, that's how it worked with Fennel. She was always fragile emotionally, and you could tell Daddy was almost literally afraid she might break if he didn't rush to look after her. To be fair, I don't think Fennel actually played on that. It's just how she was.'

'But your mother didn't respond to her in the same way as your father?'

'It was different with Mummy. She'd act tougher about it, say, "Don't worry about Fennel – she's just having one of her prima donna moments." She'd *say* that, but in many ways she was as much in thrall to Fennel as Daddy was.'

'But she's not been as affected by her death as Ned is. She's even referred to it as being a relief.'

'Yes, but you can't always believe what Mummy says. She can be quite devious at times. With her there's a lot going on that you don't see on the surface.'

Jude nodded, having received confirmation of the impression that she had of Sheena Whittaker.

'So what I'm saying is,' Chervil went on, 'I've always felt inferior to Fennel. In spite of the fact that, by any kind of public criterion, I've always been much more successful than she has. I did better than her at school, and in my business career. And my relationships with men were always better. I didn't end up with the kind of no-hopers Fennel did.'

Jude was struck, not for the first time, by how deeply ingrained childhood perceptions could prove to be in adult personalities. Family designations, like 'the pretty one' or 'the clever one' could cast long shadows into the future.

But she did pick up on one thing Chervil had just said. 'You're not describing Giles as a "no-hoper", are you?'

'How do you mean?'

'I know that Fennel had a relationship with him too.'

Chervil looked annoyed. 'Who did you hear that from?'

'Denzil Willoughby.'

'I might have guessed. There's a streak of vindictive gossip in Denzil. Anyway, Giles is far from being a no-hoper. He was a rare exception in Fennel's catalogue of masculine disaster areas. They weren't together very long, and they were always bound to split up sooner or later –' she smiled smugly – 'which was of course very good news for me.'

There was a silence. Jude asked if Chervil would like a drink, but the offer was refused. 'Maybe we could get back to the suicide note . . .?' Jude suggested.

'Yes. I'm trying to explain why I kept it. I don't know, it seemed logical at the time. Fennel had just staged another of her dramas. As usual, Daddy had dropped everything and come rushing to her aid. And once again I knew he'd smooth the whole thing over, keep it quiet, see that news of what had happened didn't spread beyond the family and close friends. And no one would believe the kind of panic and aggravation Fennel had caused us. So I kept the suicide note as kind of, I don't know . . . evidence against her, if I ever needed it.'

'And did you ever need it?'

'I don't know what you mean.'

Jude left that line of questioning for a moment and moved on in another direction. 'You realize there are certain logical consequences from your admission that you kept the suicide note . . . and even more from the fact that it was found by Fennel's dead body.'

Again Chervil said, 'I don't know what you mean.' Jude

couldn't decide whether the girl was playing for time or whether she genuinely hadn't followed the logic through.

'Well, to put it bluntly, it means that your sister didn't commit suicide.'

'Not necessarily.'

'Oh, come on, Chervil . . .' There was a rare note of exasperation in Jude's voice. 'Your father's told me that the note left by Fennel's body in the yurt was definitely the one he saw in the flat in Pimlico, the one he told you to destroy. That means it wasn't left there by Fennel herself, because even if she had wished to go down the bizarre route of leaving the note she'd written before, it wasn't in her possession, so she couldn't have. You had it, Chervil, and I'd need a pretty convincing argument to persuade me it wasn't you who left it there.'

'Well, it wasn't.'

'No?'

'No.'

'When did you last see the note, Chervil?'

'A few weeks ago. There's a file I keep in a drawer in my bedroom. It's personal stuff, things I don't want to lose.'

'Are you talking about your bedroom in your London flat?'

'No, down here at Butterwyke House.'

'And why did you look at the note a few weeks ago?'

'Er, I can't remember.' The girl's hesitation showed she was lying.

'That's not good enough, Chervil. We're talking about a murder here. The suicide note was in your possession, then it appeared beside your sister's body. The most likely explanation remains that you put it there.'

'I didn't!' came the passionate response. 'It was already there when I . . .'

The words trickled away as she realized what she had said. Jude let the silence stretch long enough for Chervil Whittaker to take in the full impact of her giveaway, then observed, 'I think you've come rather close to an admission there.'

'Admission of what?' Chervil demanded defiantly.

'Admission that you did go to the treatment yurt at Walden the night Fennel died.'

'And what if I did? I didn't murder her. She was already dead when I got there.'

'With the suicide note lying beside her?'

'Yes.'

'So what did you do? On the previous occasion when you found Fennel like that you immediately contacted your father. Is that what you did this time?'

'No.'

'Why not?'

'I didn't want him involved. I didn't want anyone involved. I didn't want anyone to know what'd happened.'

'Or rather you didn't want anyone to know that you'd been in the yurt.'

'All right, that was part of it. Look, I was in shock. At first I thought Fennel must've killed herself. She'd threatened to enough times. I thought she'd finally succeeded.'

'But then you saw the note.'

'Yes.'

'And its presence told you that she must have been murdered.'

'Well, it told me that was a possibility. As I say, I wasn't thinking straight.'

'Mm. I think the presence of the note brought another thought into your mind, the thought of who might have put it there.' The girl didn't respond, she remained stubbornly silent, so Jude changed tack. 'Who else knew you had the suicide note, Chervil?'

'No one.'

'I don't think that's true. And if it is true, then you are the only person who could have planted it by the body. So either you admit someone else knew you had it, or you are effectively identifying yourself as your sister's murderer. I do still have the number of Detective Inspector Hodgkinson, the police officer who questioned me after Fennel died . . .'

It was not the kind of threat that Jude liked using, but it did have the required effect. Chervil said, 'Yes, all right, I did show it to someone else.'

'Who? I can't think there are that many candidates.'

'Well, I . . .'

Jude was distracted by another thought. 'When you found Fennel's body, did you also find her mobile phone?'

Chervil Whittaker looked as guilty as a schoolgirl caught smoking by the headmistress. 'How did you know that?'

'Logic,' replied Jude, though in fact guesswork would have been a more truthful answer. 'Did you take it?'

'Yes.'

'Why?' Silence. 'I don't think I really need to ask that question. I know why you took it. Because you knew that the last message or text on the phone would have been the one from Fennel's murderer, the one that arranged their meeting in the treatment yurt. You took the phone because you wanted to protect the person who you thought had killed your sister.' Still no response. 'And where's the phone now?'

'Somewhere no one will ever find it.'

'I wonder where that might be . . .? Rather blessed round here, aren't we, being so close to the sea. Not to mention to the River Fether. And of course that's tidal, so anything thrown in there can get swept out a long way. Be hard to find a mobile phone in the English Channel, wouldn't it, Chervil?'

Jude was busking, improvising wildly. But she had some-times known occasions where her instinctive conjectures had proved to be right, and she felt as if she was on just such a roll at that moment.

Anyway, the actual location of the missing mobile didn't matter that much. There were more important issues to be discussed.

'So who was the last message on Fennel's mobile from?' she asked implacably.

'I didn't look.'

'You're lying. Of course you did.' The girl's mouth was set in a line of defiance. 'It's not too difficult to work out, you know, Chervil. And it's even easier to work out who you showed the suicide note to. There aren't that many people who you'd invite into your bedroom, are there?' Jude waited for a response, but once more in vain. 'Why did you show the suicide note to Giles, Chervil?'

The younger woman's shoulders sagged suddenly. All the fight had gone out of her. 'It was when we first started going out together – or at least I wanted us to go out together, but Giles wasn't so sure. Anyway, I'd met him for a drink at the

Crown and Anchor in Fethering and then we'd gone back to the Cornelian Gallery. He was still seeing Fennel, and I wanted to show him that she wouldn't be good for him, that if he kept seeing her he'd get into the same kind of emotional blackmail trap as Daddy had.'

'So you actually used the suicide note to persuade Giles to stop going out with Fennel and to start going out with you?'

'Yes,' Chervil Whittaker replied. And the note of triumph in her voice revealed the depths of the jealousy she had always felt for her dead sister.

TWENTY-EIGHT

'So Chervil didn't see Giles the night of Fennel's death?' asked Carole.

'No. She left him at the Private View. He was supposed to be joining her at Butterwyke House, but then he texted her to say that he was out drinking with Denzil Willoughby and would be a bit late. He didn't turn up till the following morning.'

'Did Chervil say why she went to the treatment yurt in the middle of the night?'

'She gave me some guff about waking up with a sense of foreboding and being drawn towards the place, which sounded like a pack of lies to me.'

'I'm surprised.'

Carole's words had Jude fazed for a moment, but then she got it. The implication was that 'a sense of foreboding' and 'being drawn towards the place' were exactly the kind of New Age mumbo-jumbo that appealed to Jude. She didn't bother to rise to the insinuation, instead saying, 'At least we now know for sure that it was murder.'

'And we know that Giles Green was the perpetrator.'

'I'm not so convinced about that. He was certainly involved, but I'm wondering whether they planned the thing together.'

'Hm. And the last message on Fennel's mobile was presumably from Giles?'

'From his number, yes. Chervil admitted that.'

They were back in the High Tor kitchen. By the cold Aga, Gulliver looked balefully at the bandage on his infected paw. In the Renault on the way back from the vet's he'd tried to chew it off, but now recognized that was a battle he was not going to win.

Carole tapped her teeth thoughtfully. 'Of course, Giles Green has in theory got an alibi for the relevant night.'

'Oh, come on, Carole. "Drinking with Denzil Willoughby at the Dauncey Hotel"? What kind of an alibi's that? Denzil's virtually told us that those two'd tell any lie to get the other one out of a spot.'

'Yes.' Carole looked at her watch. 'Well, one thing I think we can be pretty sure of is that by now Giles Green has had a full action replay of the conversation you've just had with Chervil.'

'I would think so, yes.'

'Which might of course mean that you are now at risk. That old cliché beloved of crime writers about a person who's killed once not being afraid to do so again.'

'I don't know why you're looking so smug, Carole. He knows that you were involved in the investigation too. If I'm at risk, I'm certainly not the only one.'

'So the question is: what do we do? Just wait till Giles Green contacts us?'

Jude spread her hands helplessly wide. 'What else can we do?'

'Well, now we definitely know it was murder, maybe you should get back in touch with your friend Detective Inspector Hodgkinson and suggest she reopens the official enquiry . . .?'

'Ooh.' A dubious look. 'I'm not sure that we've got enough evidence to do that yet, have we?'

Carole grinned broadly. 'I'm so glad you said that, Jude.' Handing over to the cops during one of their investigations always did seem to be a bit of a cop-out.

Jude was unsurprised to have a phone call that Thursday afternoon from Giles Green. He wanted to come and see her. She agreed, but told him that Carole would be there too. Partly she wanted a witness for anything the young man might say, but she had a safety motive too. If Giles really had murdered Fennel Whittaker . . .

He arrived much less flustered than either Ned or Chervil had been. As ever, he was wearing a pinstriped suit (Carole and Jude were beginning to wonder whether he possessed any casual clothes). He accepted the offer of a cup of coffee, and his demeanour was one of urbane reasonableness. There's been some minor misunderstanding, his manner seemed to say, which I'm sure we can sort out very quickly.

When they were all supplied with drinks, Jude said, 'I assume that Chervil has told you about the conversation we had earlier.'

'Yes, of course.'

'Well, it would seem to me,' said Carole rather beadily, 'that you have some explanations to provide.'

'I can understand why you would think that.'

'You don't deny that you knew about the note that Fennel had written at the time of her first suicide attempt?'

'No, I don't. Chervil had shown it to me.'

'And you knew where she kept it? In the file in her bedroom at Butterwyke House?'

'Yes, I knew that.'

'And presumably you have recently spent some time in that bedroom?'

'I certainly have,' he replied roguishly. To Carole and Jude he seemed far too relaxed, unaffected by the seriousness of the allegations against him.

'So you had the opportunity to take the suicide note?'

'I had. On many occasions. But the fact remains that I didn't.'

'Chervil seems to think that you did.'

'Chervil is trying to cover her back.'

'Oh?'

'Look, all this is very difficult for her, poor love.'

'I'm sure it is,' said Carole.

'She's had a lot to cope with over the last few months. Our relationship has been good, but it hasn't always been easy.' Carole and Jude exchanged looks. Was this a reference to his reputation for violence to his girlfriends? 'The thing is, for some reason I can't fathom, my mother doesn't approve of Chervil.'

'I thought the reason was that she preferred your wife,' said Carole tartly. 'She thinks you should get back with Nikki.'

'Oh yes, that's certainly true.'

'We have actually seen Nikki . . . you know, since the Private View.'

If Carole had thought she'd get a response from this small bombshell, she was disappointed. 'Yes, I know,' said Giles coolly. 'Up at Denzil's workshop.'

Of course the two men were in each other's pockets. Anything Denzil Willoughby knew was pretty soon known by Giles Green.

'While we were there,' said Jude softly, 'he got the news of his mother's death.'

'Yes, he was very cut up about that. They were very close.'

'Whereas his relationship with his father . . .?'

'Was not so close, no.'

'Their chief argument being that Addison Willoughby kept his son short of funds?'

'That was part of it. There were a lot of reasons why they didn't get on. Denzil didn't like the way Addison had treated his mother.'

'And of course,' Carole interposed, 'it's Denzil Willoughby who's supplied your alibi for the night of Fennel Whittaker's death.'

'Yes.' The smug smile had returned. 'We were drinking together in the Dauncey Hotel.'

'All night?'

'All night,' he confirmed complacently. They knew they'd never shake him on that. They also knew that the alibi was just as likely to be false as genuine.

Carole tried a different approach. 'Did you tell anyone else that you'd seen Fennel's suicide note?'

'Why on earth should I have done that?'

'The person who left it by her body must have known of its existence.'

'They did.'

'Are you saying you know who left it?'

'Of course I am. Chervil left it there.'

'What are you saying?' asked Jude. 'That Chervil killed her sister?'

'No, of course I'm not saying that. Chervil found Fennel dead in the treatment yurt. After the time in Pimlico she had no problem recognizing what had happened. Her sister had killed herself. But she thought people might misinterpret the death, might even think it had been murder, if there wasn't a suicide note there. So she collected the one that she'd kept in her bedroom at Butterwyke House and put it beside Fennel's body.'

'That's nonsense,' protested Jude. 'Why on earth should she have done that?'

'I don't know why, just take my word for it, that's what she did!' For the first time in their encounter Giles Green was in danger of losing his cool.

'And did she take Fennel's phone?' asked Carole. 'The one on which the last message had come from your mobile?'

'She took the phone. But the last message was not from me. It was from Chervil herself. She'd fixed to meet Fennel in the treatment yurt. That's why she took the mobile and destroyed it. She thought it might incriminate her.'

'You mean, if it had been found, people might have thought Chervil murdered her sister?'

Giles Green shrugged. 'It's a point of view,' he said infuriatingly.

'He's protecting someone,' said Carole when they were once again alone in the front room of Woodside Cottage.

'I think I agree with you, but who?'

'Himself? I'd still rather put him in the frame as a murderer than Chervil.'

'Yes, he has a funny way of showing his affection for her, hasn't he? Didn't worry him at all when we suggested she might have killed her sister.'

'I think that was relief that we were naming a suspect who wasn't him.'

'Or who wasn't the person he's trying to protect,' suggested Jude.

'And who might that person be?'

'You tell me.'

'Well, I was just thinking,' said Carole. 'Suppose Chervil had told either her mother or father that she'd kept the suicide note . . .?'

TWENTY-NINE

The next morning Jude was doing a little idle shopping along the Fethering Parade and trying to decide how to spend the day. She had been reckoning her morning would be taken up by a client whom she was treating for panic attacks, but the woman had rung at eight thirty saying she couldn't make the appointment. Whether the cancellation was actually a symptom of a panic attack Jude couldn't be sure. The phone call had been ended so abruptly that Jude hadn't had a chance to check out that possibility. She made a mental note to call the woman back the following week.

Normally Jude had no problem filling her time, but that Friday morning she felt a little frustrated. She and Carole seemed to have come up against a series of brick walls in their investigation. Her neighbour had even ended up the previous evening by suggesting again that Jude should get in touch with Detective Inspector Hodgkinson in order to reactivate the official enquiry. And if that wasn't an admission of failure, then what was?

Jude was assessing the rival claims of a walk on Fethering Beach, including perhaps a coffee at the Seaview Café, and pottering around in the Woodside Cottage garden, when she saw Bonita Green emerging from the front door of the Cornelian Gallery. The woman was dressed in her trademark black, but smarter black, the jeans and jumper having given way to a trouser suit and the trainers to court shoes.

Bonita carried a shoulder bag and, under the other arm, unwrapped, the Piccadilly snowscape that had hung in the Cornelian Gallery even when the space had been taken over by Denzil Willoughbys.

Jude was intrigued, and then she remembered it was Friday. The day when the Cornelian Gallery was always closed.

The decision to follow the gallery-owner was instantly made.

It wasn't too difficult for Jude to loiter at a distance, keeping Bonita in sight. There were enough people around in Fethering that morning for the surveillance to be inconspicuous. It seemed as though the woman was heading towards Fethering Station, and Jude remembered Carole reporting her conversation with Spider at the Private View. Friday, he'd said, was not only Bonita's 'special' day, but also the day when she went 'to London'.

Jude checked her watch. She knew the times of the morning trains and realized that the first one – the one she and Carole had caught the previous Monday – was due to leave in about ten minutes. Before she bought her ticket she checked along the platform and saw Bonita Green sitting down, engrossed in a book.

With her ticket purchased, Jude went to the adjacent convenience store and bought a *Daily Mail* (every now and then she enjoyed reading something that made her seriously cross). Then she lurked by the ticket office until the train was virtually in the station before rushing out to catch it. As she did so, she saw Bonita Green getting into a carriage two behind her. There was about the woman's movements an air of ritual, of a routine that she had followed many times before.

On the journey up to London, Jude read her *Daily Mail* and fumed quietly. Some of the time she just looked out of the window. It was a beautiful May day and she watched as the greens of the South Downs gradually gave way to the brick-red and grey of the sprawling suburbs.

At some stations she checked through the window that Bonita Green hadn't got off. Horsham, Gatwick Airport, East Croydon and Clapham Junction all offered opportunities to join other routes, but none of them tempted her quarry.

When the train stopped at Victoria, Jude didn't rush to get off. She waited till the oblivious Bonita Green had walked past her compartment and then eased herself out on to the platform. There were quite a lot of people getting off the train, but she had no difficulty in keeping the small black figure in her sights.

Bonita Green went through the barrier and headed straight for the Underground. Anticipating this, Jude had bought a day's travel card so she wouldn't be delayed by buying a ticket for the tube. Bonita must have done the same, because she went straight through the gate leading to the Victoria Line.

It was at this moment that she did something unforeseen. Jude had somehow assumed the gallery-owner would be going north into Central London, but she moved on to the southbound platform. Jude followed, not bothering to look too surreptitious. If Bonita Green did spot her, it wasn't the end of the world. Jude had as much right to be spending a day in London as anyone else.

Not wishing to lose sight of her quarry, Jude actually got into the same compartment, but Bonita still seemed unaware of her. She wasn't reading now, but she seemed caught up in her own thoughts. And the air of serenity about her suggested that they were pleasant ones.

Jude was surprised that they only went one stop. Pimlico. She let Bonita get out ahead of her and followed at a distance. But she had to hurry to keep up. There was a skittishness about the movements of the woman ahead. She almost ran up the escalator.

Jude, who carried more weight than she should have done, was a bit breathless by the time she reached ground level. When she emerged from Pimlico Station, she was worried she might have lost the trail, but after a moment of anxiety, she spotted the woman in black walking demurely in the direction of Vauxhall Bridge.

Before she reached the river, Bonita turned right into a narrow road on one side of which was a parade of shops and on the other a terrace of pretty little cottages. Without a backward glance, the woman took a set of keys out of her shoulder bag and let herself into one which had a door of Victorian purple.

It was by now about eleven o'clock. Jude, trailing some way behind, looked at the row of shops and was delighted to see that one sold coffee. Taking her time, she ordered a cappuccino and an almond croissant, then settled herself into a window seat. She pretended to be reading her *Daily Mail*, but she had already been over it so thoroughly that it no longer even made her cross.

She was getting towards the end of her second cappuccino (and her second almond croissant) and beginning to wonder how she could eke the time out much longer, when the purple door opposite opened.

Bonita Green came out first, and there was about her an aura of happiness which Jude had never seen in their previous encounters. The bag still hung from her shoulder, but there was no sign of the painting.

She was followed out by a tall white-haired handsome man who looked at least as happy as she did.

Jude recognized him from the websites Carole had shown her. It was Addison Willoughby.

THIRTY

J ude followed the happy couple at a distance. They walked along arm in arm, talking and giggling animatedly.

Given the time of day, it was quite possible that they were on their way out to lunch. Jude wondered how she would maintain her surveillance if that was their intention. Go into the same restaurant and scrutinize them over the top of her menu? Sit in a convenient coffee shop opposite their venue and drink more bladder-straining cappuccinos? But as was usually the case with Jude, she decided she would make that decision when she had to.

Anyway, it was soon clear that their destination was not a restaurant. In fact, they seemed to be heading straight back the way Bonita had come, to Pimlico Underground.

So it proved. At the head of the stairs down to the station the couple stopped and embraced warmly. Jude managed to be close enough, apparently removing a stone from her shoe, to hear their conversation.

'It seems awful to be going so soon,' Bonita said.

'Just for today,' said Addison Willoughby. 'Once I've sorted things out with Denzil, there's nothing to stop us being together all the time.'

'I can't wait.' Bonita Green rose on tiptoe to give him a parting kiss on the lips. 'Call me when you've done the deed.'

'Of course.'

Then he watched her as she skittered off down the stairs. When Bonita was out of sight, he turned to find himself facing a generously upholstered woman with a bird's nest of blonde hair.

'Hello,' she said. 'My name's Jude. You don't know me.'

'No, I certainly don't.' But he said it in puzzlement rather than anger.

'I know your son Denzil.'

'Ah.' He waited to see what she'd say next.

Jude, grateful that Carole wasn't there to disapprove, decided to go for broke. 'And I'm investigating the death of his former girlfriend Fennel Whittaker.'

'Are you from the police?'

'Not exactly.' Which, given the situation, was a rather cheeky answer. 'You heard what happened to her?'

'Yes, yes,' he said almost snappishly. 'And what – are you suggesting there's some thought Fennel might have been murdered?'

'It seems to be a possibility.'

'And Denzil is under suspicion of having done it?'

'Let's say we'd like to rule him out of our enquiries.'

'Very well,' said Addison Willoughby wearily. 'You'd better come back to my place.'

The interior of the terraced cottage with the purple door was immaculate and expensively appointed. But it had the feeling of a hotel suite, not a place where people lived all the time.

Over the fireplace in the front room where they sat hung the Piccadilly snowscape from the Cornelian Gallery. 'Did you do that?' asked Jude. Addison Willoughby nodded. 'It's very good.'

'Yes, there was a time when I was thought to have considerable talent. Long ago dissipated, I'm sorry to say.'

'You seem to have been very successful in the world of advertising.'

'Maybe, but I don't regard that as a talent. It is at best a skill, and a learnt skill at that. Talent is what artists have.'

'Like your son?'

'I'd say the jury's still out on that.'

'Then like Bonita?'

'She too has not fulfilled her early promise. Every year the art schools churn out another generation of aspiring artists. Most of them are at that stage described as "promising". Very few of them actually make it.'

'Is it a disappointment to you that you weren't one of those who made it?'

'A constant disappointment, yes.' There was a dry bitterness in his tone.

Jude was silent, wondering where next to direct her questioning. Then she asked, 'Has your relationship with Bonita been going on a long time?'

'Yes, a very long time. We met as students at the Slade, had a wild fling, then drifted apart and married other people. Both married too young, of course.' He sighed. 'Everyone marries too young.'

'I think they may have done in our generation. I'm not sure that they still do.'

'Maybe not. Certainly Denzil shows no sign of leading some poor unfortunate girl to the altar.'

'He told you, I assume, that I and my friend Carole visited him at his studio on Monday.'

'He mentioned it, yes.'

'We were there when he got the text about his mother's death.'

'Oh.' The intonation was so flat it was hard to tell whether this was news to him or not.

'I'm sorry for your loss,' said Jude formally.

'You don't need to be. It's been common knowledge for years that Philomena and I didn't get on. We've lived apart since Denzil was about five.'

'Did you separate because of your relationship with Bonita?'

'That was one of the reasons on my side. Not Philomena's. I worked very hard to ensure that she never knew about me and Bonita.'

'I don't see how that could have been possible.'

'What do you mean?'

'Well, if you walk through the London streets arm in arm, surely there's a very real danger of your being seen by friends of your wife or, given your high profile, being spotted by a press photographer and—'

'You don't understand. What you've witnessed this morning is something very new. Something I wish could have happened a very long time ago. Up till now our relationship has been conducted exclusively within these walls. We haven't dared go out together, even to a restaurant, in case, as you say, we were seen by someone who might get the news back to Philomena. Now the situation is different.'

'Because of Philomena's death?'

Addison Willoughby nodded. 'For that very reason. Now there is nothing to stop Bonita and me from doing what she should have done many years ago – and getting married.'

'But why did you feel you had to wait so long? It's not too hard to get a divorce these days.'

'There are two reasons why we waited. One was that, though Philomena and I didn't get on, I didn't hate her. I still had a lot of respect for her, and I wanted to spare her the pain that must inevitably be caused by her knowledge that Bonita and I were lovers. The public explanation of our marriage break-down was that I was a workaholic – which is probably true, by the way. Anyway, that ensured that Philomena was not publicly humiliated.'

'You said there were two reasons.'

'Yes. The other was that both Philomena and I are Catholics. She's considerably more devout that I am.' He was unaware of using the present tense, as though his wife were still alive. 'But it got to me too. I was taught by Jesuits. And you know the old maxim: "Give me a child for his first seven years and I will give you the man." Well, much as I resent it, that has worked its evil magic on me . . . with the result that I could not contemplate the idea of divorce. Bloody nuisance, but there you are.'

'Now, though . . .?'

'Yes. With Philomena dead, my problems are at an end. Well, some of them are, anyway.'

'Does Denzil know what's about to happen?'

'No. I am going to see him this afternoon to tell him. It is not an encounter that I relish. But once that hurdle has been overcome, the future for Bonita and me looks set fair.'

A new line of enquiry offered itself to Jude. 'What happened to Bonita's husband?' she asked.

'Hugo? He drowned on a family holiday in Greece. A merciful release.'

'Why do you say that?'

'Because he was severely crippled. He had a pretty miserable quality of life.'

'Was he crippled from birth?'

'God, no. We were all contemporaries at the Slade. Hugo was a huge, boisterous character. Very good-looking, zapped around London on a Harley-Davidson, vacuuming up all the female students. I think initially the marriage to Bonita worked pretty well. They had the two kids, with about seven years' gap between them. Bonita didn't have much time to do her art, but Hugo was becoming very successful.

'Then, maybe four years after Giles was born, he was in a horrendous crash. Came off his Harley on the M1. Hugo was smashed to bits. No one thought he could possibly survive. Somehow he pulled through, but he was condemned to spend the rest of his life in a wheelchair. A terrible fate for someone with a larger-than-life personality like Hugo. And there was no way he could continue with his painting.

'It was round that time that I met up with Bonita again and I couldn't believe it when I saw the state Hugo was in. He talked about committing suicide, so as I say, the drowning was a merciful release.'

'Do you know how it happened?'

'The drowning? They were on holiday out in Corfu and they had an inflatable dinghy with them. Not a real boat, not much more than a toy really, with plastic paddles, you know. Anyway, as Bonita told it to me, Hugo had kept saying he wanted to go out in the dinghy and she said it'd be dangerous – he had metal calipers on his legs, apart from anything else. But Hugo was strong-willed, a difficult man to argue with, so eventually he persuaded Bonita to let him have a go. The little

girl stayed on the beach sunbathing, but the other three went
out in the boat. Well, everything was fine at first, but, I don't
know exactly what happened . . . The boat capsized, Bonita
grabbed hold of Giles, and Hugo, weighed down by the calipers, went straight to the bottom. Of course they raised the
alarm, but by the time anyone got to him, Hugo was already
dead.

'I've never mentioned it to Bonita, but I wouldn't be
surprised if Hugo didn't tip the boat over deliberately. As I
say, he had no quality of life and no prospects of things ever
improving. I think he wanted to die.'

There was a silence before Jude said, 'I hope you don't
mind my asking this, but did you restart the relationship with
Bonita before Hugo's death?'

Addison Willoughby gave a shamefaced nod. 'I'm afraid
we did, yes. Bonita's a very highly sexed woman and with
Hugo she was locked into a kind of Lady Chatterley situation.
I took the role of a rather more cultured Mellors. I'm not
particularly proud of what happened, but I'm very grateful for
it.'

'And it's been confined to Fridays ever since?'

'Yes. We wanted to be together all the time, but I couldn't
do that to Philomena. After a few years I bought this place
. . . Pimlico, popular place for MPs to set up their mistresses.
Nobody takes too much notice of what goes on here. So yes,
for Bonita and me it's been Fridays ever since.'

There was a silence. Then Addison Willoughby said, 'Still,
that's all water under the bridge. You wanted to talk to me
because you suspect my son of murdering Fennel Whittaker.'

Jude had forgotten the lie she had told to engage Addison
in conversation, and was a little flustered as she said, 'I
wouldn't go that far. It's just that there now seems to be little
doubt that she was murdered.' She briefly outlined the
discovery that the suicide note dated from Fennel's earlier
attempt. 'And it was your son she bawled out at the Private
View. So he could be seen to have had a motive against her.'

Addison Willoughby smiled a humourless smile. 'My son
has few redeeming qualities. One thing he certainly doesn't
possess is any organizational skills. The idea that he is capable

of planning what sounds like a fairly complicated murder is
. . . well, frankly unbelievable.'

'You may be right.'

'I've asked him about what he was doing the night Fennel
died, and he says he was drinking all evening with Bonita's
son Giles.'

'Yes, I'd heard that.'

'Well, I've no reason to disbelieve him. It would certainly
be in character.'

'Hm.' Jude deliberately moved the conversation in another
direction. 'What about Bonita's daughter? What happened to
her?'

'Ingrid? Oh, they've completely lost touch. Never got on
well . . . you know, mothers and daughters can be a combust-
ible mix. Ingrid moved away from home at the first opportunity
she had.'

'Do you know what happened to her?'

'Haven't a clue. She had inherited Bonita's talent, was a
very good artist when she was a kid, so maybe she too is
somewhere in the art world. Another one of those who's realizing her potential rather than capitulating to mediocrity,' he
concluded bitterly. Jude was once again struck by how little
he valued his success in the advertising business. To Addison
Willoughby's mind, anyone who wasn't an artist was a failure.

A wisp of a memory came into Jude's mind and she tried to
trap it. 'Just a moment. Ingrid, Ingrid. It's not that usual a name,
but I'm sure I've heard it somewhere recently.' Her brows
furrowed with the effort of concentration. Then it came back to
her. In what turned out to be their last session Fennel Whittaker
had spoken of a tutor at St Martin's College of Art called Ingrid,
a tutor whom she had 'rated' and who had liked her work. The
link was unlikely – Ingrid was not a common name, but nor was
it strikingly unusual – but everything was worth investigating.

'Denzil trained at St Martin's, didn't he, Addison?'

'Yes.'

'He never mentioned a tutor called Ingrid, did he?'

'No. But then again we didn't see much of each other while
he was at college. He only tended to get in touch when he
needed money.'

'Yes. Fennel said he was only after her money.'

'Entirely possible. Denzil may be my son, but I wash my hands of any responsibility for his moral values – or lack of them.'

'When we met him, he expressed the view that artists needn't be judged by the same moral values as ordinary people.'

Addison Willoughby nearly choked with fury at that. 'The arrogant little shit!'

'He also complained that, given how well-heeled you are, you tended to keep him rather short of funds.'

'He said that, did he? Well, there may have been one or two occasions when that criticism might be justified, but that ignores the many times when I have bailed him out. I've just learned by experience that, however much money I give Denzil, he'll soon be back for more. So I've moved towards a policy of not giving him any.'

There was a silence. Jude looked up again at the Piccadilly snowscape. 'That really is very good,' she said.

'Thank you. It also has considerable sentimental value for us.'

'Oh?'

'The first time Bonita and I . . . when we re-met after we were both married. We'd had lunch and it was snowing in London. She came back to a flat I had then and the trains were all cancelled because of the snow, so she had to stay . . . Yes, as I say, considerable sentimental value.'

Jude understood why the picture had had pride of place in the Cornelian Gallery. And she wondered whether Bonita Green had enjoyed the irony of a work by Addison Willoughby still hanging there at the Private View surrounded by the efforts of his son.

The advertising executive looked at his watch. 'Look, I do have other things to do with my day, so may I ask if you have any further questions for me? You've already cast a bit of a damper over what should have been one of the happiest days of my life, so, as far as I'm concerned, the sooner this interview ends, the better. Which being the case, is there anything else you wanted to ask me?'

'Yes,' Jude replied. 'How did your wife die?'

THIRTY-ONE

Jude went back to the same coffee shop from which she'd done her earlier surveillance. If the staff thought her apparent addiction to cappuccinos odd, they gave no sign of it. This time, instead of an almond croissant, she ordered a toasted ham and cheese panini. As soon as she had given her order, she used the Ladies, for which her need had become quite urgent.

Her suspicions about the death of Philomena Willoughby had been quickly dashed by the ungrieving widower. His wife had been suffering from cancer for some time. She had spent her last months in a hospice. That explained why Denzil had been so preoccupied with his iPhone the previous Monday. He had been waiting to hear the worst about his mother.

Jude rang through to High Tor, and was relieved when the phone was answered. Of course, she remembered, Carole didn't even know that she was in London, so Jude didn't bother to tell her the events of the morning, instead saying, 'Look, there's something I want you to check on the laptop. Could you do that for me?'

Carole conceded that she could, and then of course had to go upstairs. The laptop's portability continued to be ignored.

'Very well. I'm there and switched on. What do you want to know?'

'It's something about St Martin's College of Art. I'm sure they must have a website. Can you get on to it?'

Carole did as instructed. 'Yes. So what do you want to know?'

'If they have lists of their tutors there, can you check and see if there's one whose first name is "Ingrid"?'

'I'll try. What's all this in aid of, Jude?'

'I'll tell you in a minute. Just see if you can find the name.'

A long-suffering sigh from High Tor preceded the clacking of fingers on keyboard. Then, 'Oh goodness, there are a lot of them. Every course seems to have its own army of tutors. Can you narrow down the search a bit for this Ingrid? What's she likely to be tutoring in?'

'Fine Art, maybe? Painting? Drawing? Watercolours? I don't know.'

'This could take some time.'

'Call me back then.'

'Where are you?'

'On the mobile.' Which, to Carole's mind, was an inadequate answer.

It was about twenty minutes later, when Jude was wiping the cheese grease off her lips, that her neighbour rang back. 'There's only one,' said Carole.

'Only one Ingrid?'

'Right.'

'She's a tutor in The Foundation Diploma Art and Design Course, and her surname's Staunton.'

'Ingrid Staunton.'

'That's right. Well, come on, Jude, who is she?'

'I'm not absolutely certain, but I think she may be Bonita Green's daughter.'

'Really? That's amazing. How have you got on to her?'

'Long story. I'll fill you in on the details later.'

'Look, I didn't even know where you're calling from,' said Carole plaintively.

'I'm in a coffee shop in Pimlico.'

'What?'

'Ooh, one other thing . . . Could you give me the number for St Martin's College of Art? It'll be on the website.'

Grudgingly, Carole did as requested. 'I wish I knew what this was all about.'

'I'll phone you back when I've got something definite. Promise.'

And the line went dead.

Jude tried the number of the St Martin's College of Art, but the girl who answered wouldn't give contact details for the tutors. Which was very right and proper, but not a little frustrating.

She was trying to think what to do next when her mobile rang. It was Carole again.

'I've just googled "Ingrid Staunton" and found her website. She's an artist.'

'What kind of stuff does she do?'

'It says,' replied Carole, contempt curdling her words, 'she "plays with the defamiliarization of everyday objects until they reach a state of figurative reciprocity".'

Jude giggled. 'You must get one of hers for your front room.'

'Very amusing,' said Carole drily.

'Is there a photograph of her on the website? Does she look like Bonita Green?'

'There isn't a photograph.'

'Oh.'

'But there are contact details for her. Including a mobile phone number.'

'Great,' said Jude.

'Now will you please tell me what the hell you're doing in Pimlico?'

Carole Seddon felt very restless after the end of their call. In terms of their investigation, Jude, it seemed, was having all the fun. It was Jude who, on a whim, had followed Bonita Green up to London and found out what happened on her 'special Fridays'. It was Jude who had met and interviewed Addison Willoughby. It was Jude who had got the lead to Ingrid Staunton. Carole felt marginalized and useless.

She vented some of her spleen by cleaning the bathroom. It didn't really need cleaning, but the task made her feel a little more virtuous. Only a little, though. There was still a deep dissatisfaction within her.

Then she wandered back to the laptop, incarcerated in the spare room. Idly, she once again googled 'Ingrid Staunton', hoping to find out more about the mysterious artist. But she drew a blank. There were other references to the woman, but only names of galleries where she had exhibited and that kind of listing. Nothing that would come under the heading 'revelatory'.

Carole's frustration grew. She had finished *The Times* cross-word at breakfast. An easy one, as it usually was on a Friday, demonstrating some psychological ploy on behalf of the newspaper to cheer people up for the weekend. But that afternoon she wished the puzzle had been a stinker, something into which she could channel her anger.

It was then that she had the idea of having another look at Denzil Willoughby's website. Once again she tutted inwardly at the number of four-letter words the home page contained. Then she clicked on the 'Artist at Work' link.

After a moment she found herself looking at the webcam's view of the converted warehouse. The artist didn't seem to be doing much work, because there was no sign of the two assistants to whom he delegated most of it. But there were two people in animated discussion at the far end of the space. Denzil was one, and the other Carole recognized from his photographs as Addison Willoughby. Their hairstyles seemed to symbolize the contrast between them, the father's expensively shaped white coiffure and the son's pale stringy dreadlocks.

The webcam was a long way away from them and its inbuilt microphone was not very good quality, so Carole could not at first hear very well. But after boosting the sound level on her laptop up to its maximum and attuning her ears to the sound, she managed to pick up most of what they were saying. It would have helped if the two men were near enough for her to lip-read, but they were not, and anyway they kept moving about.

'. . . and when I told you I was doing the exhibition at the Cornelian Gallery,' Denzil was protesting, 'you still didn't say anything.'

'Why should I have said anything then?' asked his father. 'It wasn't as if you didn't know Bonita. You'd seen her lots of times when you were with Giles.'

'That's not the point, Dad! None of those times did I know that she was screwing my father.'

'Look, there's no way I could have told you earlier, Denzil. Not while Philomena was still alive.'

'Oh, you think now Mum's dead, that changes everything, do you?'

'Of course it does. She can no longer be hurt.'

'But you were hurting every time you screwed Bonita.'

'Don't be ridiculous. Philomena didn't know that was it was happening.'

'And you think that makes it better? It was still deceit on a massive scale.'

'I think it's pretty rich, you criticizing my morals. Your own track record with women hasn't been particularly distinguished, has it?'

'Maybe not, but I've never married any of them, have I?'

'What difference does that make?'

'If you don't know the answer to that, then there's no bloody hope for you. Mum said you were still a Catholic.'

'Well, I am a kind of Catholic.'

'Then you should know about the sanctity of marriage. Has it ever occurred to you, *Dad* –' Denzil Willoughby managed to put a lot of sneer into the monosyllable – 'that the reason why I haven't got married is that I still have some respect for marriage. I wouldn't go into it with the firm intention of screwing someone else.'

'That is not how it happened.'

'Oh, no? You were deceiving Mum, that's all I know.'

'But I did it discreetly. I didn't hurt her. Would you rather I'd gone public and put your mother through the humiliation of a divorce?'

'Yes, I think I would. In many ways that would have been less deceitful.'

'Oh, for God's sake!' Addison Willoughby was by now almost beside himself with fury. Throughout his marriage, at great personal cost, he had done everything he could to avoid divorce and now, instead of being praised as a good Catholic, he was being condemned for his behaviour. By his son!

'All you need to know, Denzil,' he thundered, trying without success to control his anger, 'is that I am now free to marry Bonita. And that is exactly what I'm going to do.'

'Fine! By all means go ahead. Marry the woman who killed my mother!'

'Bonita did not kill Philomena.'

'Oh no? I'd be a bit more sure of my facts before I made a statement like that, Dad.'

'Bonita would not dream of killing Philomena. She would not commit murder.'

'Oh no?' Denzil Willoughby's mouth curled into even more of a sneer as he spat out the words, 'It wouldn't be the first time.'

THIRTY-TWO

Jude had considered various subterfuges before she rang Ingrid Staunton's mobile number. She knew that a good way of getting through to an artist was to pretend to be interested in commissioning a work from them. That would generally get them listening and even agreeing to meet.

But she would have felt rather shabby, raising someone's expectations of paid work and letting them down, so in fact when her call was answered, she just said, 'Hello, my name's Jude. You don't know me, but I believe you used to tutor Fennel Whittaker.'

'Yes, I did.' The voice was cultured and intelligent, but also anxious. 'Why, has something happened to her?'

'I'm afraid it has.'

'Suicide?'

'It looks that way,' said Jude, choosing her words carefully.

Ingrid Staunton sounded genuinely shocked by the news. Jude gave very little of the background, just the fact that the death had occurred at the Whittakers' home, and the woman needed no urging to agree to meet. She had a class to teach at two o'clock that afternoon, but would be free by three thirty. She suggested a wine bar in Theobald's Road as a rendezvous.

Before the art teacher arrived Jude was already ensconced with a large Chilean Chardonnay in front of her. She had switched off her mobile. The imminent encounter was important, and she didn't want any interruptions.

There was something in the trim build and manner of the

woman who entered the wine bar that was reminiscent of
Bonita Green. Her eyes were brown but the hair was short
spiky blonde. On the other hand, Bonita's hair had been dyed
black for so long that perhaps it once, too, had been fair.

Ingrid Staunton was probably late forties, which would have
put her about the right age to be Giles Green's sister. And she
wore a wedding ring, which might explain the change of surname.

But Jude was not going to start with the woman's family
history. Nor, had that been her plan, would she have been
allowed to. Having checked she was talking to the right person,
Ingrid Staunton immediately said, 'I've been thinking about
Fennel ever since I got your call. She was such a talented girl.
This is really tragic news. Has it only just happened?'

'A couple of weeks ago.'

'I'm surprised I haven't seen anything in the press.'

'Her parents have worked quite hard to keep the news quiet.'

'Oh yes, I remember the Whittakers. They're good at that.'

'They certainly are. Let me get you a drink.'

'Something white, please. What's that you've got?'

'Chilean Chardonnay.'

'Sounds good.'

Once they'd both got drinks, Jude gave Ingrid an edited
version of events surrounding Fennel's death. She noticed a
definite reaction when she mentioned the Cornelian Gallery,
but didn't pick up on it. Ingrid also recognized the name of
Denzil Willoughby.

'I taught him for a while. Very talented, but a distinct attitude
problem. More concerned about his image than the art he
produces. Denzil has more natural talent for drawing and
painting than anyone I've taught. But that wasn't the way he
wanted to go, he took the route into conceptual art, which I
think is a bit of a *cul-de-sac.*'

'For everyone?'

'No, for some of them it's good. For Denzil, though, I'm sure
it's the wrong direction. With his conceptual stuff he's never
going to be in the first rank, whereas with his drawing and
painting he could be. Maybe he'll see the light at some point,
start following his instincts as an artist rather than just leaping
on to the latest bandwagon.' Ingrid Staunton sighed. 'But I'm

desperately sorry about Fennel. She had a breakdown, I know, and didn't finish her course at St Martin's, and I did hear a rumour that she'd made a suicide attempt back then, but I rather hoped she'd been cured. Depression is a wretched illness.'

'Yes.' Jude judged the moment was right for a change of tack. 'There has been some suggestion that Fennel's death might not have been all it seemed.'

'What do you mean by that?'

'There's a strong feeling among some people – and I'm one of them – that she might have been murdered.'

Ingrid's hand was instantly at her mouth. 'Oh my God! What evidence do you have?'

Jude retold the story of the suicide note and the missing mobile phone. 'I'm not sure that either of those is proof that would stand up in a court of law, but it's enough to convince me.'

'Me too.' Ingrid Staunton took a thoughtful sip of Chilean Chardonnay. 'You say Fennel made a scene at the Denzil Willoughby Private View. What exactly did she say?'

Jude recapped the outburst as accurately as she could and watched the other woman's reaction.

'She did actually use the words "causing someone's death", did she?'

'Yes.'

'And you say that Fennel had also had a relationship with my brother?'

Jude managed to look more shocked by this lapse than she actually was. Ingrid Staunton immediately realized what she'd said. 'Ah, that was silly of me. But I can't deny it now, can I? Yes, I am in fact Bonita Green's daughter.'

'I was hoping you were,' said Jude with a smile.

'Why?'

'Because I thought you might be able to provide a missing link in this investigation.'

'I'm rather afraid I may be able to. I don't know if you know, but I haven't seen or spoken to my mother for over twenty years.'

'I had heard something of that, yes.'

'You might think that's a rather extreme reaction to a family row.'

Jude shrugged. 'These things happen. Particularly between mothers and daughters. The relationship can be pretty volatile during the teenage years.'

'Oh, it wasn't just me being a moody adolescent. There was more to it than that. I couldn't stay living in the same house as her. I walked out when I was sixteen. Went to London, got any kind of job – bar work mostly – and saved up enough to put myself through St Martin's. I didn't bother changing my name, because I knew my mother would never come looking for me. Then in my early twenties I got married, so I got a different name, anyway.'

'Are you still married?'

Ingrid Staunton smiled a rather girlish smile. 'Yes. To my considerable surprise, I'm still very happily married. Which is amazing, coming out the family that I did.'

'Have you had any contact with your brother over the years?'

'Virtually none. I wanted to cut all ties. I had nothing specifically against Giles, but the important thing was that I got away from that woman. And I certainly don't miss either of them. I've got my own set-up. Work I love, husband and two children I adore. I don't need to dig over past history.'

'But I wouldn't mind if you did dig over a bit,' said Jude gently, 'just to help me out.'

'Mm. I know what you mean.' Ingrid Staunton ran her fingers through her spiky blonde hair. 'Right. You want to know why I couldn't stand living with my mother any longer, don't you?'

'If you think that'll help my investigation into Fennel Whittaker's death, then yes, I do.'

'I'm afraid it probably will. You said that at the Private View Fennel spoke of "causing someone's death" and her attack seemed to be aimed at Denzil Willoughby. But of course there were other people there for whom her words might have had some relevance. My brother . . . my mother . . .'

'Yes,' said Jude quietly, not wishing to break the confidential atmosphere.

'I don't know if you know anything about my father . . .'

'As of today I know more about him than I did.'

'He was a very strong, very handsome man . . . I remember

him like that.' The woman spoke wistfully. 'Then he had a terrible motorcycle accident. I suppose I was about nine when that happened.'

'I heard about it. I also heard about how he drowned on a family holiday in Corfu. He fell out of a rubber dinghy when it capsized.'

'Yes. That was the official story.'

Jude didn't provide any prompt, she just waited breathlessly for what Ingrid Staunton would say next.

'I didn't go out in the boat with them. I stayed on the beach, reading – and watching. It was very hot, like it always was in Corfu. Mum was paddling the boat and she seemed to be going out much further than we usually did. Normally with the boat we just mucked about in the waves at the water's edge. Not this time. Mum paddled out to where I knew she must be way out of her depth. And then . . .'

Jude couldn't resist saying, 'Yes?'

'She deliberately capsized the boat. She grabbed hold of Giles, who had his armbands on, anyway, so he would have kept afloat.'

Ingrid Staunton was silent for a moment, swallowing down a reflux of emotion. Then she said, 'But my mother made no attempt to save my father.'

THIRTY-THREE

Carole Seddon had kept trying Jude's mobile number from the time that the Willoughbys, father and son, had left the workshop and there was nothing else to see on the webcam. She had so much to report. Her vague suspicions of Bonita Green had now crystallized into certainties. She wanted to share them with Jude, and then she wanted the pair of them to go to the Cornelian Gallery to confront the murderer.

But she couldn't get through to Jude, so the day's frustration continued to pile up. And of course the demands of a dog didn't stop, however dramatic the human situation around him. Gulliver needed to do his business. And though he could just be taken out on to the rough ground behind High Tor, that seemed rather mean. He'd much prefer a proper walk. And if Carole took her mobile with her, she could keep trying to raise her unavailable neighbour.

Just as she was about to leave with Gulliver, the landline rang. It was, thank God, Jude. And a Jude full of more news than Carole could have hoped for. Her words came out stumbling over each other in a rush as she recounted the discoveries of the day. Finally there was enough silence for Carole to contribute what she had witnessed – via the webcam – in Denzil Willoughby's workshop.

Everything pointed in the same direction, towards Bonita Green's guilt. Jude was going to catch a train that would get her into Fethering Station soon after seven. Carole would be there in the Renault to meet her and they would drive to the Cornelian Gallery for the final confrontation.

But there was plenty of time before that for Gulliver to get a decent walk. So dog and owner set off towards Fethering Beach. The good weather was continuing and the afternoon felt more like June than early May.

It was inevitable that their route would take them past the parade of shops and, of course, the Cornelian Gallery. As her mind imagined scenarios for the forthcoming encounter with Bonita Green, Carole was not a little shocked to see the object of her speculation outside the gallery, loading suitcases into a car.

The first word that came into Carole's mind was 'getaway'. She and Jude had solved the case, they'd fingered the murderer and now that murderer was trying to get away. The confrontation schedule would have to be moved up a few hours.

Without hesitation, Carole stepped forward to Bonita Green and said, 'I'd like to have a word with you if I may.'

The gallery-owner looked a little puzzled, but closed the hatchback of her car and said, 'Fine. Would you like to come in?'

'Thank you,' Carole replied formally. 'Do you mind if I bring the dog?'

Permission granted, Gulliver was led into the Cornelian Gallery. Carole would really have preferred Jude with her than the dog. Gulliver was quite capable of defusing the drama of this kind of situation by licking the murderer's hand.

The gallery interior looked exactly as Carole remembered it when she first came in with her photograph of Lily. She was too preoccupied to notice the absence of the Piccadilly snowscape.

'So,' asked Bonita Green, 'what can I do for you, Carole?'

'I want to talk to you about the death of Fennel Whittaker.'

'Ah. I thought that was all over. Didn't I hear that the funeral's been arranged? Poor girl. Terrible someone of that age taking their own life.'

'If that is what she did,' said Carole portentously.

'I beg your pardon?'

'Jude and I are convinced that Fennel didn't take her own life. She was murdered.'

'Really? And what makes you think that?'

Carole spelled out the details of the suicide note and the missing mobile. At the end of her narration, Bonita nodded and said, 'I suppose it's possible.'

Gulliver, who had been let off his lead, went across to lick the woman's hand. Bonita tickled the top of his head. 'And who,' she asked, 'is supposed to have perpetrated this rather ingenious crime?'

Carole wouldn't have minded more of a dramatic build-up to her denouement but, presented with the direct question, could only say, 'You.'

Bonita Green took the accusation pretty coolly and asked, 'As a matter of interest, how did I do it?'

'You heard about the original suicide note from Giles. Go on, can you deny that's true?'

'No, I can't. He showed it to me. For reasons of his own he'd purloined it from that ghastly girl, Chervil. Or maybe she'd given it to him, I don't know. But he'd showed it to me and it was in the flat upstairs, yes.'

'Well then . . .'

'What do you mean, "well then"?'

'Well then, you knew about it, so you saw a way of using it to set up a death for Fennel that looked like suicide.'

'Did I?'

'Yes. You also knew that Ned Whittaker had some of the same wine as that supplied here by the Crown and Anchor for the Private View. You laced two bottles with liquid paracetamol, so that Fennel would pass out and not resist as you slashed her wrists with the Sabatier knife which you had taken from the kitchen at Butterwyke House.'

'I've never been inside Butterwyke House.'

'Of course you have.' Carole couldn't help feeling that, as confrontations went, this one wasn't one of the all-time greats.

'Oh, one thing you haven't told me,' said Bonita. 'Just as a matter of interest . . . *why* did I kill Fennel Whittaker?'

'Because of what she said at the Private View. Everyone assumed that she was attacking Denzil Willoughby when she talked about "causing someone's death", but the person she was really targeting was you.'

'And whose death am I supposed to have caused . . . apart, of course, from Fennel Whittaker's?'

'The death of your husband Hugo.'

That did strike a deep blow. Up until then, Bonita Green had been playfully dismissive of Carole's accusations. But she almost physically reeled at this one.

'Have you been talking to Ingrid?' she asked through tightened lips.

'Jude has.'

'Ah, your fellow conspirator. Of course.'

'Ingrid remembers you in Corfu, deliberately capsizing the boat and watching your husband drown.'

Bonita Green tottered, found the edge of the counter with her hand and propped herself up against it.

'I know that's what Ingrid thinks. She's told me enough times. That's why she left. She said she couldn't bear to continue living in the same house as her father's murderer.'

'Well, you could see her point.' Carole was beginning to think that the balance of power in the conversation was finally shifting in her favour.

'But I didn't kill Hugo.'

'Well, you would say that, wouldn't you?'

'I didn't. But I couldn't tell Ingrid what really happened.'

'She saw what really happened. She saw you capsize the boat.'

'No, she didn't. That's what she thought she saw.'

'She saw you suddenly stand up in the boat to tip it over.'

'No! I stood up in the boat to try and catch Giles. To stop Giles doing what he was doing.'

'What was he doing?'

'He was pushing Hugo off the boat.'

'What!'

'Giles, five-year-old Giles, had heard his father going on about how useless he was, and how he'd be better off dead, and so Giles thought he was doing what Hugo wanted. But I could never tell Ingrid that, could I? She had her own interpretation of what had happened. Better she thought what she thought than knew her brother had killed her father.'

Bonita Green was engulfed by deep emotion. A tsunami of sobs ran through her body. 'I couldn't kill anyone,' she wailed.

'No, but I could.'

Carole turned at the sound of the voice, and saw Spider emerging from his workshop.

THIRTY-FOUR

'I'll kill anyone,' Spider went on, 'who tries to hurt Bonita. I knew about the drowning. Ingrid talked to me about it. She thought she could get me on her side against her mother. She thought I'd believe Bonita'd kill someone. I knew she wouldn't. And when I heard that girl at the Private View accusing Bonita . . . well, I couldn't let that go unpunished, could I?'

'Are you saying, Spider,' asked his employer, 'that you killed Fennel Whittaker?'

'Of course I did. I did it for you, Bonita. I won't let anyone hurt you.'

'But how on earth did you set it up?' asked Carole.

'I hear a lot when I'm in my workshop. People in the gallery forget I'm there. And I work my own hours . . . evenings, sometimes weekends. That's how I heard Ingrid accusing Bonita of murdering her Dad. Way back, that was. I knew that wasn't true, and all. Then more recently I heard Giles in here, talking to that new bit of stuff of his, the one with the silly name.'

'Chervil,' said Bonita.

'Right. A Friday it must've been, because I know you wasn't here. And from what they were saying, I think Giles at that stage was still going out with the other sister, Fennel. Anyway, that Chervil was saying her sister was, like, a loony and Giles'd be much better off going out with her. And, like, to prove what a loony Fennel was, she produced this suicide note and told him about how she'd found it.

'Then she was, like, joking about how, if her sister ever got too much for her, she could use the note to set up, like, Fennel'd committed suicide. And she spelled out how easy it would be, to lace some booze with paracetamol and use a kitchen knife to slash her sister's wrists. She talked like she'd really thought it through. And Giles said, like, what a devious mind she'd got, and Chervil said she was dangerous, and Giles said that was part of her attraction, and then . . .' He stopped, embarrassed. 'Then they, like . . . you know . . . they had sexual intercourse.'

'In the gallery?' asked Bonita.

'Yeah, right here. I didn't see anything, of course, but I could hear.'

A silence ensued, then Carole asked, 'How did you know where to find Fennel . . . on that Friday night?'

'After the party finished . . .'

'The Private View?'

'Yes. That Chervil and Giles had an argument. She wanted him to go back with her to Butterwyke House, but he wanted to go and, like, drink with his mate Denzil Willoughby. So she stormed out, but she'd left her mobile here. And I picked it up and put it in my pocket. And later I heard it bleep and, like, a text had come through. And it was Fennel, saying where she was. And I know it was a message.'

'A text message?' asked Carole, confused.

'No, a message to me, telling me what to do.'

'I'm sorry, I don't understand. The message was to Chervil.'

'The text was from Fennel to Chervil. But the message was to me. Quite often I get messages like that, messages that tell me what to do.'

'Who from?' said Carole in a very small voice.'

Spider beamed. 'Well, Elvis Presley, of course. The King is my guide in everything I do.'

Bonita Green and Carole exchanged looks, the truth dawning on both how completely deranged Spider was.

'So what did the King tell you to do?' asked Carole.

'He told me to reply to the text and tell Fennel to meet in the big hut in an hour's time.'

'So she thought she was going to meet her sister?'

'Yes.' Spider smiled at his own cleverness. 'The text came from, like, her sister's phone. The King was looking after me.'

'So what did you do with Chervil's mobile after that?'

'I took it with me to the place with the huts that night. I left it there with Fennel's body.'

'And was her own mobile phone there too?'

'Yes. I left them both. I thought that was, like, clever. Anyone who, like, found the body would think it was Fennel's sister who'd fixed to meet her there.'

So, thought Carole, Chervil must have removed two mobile phones from the scene of the crime. And probably thrown both into the sea. That way the note might still make people think Fennel really had committed suicide.

Carole thought of another detail. 'The knife,' she said, 'the knife you used, Spider – did you take that from the Butterwyke House kitchen?'

He looked puzzled by the question. 'No, it was just one I had in the workshop.'

'You used it for your framing work?'

'No, I kept it here in case anyone threatened Bonita. I won't let anyone hurt Bonita.' He turned towards Carole, moving forward, looming over her. 'That includes you, lady. I don't know that I can make yours look like suicide, but through in the workshop I've got my underpinning machine, and I've got the guillotine and . . .'

He reached out suddenly and grabbed Carole's wrist. His

grip was like a steel manacle. She tried to resist, but felt herself being pulled ineluctably towards the workshop door.

'Gulliver!' she shouted. 'For God's sake, Gulliver, do something!'

Gulliver moved towards Spider and licked his free hand.

'God, you're useless!'

Carole was in the workshop now. She could smell the paint and glue. She could see the underpinning machine and the guillotine. And she was not strong enough to prevent herself from being dragged towards them.

'Spider.'

It was Bonita Green's voice, calm now and authoritative.

Spider stopped in his tracks.

'Let her go, Spider.'

His moment of irresolution seemed very long to Carole. But then slowly she felt the iron grip on her wrist relax. He let go of her and shambled across to his seat, mumbling, 'Anything you say, Bonita.'

Gulliver, realizing that the focus of attention had moved away from the gallery, padded into the workshop. He looked around, moved across the room and licked Spider's hand again.

THIRTY-FIVE

Contacting Detective Inspector Hodgkinson the following day didn't feel like a cop-out to either Carole or Jude. Though they had come to a good few wrong conclusions, they had at least proved that Fennel Whittaker's death had been murder. And since Spider now readily confessed to the crime, there didn't seem a lot more for them to do on the case.

Carmen Hodgkinson expressed her thanks for their contribution. Spider was arrested, and, standing by his confession, was sent to prison. There his behaviour was exemplary and occasionally in the evenings he would entertain his fellow inmates with his perfect Elvis Presley mime. And he still received messages from the King.

Bonita Green and Addison Willoughby finally got married. The Cornelian Gallery was sold off and its next incarnation on the Fethering Parade was as another estate agents. Bonita moved into Addison's huge house in the Boltons, he sold his agency and they lived out their lives in great wealth and happiness.

Things turned out all right for Denzil Willoughby too. On his own initiative he came to realize the good sense in what Ingrid Staunton had said to Jude. He gave up conceptual art and explored his skills in drawing and painting. The results were highly appreciated and prices for his work ballooned very gratifyingly. He continued to be a poseur and treat women pretty badly, but he still didn't find one with whom he wanted to share the sanctity of marriage.

His friendship with Giles Green endured, though Giles went back to cohabit with his wife Nikki. Both continued to have affairs, but there seemed to be something in the marriage that both of them needed.

Whether Giles would have gone back to Nikki if his affair with Chervil Whittaker had continued, who could say? In fact, she dumped him within six months of Fennel's death.

She also rather lost interest in Walden, moved back to London and got another job in the city . . . something in PR again. The Whittakers brought managers in to run the glamping site. It was successful for a couple more years, then Ned and Sheena changed their minds and developed the site into an alpaca farm. They continued to be courted for sponsorship of a variety of charitable ventures. But however generously they gave, their money just went on accumulating. The marriage remained strong, though Ned Whittaker never ceased to miss his beloved daughter, Fennel.

Sam Torino remarried. A Russian oligarch this time, one who spent most of his life in London and who always liked to have an attractive woman on his arm. It was a good career move for her which was loved by the gossip columns, who devoted a lot of energy to inventing new 'Beauty and the Beast' headlines. Force of habit meant that she ignored Jude's advice and continued to be full-on Sam Torino all the time.

She still had a lot of pain from her back, but nobody would ever have known it.

There was no reconciliation between Bonita Green and her daughter Ingrid. But then they'd never had that much in common.

Carole Seddon had her week at the end of May with Gaby and Lily. Of course they didn't go to Walden. The friends they were coming to West Sussex with had cried off at the last minute, so they ended up staying at High Tor. An arrangement which, to Carole's surprise, worked rather well. But how could anything fail if it involved someone as gorgeous as her granddaughter? Lily was very pleased with the photograph of her that hung in her grandmother's sitting room, and she never found out what had happened to the man who framed it.

Next door at Woodside Cottage, Jude continued her work of healing. At times she felt rather claustrophobic in the confines of Fethering, but no one would have known that from the customary serenity of her demeanour.

PATRON REVIEW

Please share your ratings & comments!

CPSIA information can be obtained at www.ICGtesting.com
Printed in the USA
LVOW12s1525220615

443395LV00001B/272/P

9 781780 295176